Unknown Soul

Pam Kumpe

Pam Kumpe

Unknown Soul

DEDICATION

To *That Guy* in Houston, Texas who thought
I'd forget him, and whose name is *Brian*.
I haven't forgotten you.

**

To *Paul Jones*, a friend for life

**

To *Cindy Ross & Lenda Selph*

**

To the *Angels* who have protected me.
You asked for new assignments from God and,
after God said no, you still hung in there with me.
For that, I say, "Thank you."

**

Thank You
Choctaw Nation of Oklahoma
&
Chief Gary Batton

Pam Kumpe

Unknown Soul

DISCLAIMER

Pam Kumpe

Do you not know? Have you not heard? The Lord is the everlasting God, the Creator of the ends of the earth. He will not grow tired or weary, and his understanding no one can fathom.

He gives strength to the weary and increases the power of the weak. Even youths grow tired and weary, and young men stumble and fall; but those who hope in the Lord will renew their strength.

They will soar on wings like eagles; they will run and not grow weary, they will walk and not be faint.

Isaiah 40: 28-31 (NIV)

Choctaw Translation

Chik haklo tuk o̱? Chihowa hvt Chitokaka a billia hoke, yakni ont atahaka moma ikbi.

Tikambit hoyabli toba chi̱ kiyo, micha nan ai vkostininchi ya̱ kvnat ashatvpola he keyu.

Hoyabli vhleha ya̱ isht ahlampko ima mikmvt ilbusha ya̱ nan isht aia̱hli ya̱ ishahlichi.

Himmithoa vhleha ak kia tikambi cha yohabli toba, mikmvt hattak himmithoa yvt ashachi cha yoshoba; amba kvna hosh. Chihowa anukchieto hokmvt nan isht ahlampko i̱ himmona cha chi̱.

Okla o̱ssi ahoba hosh sanahchi o̱ hikvt ittanoho̱wa chi̱; okla baleli cha hoyabli toba chi̱ kiyo, okla nowa mikmvt hoyabla chi̱ kiyo.

Pam Kumpe

Some secrets rush down the river.

Others hide in cemeteries.

Wheelock Academy

The First Day

Rushes in with Sadness

THE CHOCOLATE EYES OF THE Indian girl gazing at me from the window on the second story of Pushmataha Hall christened me with her sadness. She's called Bright Eyes, but nothing looks bright in those eyes. I'm not staying long enough to find out why she's crying, either. I'm sitting in this cedar tree by the porch waiting for Grandma, Priscilla, and Tin Can Mahlee.

Ooooh—rue—loo-ah.

"Taddy, do you hear that? Someone's crying at the cemetery. They must be having a funeral."

He shook his head. "I don't hear anything except the girl in the window."

"That's not a little girl crying. It's too loud. Too shrill. Too something." I grabbed a brown leaf, crunching it. "This is supposed to be a fun trip. I hope it's not filled with too many tears."

"We'll have fun. I saw some ponies. We can pet them."

"I hope you're right."

This is my first day at Wheelock Academy. I'm hemmed in by one hundred Choctaw girls. Some are here to go to school, but most are orphans. They line up, follow each other in the hall, eat together, go to school together, and obey the matron, which is why I'm in this tree by the long front porch. I don't like the year 1947. It has too many rules at Grandma's manor in Texarkana and too many in Oklahoma. That's probably why Bright Eyes is crying.

Seeing this many girls has only made me wish for my daddy, Side Car Ace. If he were alive, we could ride the rail without rules, or this bossy matron. But Daddy died Thanksgiving Day in '45. I'm an orphan, too—like Bright Eyes, even though I live with my grandma. My hobo friend, Tin Can Mahlee also lives with us. She acts like my mama. But she's not.

The day Daddy fell from the train in Tennessee, he gave me my hobo name, Shoelace. My given name is Annie Grace Kree. I answer to both names, unless I'm mad at you. Then I might not answer you at all.

My best friend, Taddy, is sitting on a branch across from me. He's flapping his hand in the air.

"Taddy, quit waving at that girl."

"I can wave if I want to. She's sad. Wave to her. She might smile."

"No, I want to go home. What's today's date?"

"Why? Are you worried you'll miss something?"

"No, I just want to know."

"It's Monday, January 6. We just got here yesterday. Be patient."

"My birthday is in ten days. I'll be eleven. I want to have my party at home." I pointed to the window. "I wonder when her birthday is?"

Taddy waved with both hands. "I have no idea. You'll need to ask the matron." He waved again. "See, she's our friend. She is."

"I'm not asking the matron anything. I don't think she likes me."

Taddy grinned with all of his molars. "She does. She just doesn't know it yet."

I swung my legs on the branch, thinking about the train ride to Oklahoma. We're here to help Taddy's mama, Priscilla, reunite with her twin sister, Margo. I hope we go home tomorrow.

This is a perfect spot to sit, except there's a bird hitting his face on the bark of the tree. "Hey, get out of here. You're bothering me."

Taddy giggled. "He's doing what he knows to do."

"Well, he needs to stop."

Peck. Peck. Peck. Peck. Peck.

I waved my arm. "What kind of bird hits his face on a tree?"

"Shoelace, you need to start paying attention in class at school. We're in fifth grade now."

"I do pay attention."

"No, you don't, or you would know what a woodpecker looks like. His head is red like your face gets in class when you answer a question wrong."

I stepped along the limb, glaring at Taddy. "That bird's head is probably red from soaring too close to the sun." I scaled the trunk to the ground, parading up the white steps. This is the longest balcony-porch ever.

Squeak. Bam.

Grandma Elsie, Tin Can Mahlee, and Priscilla piled onto the porch. Grandma walked up to me. "Are you ready to meet Margo?" She ran her hand through my locks.

"Where is she?"

"The matron said she's up the road a piece. We're walking to her."

Priscilla jumped from the porch steps. "I've got to go. I've got to hurry. I can't wait any longer."

Grandma called to Priscilla and used her calm voice. "Slow down, Priscilla. Margo hasn't seen you in a long time."

Mahlee bounced in man-like steps trying to keep up with Priscilla and Grandma. "Did you bring the ring? You need to make sure she gets it. It might help her remember good times."

Priscilla patted the pocket on her skirt. "The ring is right here. I'm going to slip it on her finger myself. The ring means the world to her."

I bounded from the porch and Taddy joined me. Across the lawn, I saw basketball courts. A couple of the girls told me they like to play sports. They play a game on the grass with a tiny ball and sticks, too, running up and down the field toward a goal. Sounds like work to me. I'd rather climb a tree.

Taddy ran ahead of me. "Shoelace, stop daydreaming. Catch up. We're headed to the doctor's office beside the cemetery."

I skipped a few feet, almost falling on my next step. I looked over my shoulder at the Wheelock grounds. There were dozens of buildings and a water tower. The tower rose above the two-story, white-washed frame dorm. A huge bell hung like a moon on the top of the roof. Behind the dorm, a lake sat at the bottom of the hill.

Taddy yelled. "Come on."

"I'm coming. What's the hurry? No one has seen Margo for years. What's a few more minutes?"

I caught up with him on the sandy road and Taddy slugged me. "Stop acting like this trip is for you. We're here to bring Margo home. She's family. She belongs with us in Texarkana."

"I can always run fast and catch up." I tripped Taddy with my red PF Flyers.

Taddy dusted himself off and spun around. "Stop knocking me down. Listen. I hear someone crying. Don't you?"

Ooooh—rue—loo-ah.

"Nope. But I do hear a high pitch, it's hurting my ears. It sounds like a funeral song."

Taddy moved toward the tree by the entrance to Wheelock Cemetery. "Hey, it's the lady over there. She's wailing. What's wrong with her?"

"She's probably sad. Leave her alone." I twirled around looking at the trees, noticing the big S-shaped road twisting up the hill beyond the river. I could hear water falling over the rocks. The brown leaves crackled and the orange sun warmed my nose, but the wind was cold and my fingers ached. On my final twirl, a log house caught my attention. "What's that?"

Taddy pointed. "It's the doctor's house. Margo is supposed to be there."

I kicked at the dirt and made footprints with my shoes, stomping them to make the powder fly.

Taddy stopped and tugged on my shirt. "Look. That's Margo over there. She's the crying lady. It has to be. She looks like Mama, but she's not happy."

"I know she's not happy, or she wouldn't be crying. That's not Margo. That lady sounds crazy. Her words are jumbled like the alphabet going backwards."

"She looks just like my mama. Look at her."

"I am looking. She might favor her, but that lady is much older. She has a lot more wrinkles."

"My mama has wrinkles. Not as many though."

Taddy ran to the fence and stared at the woman by the markers. I made more puffy clouds in the sand with my shoe. A rock church to my right caught my attention. An Indian girl with long braids sat cross-legged on the roof playing a flute.

Ooooh—rue—loo-ah.

A red, sun-scorched woodpecker sat on her shoulder bobbing his head with the sad music.

I ran to Taddy. "Look, over there ... Who is that?"

Before he could answer, Priscilla's scream of awesome excitement rang out over my words. "Margo. Margo Wall. It's me. It's Priscilla, your twin." She was pointing at the woman kneeling near the stone markers.

Margo rose to attention. Her face changed colors, going from pink to yellow.

A wagon rushed down the road across the bridge. The driver appeared like a ghostly shadow in the seat. The wooden wheels crunched over the gravel, and the man yelled. "Watch out! Get out of the way!"

The man holding the reins pulled and yanked, but the muscled, black horse snorted strength into the air as he galloped straight ahead. The wagon trampled Priscilla, squashing her into the dirt. The clopping and stepping, and the dust clouded my view. One of the wagon wheels plop-plopped over Priscilla's legs. She fell silent.

The funeral song from the flute rose like sadness and felt like someone was beating their head on the bark of a tree, one called death. Priscilla lay in the dirt road like a rag doll. Her body was bent the wrong way, and blood stained the dirt under her head.

Somehow, Tin Can Mahlee had pushed Grandma Elsie into a patch of weeds. Taddy had fallen over her, landing on top of an unmarked grave at the edge of the cemetery.

The cloud of pain lingered, and the wagon disappeared up and over the hills around the bend.

I found myself crumpled in a ball on the other side of the road, with no scratches, nothing hurt. I didn't have a bruise.

I watched Margo rock from side-to-side. I've seen Mahlee rock on days she goes sad. I've also seen Priscilla rock in chairs without rocking-legs. Usually it's when she's crying and gazing at her *own* blue ring on her finger.

Taddy rushed to Priscilla. "Mama. Mama." He collapsed, his tears pouring down his face. "She's breathing. She's not dead. We need a doctor."

Mahlee hurried to the doctor's porch while I ran to Taddy. "Hold her, Taddy. Hold her. Don't let go."

Grandma Elsie took her apron off, the one she often wears with the cats on it. She wrapped the fabric around Priscilla's bleeding head.

The rushing water of death swallowed Taddy's sobs. He wailed, "Mama. Mama. Not my mama."

Margo climbed the iron fence and rushed across the dirt road. She slipped behind the church where the Indian girl had sat, but who was now gone. I ran after Margo, circling the stone church from the other end, tripping on a stump next to a tall tree.

Margo sat on the back of a painted tan horse. "Move little girl. Get out of my way." Her fingers clutched the white mane of the horse, her voice echoing in the wind like Priscilla's voice. A much older, much sadder sound.

I put my hands up, blocking her way. "Wait. Don't go. Not now."

Her leg pushed me aside and knocked me to the ground. I jumped to my feet, chasing the whipping tail of her horse. I watched Margo ride across the bridge. Should I follow her? Or should I help Taddy?

A woodpecker dove at me, circling my head. I swatted at him and he hovered in the air, doing a wing-dance-flutter. For some reason, he blocked the road. I would take a step. The bird would swoop. He must not want me to follow Margo.

The First Afternoon

Priscilla Gone Quiet

THE PICKUP SPUN OUT FROM behind the doctor's office, throwing gravel. It skidded inches from hitting me. A man shouted from the open window. "Move kiddo. I'm Doctor Rigghazel."

I jumped out of his way, tripping on rocks.

The doctor stopped sideways in the road near Priscilla and hopped from the seat, carrying a little black bag. He rushed to her and motioned for the others to move. "Get back. Give me some room." He put his hand to his face, gasping. "My goodness. Is this? Could this be Margo's twin sister? I heard she was coming. I heard … We've all heard …" He stumbled closer.

Taddy shuffled up to the doctor. "Can you help? Will you fix my mama?"

"Sure, sonny." He patted Taddy on the head.

The doctor pointed at Mahlee. "Put her in the back of my truck, and I'll treat her at the office. Keep her back straight."

Mahlee grabbed the doctor's arm. "You better make sure she lives. This little boy has to have his mama back. I have to have her, too. She's my friend."

He shook his arm free. "Hurry up then. Not to worry. I'm the best doctor in these parts. Ask the missionary at Wheelock, he'll tell you."

"And I'm Tin Can Mahlee. If you want to stay a doctor, you better save Priscilla's life."

Grandma Elsie spoke up. "Doctor, hurry. Her breathing is shallow."

Taddy dodged cemetery markers with each step, running to the doctor's office as the truck drove his mama to the front door of the log building. He called. "Save my mama. I need her. And she needs me."

Mahlee carried Priscilla into the small building. Taddy rushed up behind them. I touched his arm. "Taddy, she's gonna be fine."

Taddy whimpered, crumpling to the ground. "Why did we come? Why? I don't care if I ever see Margo now. If we'd stayed home, Mama wouldn't be hurt. This is Margo's fault."

"It's not. The wagon ran over her." I pulled his ear. "Come on. The Taddy I know is strong. Let's go inside."

"I'm not so strong. You are the strong one. You're gonna be eleven. I'm just ten."

"Together we're strong. Come on. Your mama needs you."

Inside, Taddy walked to the tall cot where Priscilla's body lay lifeless. He sat on a stool by her head.

I tugged on the doctor's sleeve. "Mr. Doctor. How long until she wakes up? Can you tell me? Hey mister, I'm talking to you."

"Get out of here. I don't need your questions."

Grandma Elsie gave me the look and I stomped off, going outside. I paced around the tombstones at the cemetery next to the driveway and headed to the spot where Margo had been kneeling. I stared at a flat stone smashed into the ground. There were two words on it. Two words. No name. I spun around and counted seven more flat markers with the same two words, *unknown soul.*

I leaned on the iron fence next to a headstone taller than me. On the front, green moss hid the name, but a witch flying backwards was etched in the stone. I shuddered. "Gosh, what kind of place is this? Wheelock has a kid on a roof playing a flute. An Indian girl crying in a window. Now Margo is weeping at a grave."

Mahlee and Grandma moved to the porch. Their voices floated in the air straight to my ears. Grandma assured Mahlee. "We'll need to stay at the orphanage a few days. Priscilla will need time to heal. We need her to wake up, too."

They hugged each other, weeping. I ran to them, edging my way between their bodies. Grandma prayed, "Dear God, Priscilla was so excited to find Margo. Please bring them both back to us. I don't understand your ways, but I know you can use this to bring us closer."

I tugged on her dress. "Grandma, say a prayer for Taddy. He's scared."

"Baby girl, I sure will." She sighed. "God, Taddy is like my own. He's family. Give him the hope he needs."

Grandma motioned to Mahlee and they slipped inside, leaving me sitting on the steps. I wondered where Margo rode off to, and why. The trail of dust from Margo's horse had drifted from the road, but above the ridge a new dust trail rose up. I watched the sky, torn between following Margo and staying with Taddy.

My PF Flyers danced in the dirt and itched to run. The wind rustled the brown leaves in the tree. Beside the doctor's office, the mallard ducks in the pond launched themselves to the roof. They tapped on the wooden shakes.

Quack. Quack. Quack.

A wind chime on the porch clinked and jingled a sound like the start of a race.

Tinkle-clink. Ping-clink.
If I waited too long, I'd never find out where Margo was headed.

I ran inside the doctor's office. To my left, a piano hugged the wall. Dozens of pictures of Indian girls were taped on the plaster. I hurried to the door to my right and peeked inside the small room. The doctor mixed white sticky stuff together for a cast. Taddy whispered to his mama. "I'm here. Don't leave me." He touched her shoulder with his fingers, wiping dirt-tears with his other hand.

Doctor Rigghazel shooed me off. "Priscilla needs quiet. Go on now."

"Why does Taddy get to stay?"

"Girl, it's his mama. Not yours."

Grandma took me by the hand. "Go out to the porch. Try to stay out of the way."

I sucked on my bottom lip to keep from mouthing at the doctor, but it didn't keep me from thinking ugly words.

Grandma spoke to me as I held onto the door knob. "I know what you're thinking. Now ... now ..."

I raised my eyebrows. "Yes, ma'am."

As I shut the front door, I overheard the mean doctor. "We've got to put casts on both legs. She needs stitches in her head. I'm not sure how bad the internal injuries are, so we wait. We'll see if she pulls through. It will be a long, first night."

I stood alone on the porch. The cemetery was to my right. The church was across the road. The bridge to my left. A stray black dog howled in the middle of the bridge like he was calling me to run with him.

Ooowwwl. Ar roof. Ar roof.

If I bring Margo back, then Priscilla will get better. I'm sure of it. The woodpecker had flown away, but I could hear him hitting his face on a tree in the woods.

Peck. Peck. Peck.

I shuffled off the porch and out to the bridge where the bamboo swayed. The water splashed over the rocks in the river. The wind howled like a dog's bark.

I took off down the road, one jog, one step, on a race to find Margo before dark. I've tracked game with my daddy on trails in Memphis. We lived in hobo camps and hunted for food. This would be no different, except I was hunting a human who wanted to hide.

The black dog loped beside me, nudged my leg with his nose, keeping pace with me. My overalls were flapping in the wind, sending a chill up my back. I should have grabbed a jacket this morning. I pressed on, my heart beating so fast I could feel a thump-thump in my hands.

Crunch-roar-creak. Crunch-roar-creak.

I skidded to a stop in the dirt to see what the noise was, and a wagon with a mule rolled up next to me. The Indian with saddle-brown leather skin tipped his hat. His wrinkles were so deep you could make a river in them. He spoke. "Are you headed to Boggy Depot in Millerton? Do you need a ride?"

I shook my head. "No, but I could use a lift to the top of the hill."

"Hop in the back. Don't let the casket bother you. It's empty." The Indian wearing a white ruffled shirt was packing a gun. His yellow teeth reminded me of mold, like the kind on cemetery markers.

I jumped in the back of the wagon, mostly out of fear. Black Dog joined me and I felt a little safer.

Unknown Soul

The Indian peeked over his shoulder. "My name's Boswell. What's yours?"

"Shoelace."

"Odd name for a girl."

"It's Annie Grace Kree. But my hobo name is Shoelace."

"Hobo? You're a hobo?"

"I used to be. I might still be. What's it to ya?"

"I was simply wondering." He bellowed out a laugh, shaking the casket beside me. "Is that your dog?"

"Nope. He's not mine. He's following me."

Black Dog nestled up to me and placed his head on my lap.

Boswell cracked the reins against the mule's back.

Pha-lap. Pha-lap.

Boswell turned and gave me a glance. "So, he's not your dog? Looks like he's found a master."

"He's not mine."

"So, what brings you to my part of McCurtain County?"

"I'm taking a walk. My friend, Taddy, told me the Choctaw Indians walked here. He said this is the *Trail of Tears*. He said our teacher taught on it, but I'm not sure she did." I rattled on, while Black Dog closed his eyes.

Boswell rubbed his brow, straightening his hat. "This road will take you anywhere you need to go and then some. It's a road filled with tears, but also with life. Depends on how you look at it. And who you run into."

"I know where I'm going. I'm not after any tears, either." I stood to my feet in the back of the wagon. "Hey, I don't think I need a ride. I've changed my mind."

"Sure, you do. Hold on." He cracked the whip on the mule causing me to fall backwards. We hurried on down the trail, bumping and scooting. I pressed my feet against the side of the box to keep from getting squashed. The wagon slowed, and I crawled up behind Boswell's seat, holding onto the casket. "Hey, I want to get off."

Boswell looked at me, grinning. "Whoa."

On the hill, Margo rode her limping horse. She hopped from his back, picking up his hoof, digging around. She then jumped back on.

If I hurry, I might catch up with her.

Late Night of First Day

Chase of the Missing Sister

BOSWELL TWISTED HIS HEAD AND gave me a peek from his seat. He pulled on the reins and slapped the back of the mule. "Slow down, mule. Slow…" The wagon rolled to the crossroad. "I'm turning left here. Millerton is a mile up the road by the railroad depot. I've got to deliver this casket before five."

I jumped on top of the wooden casket. Black Dog jumped up next to me. "I'm going straight. Thanks for the ride."

The mule kicked his back feet, jerking the wagon forward. The casket swayed, rocking back and forth. It slid from the back of the wagon, crashing to the sand and rocks.

Boswell yelled at the mule. "Whoa."

I tumbled to the dirt, landing beside the casket on my back. The lid to the casket toppled sideways, and an old Indian man dressed in a blue shirt plopped on top of me. His nose, dotted with moles the size of pencil erasers, touched my face. "Get him off me."

"Don't get scared. He's already dead." Boswell came to my rescue, rolling the man off. He pulled me to my feet, helping me stand.

"You told me the casket was empty."

"Well, you needed a lift. A dead body might have kept you from saying yes."

Ar roof. Ar roof.

Black Dog dug at the dirt beside the old man.

"Stop that. Get away." Boswell slapped the hind side of not-my-dog and rolled the body back into the casket. He pushed and propped. He pulled and shoved. Finally, he got the casket back into the wagon.

I helped, but not much. "Mr. Boswell, can you catch moles? That man had oozing moles." I trotted to the side of the wagon.

Boswell climbed to his seat. "No one can catch a mole. But you are good at catching a tumbling body." He laughed and slapped his leg.

I pointed at Margo riding her horse up a ways. "Do you know her?"

Boswell coughed, spitting green spit on the dirt road. "Yes. I know Margo. She's a few thoughts, less than one whole one. She gets mixed up and often hides in the chief's abandoned log home in the woods. Most people stay away from her."

"Does she live by herself?" I moved away from the wagon as Boswell hit the mule with the reins.

"She might. But you never know. I'd be careful."

"I can take care of myself."

Black Dog ran to the edge of the road, pouncing in the weeds like a rabbit. He darted at me and knocked me to the ground. "Black Dog, go home. I don't need you tagging along."

Boswell laughed. "You're doing a great job of taking care yourself."

"I tripped. People trip." Black Dog licked my face with a slobber kiss. His one blue eye begged for a master. His right eye, the brown one, looked sad. I rubbed his head. "You can go with me, but just for today." I stood and dusted my pants, turning to Boswell. "So, how far is the chief's house?"

Boswell put his hand on the butt of his gun, tightening his grip on the reins with his other hand. His white ruffles waved like ripples on a pond. "Why are you asking so many questions?"

"No reason. I'm a curious hobo girl. Thanks again for the ride." I ran up the hill with Black Dog. He paced his paw steps with mine.

Crunch-creak-crunch.

The sound of the wagon wheels grew faint. The thump, thump faded. I stepped to the top of the hill and Margo was, once again, out of my sight. I sat on an old rotten fence post, wiping the sweat from my head. A cold gust of wind chilled my arms.

Black Dog tugged on my right shoelace.

Grr... Ar roof. Ar roof.

"Let go. No one messes with my PF Flyers. Stop it." He yanked on the shoe and moved to the left shoe, untying them both. I swatted his head and he backed up. "Black Dog, we've got to find Margo. Come on."

I tied my shoes, trekked down the road, moving higher to the crest.

Neigh. Neigh.

"Wait. Wait here, Black Dog." I put my hand to my ear, cupping it. The neighing sound rattled in the bushes. I peeked between them. "Could that be *her* horse? Looks like the same one."

I worked my way through the thicket and the trees. I bent down, crawled under the barbed wire, catching my shirt on the fence, ripping it. I scooted on my stomach until I got to the brown grassy part of the field.

Neigh. Neigh.

The horse raised his front legs at me, neighing, snorting, and kicking. He danced around me like he knew I was a stranger. His horseshoes made a *tab-dak, tab-dak* thud.

I ran in circles while he bumped me with his nose. "Stop it." I twirled around, falling under his nudge.

From nowhere, but somewhere, the woodpecker with the red head swooped around me, like a giant mosquito. "What? What is wrong with the animals here?"

I charged to the woods and the horse galloped behind me, bumping me and snorting his hot breath on my neck. Once I got to the narrow part of the trail, the horse turned back and neighed near the trees.

Black Dog followed off to the side a few feet, growling at the horse.

I yelled at him. "Some watchdog you make."

That blasted woodpecker dove at my hair, pecking at my head. I swatted at him. "Stop it. Stop it now. Get off of me and leave me alone."

The woodpecker flew into the trees. The sun was low now, and smoke rose up with the moon. I stepped to the clearing, saw the log house, and stomped around the trees, making a new path. I could see my breath and crept to the back porch. A breezeway ran through the middle of the house.

Black Dog sniffed the ground, pawing at the steps by the porch. He curled up on the second step for a nap. I inched up to a window to peek inside. The curtain was sheer, like an old sheet worn from use. "Black Dog, there she is. She's sitting by the fire in a rocker and she's holding a baby in her arms. There's somebody else in the room. She's talking to someone." I twisted my neck to see who else was in there.

Thwack. Thwack.

I fell sideways as two wallops on my shoulder blades sent me to the porch. "Ouch! What was that? Who hit me?"

"You are not welcome at this house. You need to go back to Wheelock Academy. Go now. The time is not right for you to be here." The Indian girl who'd played the flute on the church shouted at me.

"Who are you to tell me anything?" I pushed her with both hands. She didn't budge.

"I'm Chula Kickingbird." She pulled on strands of my blonde hair, knotting it between her fingers. "I'll scalp you if you tell anyone of this place."

"Boswell knows where it is. How do you think I got here?"

Chula let go of my hair, pulled me to my feet, yanking out a knife. "I mean it. Get going." She touched my neck with the point, pricking my skin. A trickle of blood dripped to the top of my PF Flyer. "Don't tell anyone what you saw tonight. Not a single soul. The time will come. It's not what you think. You are here to save someone, but not tonight."

Ar roof. Ar roof.

Black Dog locked his jaw onto Chula's wrist and the knife clanked to the porch.

I swallowed hard, socking her in the eye. "I'm here to get Margo. I need her to come to the doctor's office. Her twin sister, Priscilla, is hurt."

Chula rubbed her face and tried to shake Black Dog from her wrist.

Grrr…

"Let go. Your dog better let go."

Grrr…

"He's not my dog. He's only with me for today."

Chula shook free. "Get out of here. And keep this place a secret, especially the baby. You cannot tell anyone. Promise me."

I touched the bloody spot on my neck. "I promise. Just don't stab me."

I looked at the knife. Chula did, too. We dove, our fingers reaching, but the knife was hung between the slats on the porch. Chula jumped to her feet, standing firm in her moccasins. She put both hands on her hips. "Leave now, or I'll get Margo's gun. Go back to Wheelock Academy. Go like the wind. Go as fast as you can."

I darted through the breezeway, crashing into an Indian lady wearing a dress, whose tummy pooched out. She wore a necklace of turquoise. "Sorry … sorry."

She called to me. "Who are you? Why are you here?"

Another Indian lady who held her round tummy stepped from the end of the porch. She wobbled toward us. "Are you all right, Pauline?"

The first lady rubbed her belly, "Yes, Eliza, I'm fine. Baby's kicking me, though."

I tumbled from the porch and ran to the woods. I had to get away before the Indian girl, Chula, came after me with a gun instead of her knife. I had to keep this a secret. I had to forget the baby. Or so Chula said.

I didn't stop running until I got back to the road. In the middle of the dusty path, Black Dog lay asleep like he was waiting for my return. "Some help you were. You disappeared on me."

I inched down the hill, and a woodpecker perched himself on the old fence post where I'd sat earlier. The crackling sounds in the bushes behind me sent a chill down my spine.

I'm being followed.

The First Day Ends

Margo Makes the Moon Cry

I RECITED A CHANT TO keep from crying and getting scared. I tripped and stumbled down the dirt road, the shadows lurking and cracking in the night. I stepped with one foot and then the other, working my way toward Wheelock. "Four more steps. Five more minutes. Four more steps. Five more minutes."

My throat hurt, my chest ached, and my arms felt heavy. I wished my daddy was here to save me, but he wasn't coming home—ever. The sadness at thinking I'd never see him again almost made me collapse, but he'd want me to run. He'd want me to get home. He'd want me to get out of this icy-night air.

I ran past the doctor's office and thought I'd check on Priscilla, but knowing how mad Grandma Elsie gets, my feet kept running.

The moon had followed me on my escape from Margo's Mountain. It shifted in the sky like a light bulb, shining a spotlight for me to find my way. I could see the road the whole time, but I kept hearing crunching steps behind me. I couldn't see anyone, though.

Krunch. Krunch.

"Who's there? What do you want?" I screamed this for the fifth time. No answer. Every time I yelled, the crunching noises stopped. "If you're behind a tree, show yourself. I'm not scared."

Nothing. No answer.

29

I took off running and the crunch-echo faded behind me. I made it to the spot that leads to the road. Black Dog chased a rabbit into the weeds, jumping into the thicket. He bounced between the bushes, and I followed the road toward Wheelock. Soon Black Dog disappeared for good. He's not so brave. His attack on Chula was more like a play-bite game. He's probably playing tag with that rabbit.

The moon lit up the front gate to the girls' school. The driveway welcomed me. I stopped under the giant letters, bending my head back. I'm not too happy we're in Millerton, Oklahoma. So far, I've not had any fun.

I ran down the long driveway with my eyes on the lights at the dorm. I'm safe, nearly out of this cold. I jogged, shivering and shaking.

Whizzle snap. Whizzle snap.

"What? Ouch …" I toppled face forward like a bullet, hitting my nose and chin in the gravel. I rubbed my nose. "I'm bleeding. What has my feet tied?" I grabbed my ankles. "Rope? I've been lassoed? Chula? Are you doing this? I'm not going to tell anyone about the baby. I promise. Just let me go."

The shadow grabbed me by the neck, pushing my back against a tree. My shoulders were crammed against the trunk. Chula was strong, but not this big or strong. A person leaned in close, and the raunchy breath made me choke. The shadow inhaled, tossing out hate. "Stay away from my house. You get caught on my porch or on my property again, and you won't find your way home."

"I won't be back. I promise."

"Watch yourself, too. There are ghosts at Wheelock. And some of them are already dead."

I felt the rope unravel from my feet, and the hands lift from my shoulders. My tears fell while my heart beat so loud my ears hurt. I yelled into the night. "Why don't you like your twin sister? What is wrong with you?"

No answer. Nothing.

I'd come face to face with Margo. As fast as she had lassoed me, she was gone. I put my hand to my face, my nose was dripping blood and my sobs echoed for help. "Grandma. Grandma. Mahlee. Someone. Anyone. Help me."

I could see the lights of the dorm at the end of the driveway. "Four more steps. Five more minutes. Four more steps. Five more minutes." I charged the rest of the way, and it felt like a mile-run across the Harahan Bridge in Memphis.

Whizzle-snap.

"What? Ouch. My wrist." I grabbed my arm, tumbled forward, hitting the gravel.

Margo yelled at me from a tree. "You tell anyone you saw me, I'll make sure Taddy never sees his mama again."

I curled up in a ball, like the night the Phantom Killer pushed me from the boxcar. I needed to forget this night ever happened. I whispered to Margo, hoping she heard me. "I won't say anything. Just let me go."

Margo jumped down from the tree, pulled the rope from my wrist, disappearing into the night.

I hurried to the steps at the side of the dorm. I turned the knob on the door, tumbling to the floor inside the dining hall.

"Shoelace. What in the world?" Mahlee rushed to me, kneeling down. Her eyes were filled with questions.

"I ... I ... took a walk. I got lost. I couldn't find my way back and ended up in the woods. I fell over some rocks." I lied to save Taddy. I lied to save myself.

The orphan girls held their spoons in mid-air, watching me like I was the first blonde girl wearing overalls to ever fall into their lives. Well, I might be the first hobo girl, but if they knew how Margo lurked outside in trees with rope, the girls wouldn't be staring at me. They'd be watching the windows and doors, calling the police.

Grandma sat me down, putting a cold rag under my nose. "Here, your nose is bleeding."

The silence of no one eating made me stare back at the girls. Bright Eyes took an extra roll and stuck it into her pocket on her dress. I used to sneak extra food on the rail too, when Daddy and me ate at missions. And when Mahlee and me ate there, too.

The matron spoke, clapping both hands. "Girls, our guest was missing tonight. She's fine now. Eat up. Lights out in an hour."

The girls answered in unison, "Yes, ma'am," and dove into their food. The clanking of spoons played music like a song without a tune.

Grandma sat across from me, running her fingers through her gray hair. "Annie Grace Kree. We were fixing to borrow Boswell's wagon or take his pickup to come look for you."

I spoke to the rag, using my sad voice. "Sorry. I was lost."

Mahlee handed me a fresh cloth for my face. "Wipe your face. A mile of dirt is stuck on you."

I sniffed and washed my face, turning to Grandma. "You know Boswell? How do you know him?"

"He's the groundskeeper and lives in the back of the barn with the mules. He's also a carpenter. He told me earlier you hitched a ride toward Millerton. Girl, we just got here, don't go wandering off and getting into trouble."

I leaned on the table and Mahlee handed me a glass of water. I gulped the whole thing in one swig. "I didn't mean to get lost. I don't know these parts. Is Priscilla any better?"

Grandma wrapped me up in her arms. "She's still unconscious. Taddy won't leave her side. He's staying there with her. She has casts on her legs and blood keeps gushing from her right ear. The doctor put 35 stitches in her head. We can only pray and hope, right now."

Mahlee sat next to Grandma. "I hope this trip wasn't a bad idea. But the letter came to Priscilla. She thought Margo wanted to come home. Maybe she didn't send the letter. I can't help but wonder if we should have stayed home."

Grandma interrupted. "Ms. O'Malley is taking care of the manor for me. This has been a horrible first day. For now, we're going to stay. Margo may come around."

I put my head on her shoulder and kissed Grandma's face. "I'm sorry. I didn't mean to scare you."

"Just behave while we're here. We don't need any more trouble."

Mahlee handed me a bowl of stew. I gobbled up my food, while replaying the threats from Margo in my head. The Indian girls laughed and chatted, most whispered at some point. A group pointed at me, giggling.

Scratch. Scratch. Scratch.

I rushed to the door, opening it. "Look at you. How did you get tangled in that rope?" Black Dog's neck held the type of rope Margo used on me, but the end was frayed, like Black Dog chewed loose from being tied up.

Mahlee rubbed his ear by the blue eye. "Who is this?"

"This is Black Dog. He found me on the road, or maybe I found him. Someone must have tied him up, and now he's loose. I'm getting him some water."

The matron strutted up in her big black boots. "We don't have any pets here."

I smiled. "He won't bother you. He doesn't know how to bite."

Black Dog growled at the matron and I petted his head. "Be nice. She might let you stay."

"We'll see. We'll see." The matron ordered the girls to their rooms to wash for bed. The older girls gathered up the dishes and cleaned the kitchen. After I sat with Grandma and Mahlee for a while at the table, Grandma showed me where I'd sleep, but I wasn't so sure sleep would come tonight.

Upstairs, in the giant dorm bedroom, the cots were lined up in rows with a chair beside each bed. The girls wore the same haircuts like someone put a bowl over their head and whacked their black hair. The little girl from the window this morning was curled up on the cot next to mine by the wall. Her black hair was long. I wondered why she didn't have short hair.

"Halito. Why are you staring at her?" An Indian girl close to my height sat on a cot across from mine.

I turned to her. "Who are you? What does halito mean?"

"It's 'hi' in Choctaw. I'm Eleanor."

"I'm Shoelace. I'm here with my grandma to bring Margo home."

Eleanor smiled. "We heard Margo has a twin. We're glad you're here. You're the most excitement we've had in a long time. But watch out, Margo is wild."

"I know. I met her today. She's crazy." I pointed at the cot where Bright Eyes snuggled with her pillow. "Hey, why isn't her hair cut short like yours?"

"Oh, her. Well, she bites and she hits. She's not easy to handle. They were afraid they'd cut her with the scissors. She's only three. They are letting her get used to being here. Bright Eyes arrived with a group of girls from Memphis a few weeks ago."

"My grandma told me everyone calls her that. But her eyes look sad to me."

Eleanor tapped me on the arm. "This is why we call her a happier name, so maybe she'll brighten up one day. Don't try and talk to her, she doesn't speak. Well, she might, but we've never heard her."

I crawled onto my cot. "Night, Eleanor."

"Night. The bell rings at six, you better get some sleep."

In my nightshirt, I counted the windows leading to the upstairs balcony. "One, two, three, four … ten, eleven, twelve." The matron switched the lights off. The girls didn't whisper or talk to each other in the dark. They obeyed the matron like she was a drill sergeant. I wasn't going to be the matron's favorite since I break rules and don't listen to grownups like I should.

Grandma and Mahlee were sharing a bed downstairs in a private room. The night grew late, the day was long. I could hear a flute playing outside window number five. Bright Eyes crawled from her cot and shuffled to the window. She waved at someone on the other side of the window pane.

I sauntered up to see … and stood with her by the glass. Chula was wrapped in a red-plaid blanket, playing her flute in the tree. On her shoulder, the red-headed woodpecker bobbed his head along with the music. Who is this Indian girl, and why is she sitting in a tree at night?

I opened the window, stuck my head out, and started to climb onto the balcony-porch. Bright Eyes took my hand, her chocolate eyes begged me to wait. She used silent words to say nothing and silence to explain everything. She held my fingers like we'd been friends forever, like we could be sisters.

The matron came into the room. The lights popped on. The Indian girls stared at me, and Bright Eyes cried. The yelling was soon to begin, so I shut the window. I turned to give the matron my Annie Grace Kree smile.

Night of First Night

Dog Gone Fun

THE MATRON STOOD IN THE doorway of the dorm room in her blue robe and furry slippers. She looked like the witch on the marker at the cemetery. All she needed now was a broom. "Annie Grace Kree, come with me. Come see what's in my bedroom."

"Why? Where's my grandma?"

Bright Eyes let go of my fingers, scooting to her cot. She folded herself in a ball.

The matron called to me. "Come with me. It's in my bed."

"What's in your bed?" I moved toward the matron, unsure if or how I could solve her problem.

"It's your dog. You left him in the kitchen and now he's perched upstairs in my room on my mattress—on my family quilt."

I rushed across the giant room, following the matron across the hall to her bedroom. The whispers of the forty or so girls shuffling for a better look grew louder.

In the matron's room, a black statue stood in the middle of her bed. I scolded the statue. "Black Dog, what are you doing? You aren't supposed to be on the bed." I dove onto the mattress, reaching for his black legs, but he danced around my hands. He jumped and play-growled. "Stop jumping. You're gonna get us both put in the barn if you keep this up."

The matron swatted at my dog with her hand. "No dog is sleeping in my bed."

Black Dog slid off the mattress with part of the quilt between his teeth, tearing a corner of the fabric. The matron shouted. "This quilt has been in our family for years."

I chased Black Dog and he darted out of her bedroom down the long hallway. He skidded with his legs. They went every which way on the hardwood floor. He slid into the bedroom where the girls sat on their cots.

"Ahh!! It's a dog. We have a dog." Eleanor clapped her hands with excitement.

Most of the girls jumped to their feet on their cots, screaming and laughing. A few cried in fear of the dog, but most were trying to pet him as he ran up and down and in-between the cots.

I yelled at Eleanor. "Get some of the girls and block the stairway so he doesn't run off."

"We'll block him and send him back to you."

The matron ran into the room, sliding in her slippers and falling to the floor. "Oh my, this is not happening."

Black Dog licked her entire face in one swipe and raced into the hallway. I ran after him, barreling by the matron. At the top of the stairs, Black Dog slipped on the floor and toppled to his side. He became a dog-sled in a snowstorm of fun, sliding toward Eleanor and her friends.

He plowed into two of them, broke through, bouncing down the stairs again. He must have had so much fun, because he darted back up the stairs, sliding down the hall. He crashed into the wall. Then he turned around and ran to the girls, taking out three of them this time.

Eleanor laughed as she rolled onto her stomach on the floor. "I've lived here for three years. This is the most fun we've ever had at the school. I've never seen the matron swat at a dog before. We'll pay for it tomorrow, but for now, it's grand."

Black Dog jumped on the cots, bouncing on them. He then padded back to the matron's mattress, leaping on her bed. He drooled on her sheets. She chased him. I chased him. The girls chased him.

The matron yelled. "This is why we don't have pets at the academy. They are too much trouble. He'll stay outside from now on."

I defended my dog. "He's not trouble. He wants to sleep with someone. He's lonely. Dogs get lonely, too."

While I argued with the matron, Black Dog snuck off to the room with the girls. I watched him back himself out of the hall like he understood the matron. I apologized for him. "I'm sorry, Ms. Matron. I'm sorry. Don't tell my grandma."

"Don't tell me what?" Grandma's voice rose up behind me in the hallway. Giggles from the girls hanging onto every word told me they were listening to us, too.

I spun around. "Grandma. It's not my fault. He was in the kitchen and came upstairs. He jumped into her bed. I had nothing to do with it."

"Shoelace, we won't be allowed to stay here if this keeps up. It's only the first day and already …" She paused, rubbing her face. "Already … so much has happened."

The matron stepped between us. "Elsie, our families go way back with Wheelock and the missionaries. This stray dog isn't going to come between us." She hugged Grandma.

Eleanor looked around. She whispered. "Where did the dog go?"

Bright Eyes stood in the doorway to our room and pointed toward the window.

I touched her shoulder. "What? Where is he?"

She took my hand and guided me across the room. We passed four rows of cots. I shouted louder than I should have. "There's Black Dog. He's asleep under your cot."

Grandma and the matron showed up. The matron whispered, "Bright Eyes may have gotten herself a sleeping buddy. The dog can stay one night, then it's back outside for this mutt."

Bright Eyes crawled into her cot, smiled, and covered up. I slipped into my cot, wishing for a sister or even a dog. Listening to the girls snicker made me think that Wheelock might be fun—sometimes.

The matron snapped her fingers and the thud-thud of bare feet running for bed sent the look-alike Indian girls to their cots. Some of the girls from downstairs shuffled in the hall, hurrying off to their beds.

Grandma strolled over to my cot. "Do you want to snuggle up with Mahlee and me? She's already asleep. It's a big bed."

"No. I'll sleep in here. Mahlee snores. Besides, I can keep a watch on Black Dog."

"Get some sleep, and stay in bed."

"I will. I'm writing a poem first, but then I will sleep. Taddy's sad tonight. It's a sad poem night."

"We'll check on Taddy first thing in the morning."

With everyone back in bed, Eleanor called to me from a few cots away. "I'm glad you are here. This is the best fun we've had in forever. I'll never forget this. Goodnight."

"Night. I don't plan the fun. It can surprise me, too."

The lights went off, the room fell quiet. In the dim light from the window I could see Bright Eyes. At her feet, Black Dog snuggled in the blanket. He must have jumped into her bed when the lights went off.

I scribbled my poem on paper from my satchel. I'll call this poem, "Dog Gone Fun, Gone Sad."

> *We came for Margo*
> *On the first day at Wheelock.*
> *I don't know what to say.*
> *Priscilla is hurt.*
> *I fell in the dirt.*
> *Taddy is sad.*
> *And I'm flat out mad.*
> *Because once again.*
> *I've torn my shirt.*
> *I found a dog.*
> *Or he found me.*
> *He is asleep.*
> *I hope he's for keeps.*

I placed the poem in the satchel under my bed with my other clothes and pulled the blanket up to my chin. I closed my eyes, listening to the wind howl outside. I fell asleep faster than most nights, but then Black Dog drooled on my face. I could see the moon swinging from a rope in the tree outside window number five. The clanking of metal hurt my ears. I had to see what was lurking outside.

"No. No. Daddy. Put the mask down. It doesn't belong to you. It belongs to the man on the train in Texarkana. The one they call the Phantom Killer. The one who got away."

I felt my legs go numb and my heart stopped, then it started again. Margo was tying me up with rope, first my legs, then my hands. She pushed me over the edge of the bridge. I sank to the bottom and a knife floated by as I choked on water.

The knife cut me loose and I popped to the top like a raft, floating.

Margo passed by in a fishing boat and she had Taddy, who was screaming for me. "Shoelace, save me!"

Then Margo reached over and grabbed my hair. "I told you to stay away from my house. I told you to leave me alone."

My legs jerked. I was suffocating. I ... I ... fell to the floor, and woke up with my blanket wrapped around my head.

Eleanor called to me. "Are you having a nightmare?"

"I guess so. I have them when I'm tired."

She marched over, helped unfold me, and handed me a round thing with beads on it. "Sleep with this at night. It's a dream catcher. It will protect you from nightmares."

I took the gift, not sure I believed her. "Thank you. I'll keep it under my pillow."

"No. You need to hang it on the wall. Dream catchers trap the bad dreams before they can get into your head."

"Can we do it in the morning?"

"Sure. I'll tack it on the wall tomorrow." Eleanor shuffled to her cot, a few rows over, glancing back at me. She smiled. "Thank you for coming to Wheelock. Sixth grade has been tough this year. I feel so alone sometimes."

I crawled under the covers. The cot felt warm and safe. The rest of the night my dreams were of Taddy and me riding a boxcar for his birthday and eating cupcakes. I rested ... and then, I woke up to a bell ringing.

The sun blared in the windows along with Mahlee's wild voice, piercing my ears.

Flying into Day Two

Breakfast for Everyone

I SLIPPED ON MY PF FLYERS, leaving them untied. The hullabaloo coming from downstairs beckoned me. The blasts of screams and laughter rose to the second floor like a smokestack of chaos. I ran to the hallway, deciding to get my lucky rock. I should have taken it with me yesterday.

I dashed back to the room, pulling out my satchel from under the cot. I grabbed my red rock, touching the smooth surface. Skip, my hobo friend, gave me this rock. He's dead, now. I sure miss him. I say goodbye to people more than I want to. God should let my friends live longer. I wonder if God cries when I cry?

My eyes landed on the wall above my cot where the dream catcher dangled on a nail. The red and orange beads were strung together, and the yellow bead was glued to a tiny feather. Eleanor must have put it up there.

I ran to the stairs, sliding my hand down the shiny wooden rail. I hopped down most of the stairs, hurrying to the kitchen. I could tell the grownups were talking. There was so much noise, so much screaming. The girls were already awake and in the kitchen.

Across the dining hall, Mahlee held her arms out like a giant arm-gate. She positioned herself at the end of the long table. "Black Dog, get down from the table and stop eating the eggs. The matron is going to send you on down the road."

Grandma reached for Black Dog as he pounded on the wooden tables. He knocked glasses of milk over and plowed through plates. He paused, every few steps, lapped up milk and chomped on food.

I pulled on Eleanor's arm, who was giggling at the mess. "Where's the matron? She's gonna think this is my fault."

"She's gone to Millerton with Boswell for supplies. They'll be in town for hours, but our teachers will be coming to Wilson Hall soon. They live in the two-story house in the curve by the driveway. We have to get your dog before they come for breakfast."

"He's not my dog." I burst to the stove, picking up some bacon. I dangled the bacon in front of his nose. "Black Dog, look what I have. It's bacon. Come and get it."

He screeched to a stop at the end of the table, plowing right into Mahlee. She wrapped her arms around his body, but he slipped from her grasp. Black Dog took off like a rocket toward me.

Ar roof. Ar roof.

I moved to the side door. "Come on. Come on, boy." I opened the door, tossed the bacon out to the grass, and Black Dog dove to the yard. He chomped on the bacon by the rose bushes.

I hurried inside and slammed the door. Mahlee ran to me. "Thank you. We've been chasing that mutt all morning. He's a handful. You may need to get rid of him."

I sighed, followed her to the sink, mouthing at her. "You don't get rid of me when I'm too much trouble."

Mahlee slapped a playful swat on my backside. "Your grandma and I have talked about it."

Grandma came between us. "No, we haven't. Mahlee's playing with you. She's like a second mama to you."

"But she's not my mama. Mine's dead in the grave, like my daddy. Like Skip. I wish people didn't die. I wish there were no graves and no cemeteries."

Bright Eyes carried her plate to the sink, watching me. It was like she was hanging onto my every word.

Eleanor was on her heels and she put her dishes in the sink, too. I called to her. "Thanks for hanging my dream catcher on the wall."

"I didn't do it. Bright Eyes did it. She beat me to it."

I rushed to Bright Eyes and turned her around. "Thank you. Now, my nightmares won't be so scary."

A small smile slipped from her lips.

The girls picked up silverware, wiping down the tables. They cleaned up the disaster, one I had nothing to do with this time.

Eleanor danced by me. "We have to go to class, but I hope we can play some basketball or stick ball later, or I could show you a secret passage. No one knows where it is, except me and a couple of other girls."

I called to her. "A secret passage? Where?"

Mid-Morning of Day Two

Lullaby of Death

MAHLEE, GRANDMA, AND ME, TOOK to the driveway after breakfast, walking in silence. We were headed down the dirt road to check on Taddy and Priscilla at the doctor's office.

A silent fear shouted in my heart. What if Priscilla dies? What if Margo doesn't leave Taddy alone?

I rushed ahead of Grandma and Mahlee, sailing in the road on my tiptoes. I flew up and down the road with my arms out like an airplane.

Zoom. Zoom. Zoom.

Mahlee hollered. "Little hobo girls can't fly."

I yelled in the wind and at Mahlee. "I can fly. I can run. I can do whatever I want."

Grandma added her two cents. "No, you can't. You are not leaving our sight today."

I laughed in the breeze, whispering to the air. "I don't plan to break the rules."

My flying-thoughts drifted to the tree where I first met Taddy by Grandma's manor last year. I've never known anyone who's allergic to cats and peanuts. So far he's not allergic to me.

I whispered a prayer to God, *"Please don't let Margo hurt Taddy. Please God, let Taddy stay on earth for a long time. And his mama, too. Amen."*

I ran to the porch of the doctor's office, bumping into Mahlee, who had put her hand on Grandma's shoulder. It's like they were afraid to go inside. Mahlee frowned at me. "Watch out. Behave when we go inside."

"I will. I always try to behave."

Grandma took a big breath. "Let's be brave. Taddy needs us. He is like my own."

In the front room, by the piano, a woman in a gray dotted dress sat with her arms across her tummy. She sighed, not looking at us.

The doctor popped his head from the second room on the right. "Ms. Elsie and Ms. Mahlee, I've got a patient this morning. Go on in. Taddy's in there." He pointed to the other door. "I'll be busy for the next hour."

Grandma looked at him. "Thank you, Doctor Rigghazel. Thank you."

We hurried into Priscilla's room. Taddy rushed to Grandma, crying. "Mama moaned last night. She twitched, too. Doctor Rigghazel let me sleep on a pallet next to her, but I heard every howl from those coyotes last night. They kept me up."

Grandma tipped his chin up. "You may need to stay with us at the dorm. They have a room across from mine downstairs. The doctor will take good care of your mama."

He backed up. "No. I want to be here when she wakes up."

Mahlee handed Taddy a sack with bacon and biscuits. "We brought you something to eat."

Taddy placed his food on the windowsill. "I'm not hungry. I'll eat it later."

I scooted up next to Taddy, putting my hand in my pocket. "I brought you my red rock. You could use some luck."

Grandma scolded me. "Luck. I don't believe in luck. I believe in the grace of God. God will bring Priscilla through this. We have to believe."

Taddy put the rock in his pocket. "I'll keep it, but try praying for Mama. Grandma Elsie is right. We need more than luck."

"I did pray. Earlier. I was an airplane. A talking and praying airplane."

Grandma nodded. "I'll be praying, too. Taddy, would you like one of us to sit with your mama and give you a break?"

Taddy looked at Priscilla and then me. "I want Shoelace to sit with her. Grandma Elsie, if you'll show me where my bag is at Wheelock, I can change into clean clothes."

I jumped to the stool by Priscilla's bed. "I'll be right here. I'll recite some of my poems for her. Maybe she will hear them while she sleeps." I bent down to her ear. "Hi, Priscilla. It's me. I'm here. Don't get scared. I'm here to protect you."

Mahlee and Grandma left, mumbling about me under their breath. Taddy walked with them, arm in arm. They planned to return in a couple hours.

Taddy had rolled up his pallet and had it neatly placed by the wall. I sat on the stool, listening to every inhale and exhale of the sleeping Priscilla. Her head was covered in white gauze. Her legs were covered in hard plaster. Most of her face was bruised and her lips swollen. It hurt me to see Taddy's mama like this.

I spun around to look out the window. A bunch of mallards swam in the pond. I opened Taddy's breakfast sack, the one he forgot, and chomped on a biscuit. Bored, I wandered around the doctor's office, peeking into the front room. The lady with the sick tummy was no longer there.

Creak. Creak. Creak.

The floor squeaked under my shoes. I spun around, looking at the piano, touching a key. I counted the chairs. I counted cracks in the floor. I twirled in circles.

Doctor Rigghazel poked his head through the second door. "What are you doing?"

"I'm watching Priscilla. Grandma and Mahlee went with Taddy so he could change clothes."

"Get yourself back in Priscilla's room. Don't be going through my office. Mind your own business, little one."

"I am not little, but I will stay in there, I promise." I wrinkled my nose. I was pretty sure I had no plans to obey him. He may be a doctor, but he gives me a creepy feeling in my throat like I could throw up. He's made my tummy hurt, too.

A lady's voice cried out from behind the doctor. "I've changed my mind. I can't go through with this."

The sick lady in the next room must not like the doctor, either. The doctor shook his fist at me, closing the door.

I ran to Priscilla's room, stopping at the window by her bed. I counted the ducks, but my feet itched inside my shoes. I had to listen in. I stopped myself from leaving her room. Then I took a couple of steps, but the doctor's voice shouted inside my head, *Don't be going through my office.*

I sat on the stool, patting Priscilla's arm. "Taddy will be back soon. I hope you aren't in any pain."

A scream from the next room knocked me from the stool. "Stop what you're doing. I don't want to have this procedure."

I looked into the hallway, moved down the wall. I pressed my ear to the door where the shouts rattled the pictures over my head.

Creak. Squeak.

Unknown Soul

I leaned on the door. It cracked open. I tried not to fall, but I tumbled to the floor. A blur of *medicine-doctoring* unfolded in front of me. The sick lady on the bed whimpered. She reached for the doctor's neck, shouting, "It's too late. You should have listened. I didn't want to … but it's too late."

I crawled on my knees, backing out of the doorway. Blood dripped from a sheet. The lady squirmed on the bed. A bucket with what looked like guts sat on the floor. I gagged, put my hand to my face, coughing.

From the corner, a shadow blocked my view. It was Margo and she picked up the guts, turned and glared at me. "Get out. Get out of here."

The doctor escorted me out of the room, slamming the door behind me. I charged back to Priscilla's room, closed her door, and shivered, almost forgetting to breathe. I wobbled and nearly fell to the floor. I shuffled to the window, pushing the window pane up, letting the cold air hit me in the face.

I gagged and lost my second breakfast out the window. I wiped my face on my sleeve, plopping down on the stool. I got up and walked in circles, going back to the window. I threw up again. I sat back down. I got up. Priscilla's lips were turning blue. The wind was too cold for her. Too cold for me, too. So I shut the window.

What is Margo doing here? What is wrong with the lady on the bed? Why was there so much blood? Why a bucket? I was scared to stay. Scared to leave. I told Taddy I would sit with his mama. I rubbed my ears and closed my eyes, disappearing to the place in my head where no one cries or dies.

A few minutes later, the piano in the waiting room played a song. It was a children's lullaby and the man's voice sang, "Rock-a-bye baby, in the tree top. When the wind blows, the cradle will rock."

I eased the door open, peeking into the front waiting room. The doctor sat at the piano, tapping keys. Margo was nowhere to be seen. I shut the door, and locked it. I slid with my back against the door and hugged the floor.

I will wait for Grandma to return. For Mahlee to stomp into the office. For Taddy to step inside. I should have kept the lucky rock.

The music stopped.

I put my ear to the door.

Bang. Bang. Bang.

I couldn't move.

Bang. Bang. Bang.

I'm not unlocking the door.

Before Noon on Day Two

A Grave for Two

I HELD MY STANCE, AND PRESSED against the door. I wasn't letting anyone into Priscilla's room.

Taddy's whine slipped into the room through the key hole. "Shoelace, are you in there? Doctor Rigghazel, are you with Mama? Someone open this door. I need to get in there with my mama."

Grandma and Mahlee's words muffled a duet of questions. Mahlee's bossy question came through like she had her mouth on the key hole. "Open this door. Why is it locked?"

I called to them through the hollow wood. "Mahlee? Grandma? Taddy?"

Taddy yelled and the door knob jiggled. "Shoelace, unlock this door. Let me in."

I stepped away from the door, wiped my mouth, sighing with relief. I twisted the little lock piece to open.

Taddy pushed me aside. "Why did you lock the door? You only lock doors when you get scared. Is she awake? Is she ..."

"No. She hasn't moved. And I never get scared." I lied to him while rubbing my hands together. I caught Mahlee looking at me. "I'm sorry the door was locked. I don't know how it latched itself."

Taddy kissed his mama's cheek. "Mama, I've washed up and put clean clothes on. My socks are fresh, too. Wake up. Please wake up." He wiped a tear from his eye, sitting on the stool like a little boy holding onto hope and wishing he was right.

Grandma and Mahlee moved to the two chairs by the wall and sat down. Grandma wiped her forehead. Mahlee tied her shoe and wiggled in her chair. They both glanced at Priscilla and wiggled some more, not paying any attention to me.

I inched to the door, glancing into the waiting room. No doctor, and no Margo. The piano sat quiet. The chairs were empty. I moved to the corner by the piano, sliding down the wall, cradling my knees. I whispered under my breath. "I don't know what to do. I can't say anything, but I should say everything. This doctor is no good for Priscilla. He's no good for the sick lady, either."

Mahlee peeked into the waiting room. "Who are you talking to?" She glared at me like she does when she thinks I'm up to something.

"Leave me alone. You're not my mama."

Grandma stepped from behind Mahlee. "Shoelace, stop talking back to Mahlee. We have enough worries right now."

"Yes, ma'am."

Mahlee leaned closer. "I might as well be your mama, since you need one. We've been here for one day. You've already disappeared and brought in a stray dog."

"You and me are strays and Grandma took us in when Daddy died."

Mahlee nodded. "Your grandma did, but she doesn't need a dog."

"Black Dog lives here. Go away. I'm just sitting here."

Mahlee nudged me. "Since when do you sit and do nothing?"

Ar roof. Ar roof.

I started to answer her, but instead ran to Priscilla's room to see if Black Dog was outside the window.

Ar roof. Ar roof.

Black Dog jumped on the windowsill with his paws.

I pressed my hand on the glass. "I'll be back in a minute." Grandma gave out an order. "Stay close. Stay out of trouble."

Mahlee followed me to the porch, spinning me around so I could face her. "What's got you scared? I know the look. It's like the one you used to get when your pa stayed gone too late or when he spent the night in jail."

"Nothing. I'm not afraid. I'm … I'm just sad."

"I don't buy it. You have something twirling around in that head. I know you. You are hiding something." Mahlee tugged on my sleeve. "Don't go far. Grandma Elsie has enough on her mind without worrying about you."

"I can take care of myself." I bounded off the porch. "Black Dog, where are you?" I gagged. "Black Dog, stop rolling in my vomit. You're gonna stink."

He pounced at me and I dodged him.

Ar roof. Ar roof.

"You're filthy. Let's see if the doctor has a water pump out back."

Ar roof. Ar roof.

Black Dog licked his leg, took a step, and wallowed around on the ground.

"Stop. That's nasty."

Black Dog rubbed up against my leg, whining.

A voice cried near the shed. "I'm sorry. I wanted to save you." Margo was talking to the gut-bucket. She grabbed a shovel by the metal can next to a rake, clutching the bucket to her side.

I leaned against the side of the back porch. I wanted to listen, but I stayed far enough to hide. I pushed Black Dog to the ground, whispering, "Sit, boy. Sit."

He darted off the other way, landing right in the puddle of vomit behind me. He rolled around in the dirt and muck.

Margo's voice soared to a high pitch. She spoke to the bucket again. "I tried to talk your mama out of this. She wanted to change her mind. Now, it's too late."

Margo carried the bucket, a small blanket, and the shovel. She walked past a trash barrel filled with ashes and old smells. She glanced at the ducks in the pond as they flapped in the water.

Quack. Quack. Quack.

She stepped toward the cemetery. "You will not be forgotten. I'm giving you a proper burial." She lumbered to a cemetery plot, near the same spot where she cried yesterday.

I ran behind a tree, spying on Margo.

She hunkered down on the ground, pouring the guts into the blanket. She rocked, holding the bundle. "I'm sorry, baby. I'm sorry." Margo put the blanket on the ground. She dug a hole, and gently placed the package of sadness into a small grave.

I cried with Margo as she patted the dirt. She collapsed into a ball, dropping the shovel. "Baby, go to heaven little one. God is waiting for you."

I fell to the ground by the tree, sobbing. *What is this doctor doing?*

Margo's pitch reminded me of Mahlee when she cries on Halloween night. I will stay out of Margo's way. I did follow her without having permission. I did trespass. Mahlee does crazy things when she gets scared. I have too. I act one way, but I want to act another. It can get confusing.

A woodpecker made dots on the tree above me. I shooed him. "Scat. Go away. Don't bother me."

He dove and fluttered in my face.

"Get away from me. Go away." I forgot to whisper this time, and slapped both hands over my mouth. I peeked around the tree.

Margo swung the shovel in the air. "Who is there? I know you're there."

I leaned on the tree, afraid to look around the trunk.

Margo ranted, her words shrieking. "I know someone is there. I know it."

From the back of the cemetery a lone voice called. "It's me, Margo. We've got a funeral today."

"Mr. Lewis. Sorry." Margo's tone changed, flipping like a somersault to a new personality. "How are you today? I've got to get back to the doctor's office. Plenty of work to do." She headed my way.

I ran to another tree near a cluster of bushes, moving myself closer to the doctor's office.

Peck. Peck. Peck.

I swatted at the bird. "Stop following me." I darted to the next tree, falling into an open grave. "Ouch! Yikes!" I spit dirt from my mouth, landing on something hard but soft. It placed its hand over my mouth.

"Be quiet, Margo will hear you."

I screamed in silence. I shook. I wiggled and jerked. What had grabbed me?

Margo called to someone. "Did you say something?"

Mr. Lewis answered. "No ma'am, I'm whistling while I work."

I pulled the hand from my face, rolling to the dirt. "What are you doing?"

Chula dusted her moccasins off. "I'm here to help. I made sure you fell into this grave so Margo wouldn't catch you."

"What? I fell. Period."

"No. I guided you here with my bird."

"No, you didn't." I pointed at Chula. "Who are you? What do you want with me? Yesterday, you pull a knife on me and today, you say you're helping me. Which is it? Are you my enemy or my friend?"

"We will find out soon. I saved you from Margo. She waves things at people and sometimes they get hurt."

"But where do you live? You were in the tree last night."

She pointed to nothing and everything. "I live in the trees. I ride the wind. I soar with eagles."

I wiped my face. "I should have known you'd give me an answer without an answer." I leaned my head back, looking up at the tree branches, wondering how to get out of the grave. "So little Indian-girl-who-soars-with-eagles, how are we getting out of this hole? Do you have an answer for that?"

Chula pulled out her flute while the woodpecker sat on her shoulder, bobbing his head.

Wooo....wooo.

I waved my hand in front of her face. "Hello, is this a good time to play the flute?"

She ignored me.

Crunch-roar-creak. Crunch-roar-creak.

The sound of wagon wheels on the gravel road grew louder. Chula stopped playing and smiled. "Boswell is here."

I ran to the end of the grave. "Help us. Over here in the ground."

Unknown Soul

Before Lunch

Stinky Day, Stinky Dog

BOSWELL'S FACE HUNG LOOSE FROM his jaw and his black braids dangled over our heads. "What are you two doing in that grave?"

A white man with no hair, whose skin stuck to his face, bent over, too. He scolded. "You shouldn't play in the cemetery."

I defended myself. "I fell in the hole. I'm not playing. She might be playing, but I almost got hurt."

Boswell shook his head. "This is a cemetery. They dig graves and have funerals here. Mr. Lewis works hard at keeping the grounds in order."

I rubbed my forehead. "I was watching something important. I didn't hurt any of his tombstones."

Chula put her hand over my mouth.

I pulled away, backing up, folding my arms.

The bald man muttered. "Something important? You were spying on Margo."

Boswell tipped his hat. "I'll take care of this, Mr. Lewis. You can get back to work."

"Good, I've got better things to do."

I reached up with both hands. "Can you hurry up? I need to get out of this hole. It sends bumps up my arms, and down my back. They are running all over my whole body."

"I've got a rope in the wagon. I'll be right back."

I pulled on one of Chula's braids. "You just thought you saved me. It looks like Boswell is the one in the saving business."

Chula pushed me. "I did save you. Biskinik pecking the tree kept Margo's shovel from hitting you in the head."

"So now your bird has a name? What kind of name is that?"

"It's Choctaw. It means woodpecker."

"Well, that's original."

"Hey, I may need to give you a Choctaw name."

"I have a hobo name. It's Shoelace. I'll keep that."

A rope with a loop tumbled down the side of the dirt wall. Boswell looked over the edge. "Put your foot in there and hold onto the rope. My mule will pull you out."

Chula shoved me back. "I'll go first." She stepped into the rope, swung her head at me. Her two braids waved in the air. "See you later."

"Not if I can help it."

Boswell clapped his hands and called to his mule. "Giddy up."

Seconds later, I tumbled from the grave onto the grass. Chula looked at me and spoke to Boswell. "Watch out for her. A chekusi nukhobela hinla."

I ran and pulled Chula's braid. "What did you say? You're talking Indian talk. What did you say?"

"Let go of my hair. I told Boswell you are a little on the hot-headed side. It's not just any Indian talk, it's Choctaw."

"Whatever. I am not hot-headed. I can be quiet and kind, but not to you. You've ratted on yourself. You're the one who is hot-headed and mean."

Boswell stepped between us. "We've got two girls with the same hot-headed personality."

58

Together we answered, "I'm not like her."

We looked at each other. Chula stormed off one way around the wagon. I bolted the other way. We met on the other side and put our backs to each other.

Mahlee watched from the doctor's porch. Her head shaking told me I had some explaining to do.

I ran to the porch, my words pouring through my lips like hot syrup on a stack of Grandma's pancakes. "I was playing with Black Dog and he got away. I thought he ran to the cemetery.

Mahlee didn't like my explanation. She dusted the dirt from my shirt, running her fingers through my bangs. "You are one big dirt-clod. Dirt just finds you."

"I was … I was … Oh, never mind. You never listen to me anymore. Taddy would hear me. He listens. I wish I could talk to him."

Mahlee put her hand on my shoulder, turning me around. "And by the way, Black Dog has been asleep on the porch. Don't get too close. He smells like he fell into a barrel of spoiled milk and rotten eggs. So, tell me the truth, what were you doing at the cemetery?"

"Nothing. I was playing." I took off toward the orphan school. I stopped in front of the church, yelling back at Mahlee. "I'm going to change clothes. Tell Grandma where I am."

Mahlee called to me from the road. "Stay out of the way at Wheelock, and hurry up."

With each step, my thoughts kept going back to the face of Margo holding the bucket. To what happened in the doctor's office with the lady. I wish I could talk to Mahlee about it. I can't talk to her when she acts like a grownup. I don't know what to do. I don't know what is happening. Margo has secrets. The doctor has secrets. And now I do.

Ar roof. Ar roof. Ar roof.

I spun around and Black Dog jumped on me, knocking me down. He licked my face. "Yuck. Nasty tongue. A worse smell."

He chewed on my shoelace, tugging until he yanked my shoe from my foot.

"These shoes are my favorite. They are the fastest running shoes and now, you've slobbered on them."

Ar roof. Ar roof.

My shoe dropped from Black Dog's mouth. I picked it up, shaking my head. "Silly dog. Stinky dog." I put on my shoe and tied the laces in a double knot.

My temporary dog raced me to the flower arbor. He jumped to the top of the steps by the dining hall door. The matron barreled out the door, bumping Black Dog from the steps.

Roof-ow. Roof-ow.

The Matron moved to him. "I'm sorry dog. I didn't see you."

I came up beside her. "He's not hurt, is he?"

"No. He's fine." She pinched her nose. "He sure does stink. What in the world have you two been doing? You're covered in red dirt and he's covered in something from a trash pile. He smells like an outhouse."

"He rolled around in a stinky mess at the doctor's office. I got into my own stink, too."

"Come with me." The matron moved to the back of the building down the sidewalk. "The water pump is by the water tower. I keep a washtub for stinky messes."

Black Dog danced in circles around the matron, following her, tugging on her skirt with his teeth.

Grrr. Grrr.

She swatted his head. "Stop. You are two growls away from not having a home."

I rolled the tub from the side of the building, pumping water into it. The matron went inside, returning with soap powder and a rag. "Here, put this in the water. A little soap will clean up the stink."

"Yes, ma'am." I took the cup and sprinkled in the soap.

The matron went to Wilson Hall, leaving me with Black Dog. I splashed water onto his matted hair and mixed the rest of the soap into his fur. Bubbles floated in the breeze. He shook more times than I could count. "Black Dog, I was just dirty. Now, I'm muddy-wet. Yikes!" I slipped into the tub and Black Dog fell on me. "Black Dog, now I'm soaking wet. I'm freezing."

He licked my nose and twirled around, swiping his tail across my face. He spun back around, taking the rag from my hand with his teeth, playing tug-of-war. He jumped from the tub, loping across the grass toward the double doors leading into Wilson Hall.

"Come back here." I pinned him in the corner on the small porch leading into the school's classrooms. The door swung open as my grip slipped from his soapy hair.

Black Dog jogged past three girls. One of them screamed. "This dog is wet. He's soapy, too. You better catch him."

Black Dog darted down the hallway. The doors on the right were shut, but at the second door on the left, he raced into a classroom.

Ahhh! Yikes! Ahhh!

He ran up and down, past the desks. He circled the teacher who was standing in her chair. The girls were hollering. "Catch the dog! Catch the dog!"

Eleanor clapped her hands and called to him. "Come boy. Come to me."

Black Dog skidded to a halt, his tongue hanging like he thought he'd obey her, but his paws slid on the hardwood floor. He took out Eleanor, sending her crashing into the wall. She giggled with her whole body. "Black Dog. You're a thunderstorm of fun."

He charged into the hallway, skirting past the quilts on the wall. I trailed him down some stairs leading to a basement, but he rebounded right back up. He knocked over a loom and some baskets at the top of the stairs. He headed for the front door while dozens of wanna-be-dog-catchers chased him.

One girl called, "Come here, puppy!"

Another Indian girl put her back to the wall. "I don't like dogs. I don't ..."

Black Dog stopped next to her like he was trying to show his good side. He licked her hand. Then he resumed his race, knocking over some of the smaller girls.

Eleanor had joined the chase. "This is great. School was boring. Now we're having fun."

Black Dog was trapped, his wild doggy legs shot in every direction. He toppled toward the closed doors, rolling like a wet ball into the corner.

Ar roof. Ar roof.

A teacher scolded me. "Get that dog out of Wilson Hall. We have work to do. You have wreaked havoc in our school."

I inched up to her, scowling. "I haven't done anything. The matron is the one who gave me the soap."

The teacher pointed to the door. "Take him outside. We have to finish our history lesson."

I muttered under my breath while Black Dog nudged my leg with his nose. I touched his ear, mocking the teacher. "We have *work* to do. We have *work* to do." I scratched his head. "And I don't. I'm out of school until we go home."

Eleanor tapped me on the shoulder. "Meet me tonight at the top of the stairs after lights out. I want to show you something."

The Noon Sun on Day Two

Run Away Margo

BLACK DOG NAPPED ON THE steps by the dining hall. I stepped over him, went inside, changing clothes. I put my shoes by the wall furnace in the kitchen to dry. I plopped down in a chair. I glanced to my left, and counted 33 chairs on one side. Across the room, Bright Eyes sipped on a glass of milk, hiccupping in-between leftover sobs.

I moved from my chair, danced to her table, and sat down.

One of the kitchen ladies spoke to me. "She is having quiet time to think on her actions. She hit one of the other toddlers in the front room with a rag doll."

I mimicked the lady's words. "Quiet time? She's pretty quiet."

Bright Eyes grinned at me, her milk mustache widening.

The kitchen lady introduced herself. "I'm Mrs. Motes. My husband is the missionary here at Wheelock Academy. We live in the house next to the staff quarters. We're Presbyterians."

I raised my eyebrows. "I'm Baptist. But we like *Pedestrians*."

She laughed, patted my head, and moved to the stove where a large pan held crusty food with something purplish-blue. "Would you like a sandwich and then a slice of my blackberry cobbler?"

"Blackberry cobbler? I love chocolate cake better. My grandma bakes. Your cobbler does look yummy, though."

"I make pudding and cobblers when not cooking meals for the girls. Most of the younger ones like what I muster up, but the cobbler's a hit with all of them."

I looked at the saucer with purple streaks sitting in front of Bright Eyes. I spun the plate around. "If you get in trouble here, do you get dessert?"

Mrs. Motes put her finger to her lips. "Shhh. The matron and the other staff are tougher than I am. I tend to think if you're in trouble, a little extra love is what you need."

I smiled. Mrs. Motes' words were firm, but she was kind like a fly swatter without the sting. Her brown hair was pulled back in a clasp. Her freckles reminded me of Sally O'Malley, my cousin, who has freckles from walking too close to cows.

Mrs. Motes slapped a piece of bologna on bread and handed me a glass of milk. "Eat up. Supper will be late tonight. We're having chicken and dumplings."

"Thank you. I got sick earlier. My tummy's growling now."

Bright Eyes scooted her chair closer to me. She smiled with a berry-blue grin and ran her fingers down my arm.

I pointed at her face. "Your mouth is the same color as your cobbler."

Bright Eyes put her hand over her mouth, but I could tell her eyes were smiling.

I took a bite of cobbler, smacking, and swallowing. I grinned at her. "Are my teeth blue?"

A small giggle slipped out from Bright Eyes and she nodded.

**

Creeeeakkkk. Bam.

The dining hall door slammed with a blur rushing inside. The curtain on the window waved like it was surrendering from the fight. Black Dog had crept in behind Mahlee. He crawled under the table.

Mahlee stormed in a circle by the wall. "I'm done. I'm packing my clothes and taking the next train out of Millerton. I'm going back to Texarkana. I'll get Boswell to run me to Boggy Depot to check the times and get a ticket. Margo is nuts. I'm not staying here so she can hit me with that shovel again." Mahlee stormed in her boots, mouthing and repeating her words until they became a squeal.

I ran to Mahlee. "Did you see Margo? Tell me what happened."

Mahlee snorted, wiped her face, and shook her head. "See this bruise on my arm? Margo walloped me with her shovel. Who carries a shovel inside a doctor's office?"

"Margo hit you?"

"Yes. She's crazy. Flat out crazy. Worse than me."

"Why did she hit you?"

"It wasn't my fault. I was in the waiting room at the doctor's office, standing by the piano. I was looking at the pictures of the little Indian girls. She roared into the room. When she saw me, the color in her face drained. It was like she saw a ghost."

"Do you think she remembered you? From the hospital in Memphis?"

"She may have. She could have. I don't know."

"So she just ran at you with her shovel?"

Mahlee sat down. "No. I asked her why she ran off yesterday. I asked her why she wrote Priscilla a letter if she didn't want to come home. And then ..."

66

"What did she say?"

"She shook her head and yelled at me."

"But why did she hit you?"

Mrs. Motes set a bologna sandwich in front of Mahlee, but Mahlee pushed it away. The cobbler lady motioned to Bright Eyes who got up, and they quietly left the room.

Mahlee started pacing in circles again.

I grilled Mahlee and paced with her. "What did Margo say?"

"…She said that she didn't send the letter. She accused me of lying. I told her Priscilla got a letter from her. I reminded Margo about the blue ring, the one from her daddy, the one she gave me in Memphis. I told her how Priscilla saw it and thought I'd stolen it. I told her how I gave hers to Priscilla, how this one, the ring on my finger, is mine. I told her that Priscilla and me made up when she found out I hadn't taken it. How she gave me my own ring for Christmas. She kept calling me a liar."

I leaned in for more details. "But why did she hit you?"

"Because … because … I slapped her after she swung that shovel at my head. I lost my temper, and I walloped her."

"But Mahlee, you can't go around hitting people. It doesn't help. You have told me that yourself."

Mahlee rubbed her bruise. "Last year, I argued with Priscilla over a ring … and now I'm arguing with her twin sister over things that don't include me."

"So you started the fight?"

"No. I was standing by the piano, but I did finish it. My hands swung at her face. I know I shouldn't have. Now I can't stay. I'm making things worse."

I gave Mahlee advice. "You have to stay. You're big, tough, and strong. We can use you."

Shalung. Bam.

Grandma fell through the door, breathing hard. "Mahlee, what happened? Why did you and Margo have a fight?"

Mahlee pulled a chair out for Grandma. "Sit down. You're gonna have a stroke. Margo is crazy. I'm going home."

Grandma wheezed, her hand going to her throat. "So did you hit Margo?"

"Yes, but it got mixed up in my head like things do every Halloween. Margo called me a liar. I don't lie."

Grandma took Mahlee's hand. "We'll figure this out. Margo's run off again. We can sort this out. We can."

Mahlee put her hands on her hips. "I'm packing. I'm not staying another day. I'm going to the manor."

I jumped in front of Mahlee. "Mrs. Motes said love can ease our hurting. She said dessert helps, too. Do you want some cobbler?"

Mahlee pushed me. "Girl, you can't solve this kind of problem with sweets."

Grandma moved next to me. "Sweets won't fix this. But if we stay together and work on our problems, we'll find a way to make sense of the confusion. Mahlee, you can't run away every time things get hard. Margo needs us. And maybe … just maybe … we can help her."

Mahlee gritted her teeth. "But she says she didn't send Priscilla the letter."

Grandma rubbed her face. "Then someone cared enough to send it for her. We have to find a way to take her home with us."

Mahlee toppled back and landed in a chair, shaking her head. She exhaled a sigh like a squeal, picking up her sandwich. She then ate the rest of mine, gobbling the food down in four bites. She got up, pouring herself a glass of milk.

"Cobbler. I need some cobbler. Maybe a little sweet dessert will help after all."

I stepped next to Mahlee. "So, you'll stay? You're not leaving?"

"I'll stay. Your grandma needs me. I guess I need her, too."

I twirled in a circle. "What about me? Anyone need me?"

Grandma grabbed me. "I need my Annie Grace Kree. She's the fastest runner in our family, among other things."

Mrs. Motes returned to the kitchen counter and shuffled plates and glasses in the sink. I pointed at her. "She's married to the missionary. She's a *Pedestrian*."

Grandma giggled. "You mean Presbyterian."

"That's what I said …"

Mahlee rubbed her arm again. "This reunion is going to be tougher than we thought."

I laughed at Mahlee. "Your teeth are blue."

Grandma gave a belly laugh. "I may need some cobbler, too."

Mrs. Motes turned around. "I'll get you a piece. Cobbler is my specialty. Well, vanilla pudding is, too."

I walked to a window and gazed outside, thinking about the crazy things happening, the crazy things that felt scary. Just thinking about Margo's threats made me shiver. I wanted to tell Grandma. I wanted to let Mahlee know how dangerous Margo might really be. But somehow, telling them might put Taddy in more danger. I can't do that to him.

Black Dog scooted up next to me, licking my fingers.

Ring-a-ling. Ring-a-ling.

The matron flew in from a side hallway, stumbling on my shoes by the furnace. She hurried to the phone by the ice box. "Hello. Yes. Yes. I'll tell them. Thank you so much." She hung up the phone, turning to us. "Doctor Rigghazel said Priscilla is stirring … she might be waking up."

The Afternoon of Day Two

Margo's Reality

THE MATRON TOSSED THE KEYS to Mahlee, but she didn't keep them long. Grandma snatched them from her hand. "You're not driving. You scare me when you get behind the wheel."

The matron spoke. "Watch the brakes. They're touchy."

Mahlee argued. "What's wrong with my driving? I haven't run over anyone yet."

Grandma mocked her. "Not yet. And not today, either."

The three of us rushed to the side door of the dining hall, but the matron called to us. "You need to go this way." She pointed the opposite way down the hall. "The car's in the driveway on the east side of the dorm."

We bounced off each other and ran across the kitchen. *Creak. Creak.*

I stopped in the doorway, looking back. The dining hall door opened, and the orphan girls piled into the kitchen. They each took a seat while Mrs. Motes put some of the older girls to work making sandwiches.

Eleanor waved at me. "Hey, Shoelace. Come sit with me for lunch." The room was filling up with giggles and chatter.

I yelled. "I have to go. Taddy's mama might be waking up."

Bam-slam.

I ran into the wall, hitting my head.

I read Eleanor's lips. "Watch out for the wall. I'll see you tonight. You don't want to miss the fun."

I called to her. "I'll meet you later. I'll be there."

In the car, I leaned forward with my chin on the front seat. "Taddy will be so excited. I can't believe Priscilla is waking up."

Grandma steered the car, holding the wheel with a death grip. "This is great news."

Mahlee agreed, patting Grandma's leg. "Yes, Taddy needs his mama."

I listened to the gravel being spit from behind the tires. Every pebble. Every crunch. Every noise. I looked out the window. "Hey, Black Dog is chasing us."

Mahlee turned her head. "Yep, he's a fast runner like you. He's cutting across the front of the grounds. He'll beat us there."

Grandma drove like she was in a get-away car, a slow one going twenty miles per hour. She pulled into the driveway between the cemetery and the doctor's house. She turned off the car, bounding to the porch. Mahlee was right behind her, and I was on their heels.

Black Dog sat at the end of the porch facing the pond, growling at the ducks.

Grrr. Grrr. Ar roof. Ar roof.

The ducks flapped their wings and flew to the roof.

Quack. Quack. Quack.

I called to him. "Black Dog, what are you doing? Come here."

He rushed to my side, with his tongue hanging out.

"Good boy. Stay. I'll be right back."

I rushed into Priscilla's room, expecting to see Taddy smiling and hugging his mama. Instead, Grandma held him in her lap, whispering, "Your mama's going to wake up soon. Her head will heal. Her legs, too. She'll be as good as new." Mahlee hovered close, not talking, just standing. She rocked in her shoes, wiping a rare Mahlee-tear from her face.

Doctor Rigghazel came into the room. "I'm sorry to get your hopes up. It was a false alarm."

Taddy cried. "You heard her. She spoke. She called for Margo."

The doctor moved toward Taddy. "She did, but it was a fretful cry, like a nightmare. It was probably a subconscious reaction to coming here. It happens sometimes when the brain gets injured."

Taddy sat up and cried. "Her brain is hurt? Will she wake up? Will she know me? What will she remember?"

"Of course, she'll know you. She will, you'll see. For now, she needs rest. The accident was only yesterday." Doctor Rigghazel placed his hand on Priscilla's arm. "She's a fighter. She'll make it."

Grandma ran her fingers through Taddy's hair. "You need to sleep at Wheelock tonight. A good night's rest will be good for you."

"But I don't want to. I want to stay here."

"Tonight, you can sleep in a featherbed, wrap up in a warm quilt, and pretend you're home."

Taddy whined. "But I'm not home. I wish we'd never come here. I wanted to learn about Choctaw girls and what they teach them here. I was going to write an extra credit report to take to Ms. Reece at school, but I don't care anymore. I don't want to go to school if Mama doesn't get well."

I scolded Taddy. "You will want to go to school. You're a living encyclopedia. You love to learn, and your mama will get well, I promise."

"You know how well you keep promises."

"I know, but this one is for real. She's going to be fine."

Mahlee bolted over to the doctor, her hands rubbing together in fists. "Mr. Doctor, I have some questions for you. What was Margo doing here today with a shovel?"

The doctor rubbed the stubby hair on his chin. "Why? What do you mean? Margo works here. She does errands and cleans up the rooms."

"But a shovel?" Mahlee pressed him for an answer.

"She gets confused sometimes. She tends to bury things. But on a good day, she's a hard worker. Today, you scared her. She wasn't expecting to see you."

Mahlee mouthed. "She saw us yesterday on the road. She knows we're here. It's not like we just got here."

The doctor sailed through a long explanation while twitching two fingers together. "Today we had a sick patient in the other room, and a lot of blood causes Margo to react without reason. I've gotten used to her. I don't ask many questions. Questions just get her riled up."

I moved closer to take mental notes like I was doing a 'vestigation. The doctor knew more, but he wasn't telling Mahlee the whole story.

I burst out with a few questions of my own. "So where did she go? Why does she run off? Why was she crying at the cemetery yesterday? Why was she crying at the cemetery today? What is wrong with Margo?"

The doctor shook his head. "Margo has a past that haunts her in the present. She has trouble distinguishing between reality."

I looked at Mahlee. "Are you having trouble with reality, too?"

"Mind your own business, little lady. I get mixed up, but I figure it out." Mahlee turned away from me and faced the window.

I pressed the doctor for more answers. "Will she come back today?"

"Probably not. She's known for disappearing for days. Not long back, I didn't see her for six months."

Mahlee turned around and interrupted. "She just showed up to work? Why would you let her return?"

"When she works, she has structure. When she has structure, she has good days. With you coming, well, having visitors took away her structure. She got rattled with all the rumors." Doctor Rigghazel turned to the doorway. "I'll check on Priscilla later. My room is the door on the left in the back if you need me."

Mahlee quizzed him, blocking the doorway. "But wait, she sent Priscilla a letter. Or someone did. The letter said for Priscilla to come. If she didn't send the letter, then who did?"

"I couldn't say. She hasn't many friends." The doctor brushed by Mahlee, leaving the room.

Ar roof. Ar roof.

I scooted to the front porch to check on Black Dog. He was yapping at Chula, the *little savior* who hasn't saved anyone yet. She played her flute, as she sat on the church roof.

Woooo...looo...coo.

I'm going to ignore her. I am ... I'm going to pretend I don't see her. I'm not walking across the road to her. I'm not.

I am.

Late Afternoon Lessons

Leaning Posts

I MARCHED FROM THE PORCH across the dirt road, my shoes plopping in the sand. "Why are you spying on me? Why do you sit up on the roof? Is it so I can't sock you?" I stepped forward, twisting my foot on a rock. The blood on the ground from where the horse trampled Priscilla the day before reminded me of the pain this trip is causing. I moved to the side. "Tell me why you are watching me."

"I'm not spying on you. I'm sitting. This is my spot. My music floats in the breeze and the woodpeckers dance with my tunes." Chula placed the end of the flute in her mouth. With each breath, the squeaky toots became a poem of notes.

I shook my head. "Your music doesn't make me want to dance. I'm not listening to you play." I put my hands over my ears. I wasn't going to enjoy her music. But I did.

A zoom-zoom flutter of wings came too close to my face and the woodpecker tried to peck me with his beak. "Stop. I'm not a piece of wood." I swung my fist at the red-headed bird, but he soared in circles so high I lost him in the sun's glare. Then he appeared like a shadow against the ball of light in the sky, landing on Chula's shoulder. He bobbed his head with her music.

Chula finished playing, held onto the tree branches hanging over the roof, and stood near the edge. She called to me. "This is your lesson for today. Look for the leaning fence posts. Follow a post whenever you get lost. Follow the lean and you'll know which way to walk."

"I'm not doing what you say. I am not in school. Besides, you aren't my mama. You're the same tall as me. I am not listening to you."

"I'm here to help you." Chula put her flute in her pocket, and swung her hand like she was drawing a picture in the wind. "When you come to the pole at the end of the trail you'll find one standing alone and upright. Watch for it. They are rare, but they are the best."

"You are talking in circles. I'm with my grandma and with Tin Can Mahlee, and my best friend, Taddy. We are here to bring Margo home, not look for posts."

Ar roof. Ar roof.

Black Dog scampered in the soft dirt, causing cloud puffs of sand to swirl in mini-tornadoes around his paws. I danced with him in the road and yelled to Chula without looking at her. "Your lessons aren't for me. I'm not here to learn anything."

Silence.

I looked at the church. Chula was gone, again.

Ar roof. Ar roof.

Black Dog barked at the water rushing under the bridge. I ran to him and heard rustling, like someone stepping on crunchy leaves. I moved to the edge of the bridge, leaned over, and peeked between the trees and the bamboo.

Chula called from somewhere. "This is Cry Baby Bridge. Many who cross it never return."

"I know you're hiding in the bamboo. Stop with the riddles."

"They are not riddles. Remember, I am here to save you. And you are here to save others."

Crunch. Crunch. Swoosh.

"Chula? Are you there?"

Silence.

I inch closer to the bamboo. I want to follow Chula, to see where she hides, but Grandma's face keeps popping in front of my eyes. Her scolding in my head shouts louder than the swaying bamboo. If I stay close to the river, I can hurry back. Or follow it to Wheelock. I shake Grandma from my thoughts, and scamper like a rabbit down the trail. I holler for Chula. "Where are you?"

She didn't answer, but the wind whispered a sound like a chorus of owls hooting in daylight.

Shoooow. Shoooow.

"Where are you?"

No answer.

I marched beside the river, and the bamboo forest blocked the sun. I moved along in the shadows. Chills ran up my back, and crawled down my arms. My shoes sank in the mushy ground, and I grabbed for trees and bushes to balance myself. I whispered to the bush poking me in the face. "Wheelock can't be too far."

Skrack. Skrack. Skrack.

The noises clanked above me in the branches, and the wind howled around the bare limbs like they were having a sword fight.

Swoosh. Swoosh. Slamp. Snap. Skrack.

I spun around. "Who's there?" I put my back against a tree. A tall shadow hid behind a bush. No, it was a short shadow. No, it's tall now. Could Chula be playing tricks on me?

Hooooooowl. Hooooooowl. Skrack. Skrack.

The branches high above me fought in the wind, and two limbs close to me beat together like drum sticks on a drum. A group of birds sang sour notes, and a long howl reminded me of a wolf's cry. Whatever or whoever is howling in these woods was behind that bush. I ran the other direction, and the mushy ground got muddier. My PF Flyers stuck like suction cups.

Splat. Splat. Skrack. Skrack.

I stopped, and it felt like my heart might stop, too. I'm going back to the doctor's office. But the trees all look alike. The paths look the same. I have no idea which way to go. I'm stuck in the middle of shadows and noises, and afraid to move.

Hoooooooowl. Hoooooooowl. Slamp. Skrack.

"Who is following me? Chula, are you there?" My shoes were fixed to the mud. I toppled forward, landing on my knees. To my right … a wooden post leaned toward a narrow path behind a tree.

I pulled myself up and decided to follow the post. I could hear wolf-paw splats behind me. Something was tracking me and bearing in for the kill.

A patch of weeds taller than me blocked the path. I couldn't go forward. I shook. I sank to the ground, sitting in the mud.

Skrack. Skrack.

I rolled to my side, and edged my way under the bush. I hit my head on a wooden post. It leaned to the left. Toward a new way. I crushed the weeds with my knees, and tumbled into a small clearing, where the sun lit the ground. I got up, rushed ahead, and jumped over bushes. I dove under patches of tall spindly weeds, and ran up a hill.

Skrack. Skrack.

At the top of the hill, the woods thickened, and I fumbled around in circles. I found myself standing in a muddy spot by a tree where I'd already left my footprints.

The trees draped over me like a roof that was caving in, and the branches clung together like bars on a jail. A curtain of fear hung behind the tree trunks, and the forest was ready to grab me by the neck. I need to find another wooden post. And I need to find it now.

Zip. Zip. Snap.

A high-pitched voice called out like a wolf. "Get out of my woods. Get out of my life. Go home. Leave now. And never come back."

Whipple. Snap.

I fell to the ground, and my hands went to my throat. I tried to get the rope over my head, but it tightened around my neck. My breath got stuck inside my chest, and I gagged.

A voice cried. "It's a day to live. Not die. It's a day to leave, too. Get out of my town."

The rope rippled, slapping me in the face. I yanked the now loose rope from my neck and tossed it to the ground, and rushed to a patch of trees. A leaning post beside my leg next to a thicket of tall weeds showed me the way.

I shouted. "Margo, if that's you ... If you are trying to scare me, it's not working. You better leave me alone." I yelled like a bear ready to claw her, although my shoulders shook like a kitten lost on a trail.

Four trees later, a rope dropped from above and dangled in my face. I froze, and clutched my neck.

Margo warned. "You best leave. Be on your way. Don't tell a soul about today, or Taddy will be the one with the rope burns. I can lasso anyone. You won't see me coming. He won't, either."

I cut through a patch of thorn bushes, tore my overalls, and cut my leg. The blood soaked my sock, and the scratches on my arms burned. I staggered, kept moving, and lost track of time. It felt like hours trudging inside the thicket, listening to the howl of Margo in the trees behind me.

She hollered. "I don't need a family. I never asked you to come."

A streak of light shone on the path in front of me, parting the way to Wilson Hall. To my right, a tall, upright post pointed to heaven. I was going the right way.

I hurried past the shrubs and weeds, running to Wheelock. I jogged up the slope, and Chula sat in a tree. She wiggled her moccasins in the wind, grinning. "Did you get lost on the trail?"

I wanted to slap her, but I yelled instead. "I didn't get lost. I got ... got chased. Margo is crazy. She chased me in the woods."

"She can be, but did you see the leaning posts? They helped you find your way, didn't they?"

I frowned.

"Come sit up here. We can see the lake."

I climbed the tree thinking that if I got close enough to her, I could knock Chula out. I sat with the flute-playing girl, and my hand went to her shoulder.

Chula pushed my arm away. "Knock me off, and you'll not find another post of safety. I'm helping you. You need me."

"I don't need you." I could smell her breath. "Do you smoke?"

She patted a small leather pouch on her hip. "Maybe. A little. I have a pipe. Boswell taught me."

Ar roof. Ar roof.

Black Dog raced up the hill, howling at us.

Hooooooowl.

Chula swung from the branch, landing in a ball on the ground next to Black Dog. She waved her arm at me. "Follow the wooden posts, and you'll always find your way home.

"I won't get lost. I'm not going in those woods again."

Chula ran down the slope toward the water, taking off across the stone bridge.

I climbed down from the tree and looked at the cut on my leg. It's not too deep, no need for stitches. No need to tell Grandma about it, either.

"Shoelace. Hey, over here."

I spun around and saw Eleanor waving and jumping up and down. I waved back, and noticed her smile stretches longer than the trail of tears in the woods. Longer than Margo's rope. Longer than a rushing river. Longer than anything. When I'm with Eleanor, life feels good.

We'll be friends for life.

Night Ends on Day Two

When Life Pierces

THE GIRLS WERE DISMISSED FROM their classes for the afternoon and they scampered to the grassy areas to play. Some carried sticks with little baskets on the end. They formed teams and started chasing a small ball up and down the field.

Another group of girls picked teams for basketball. Eleanor was on one of them. "Hey. Come play basketball with us."

I stood next to the concrete court. "I've never played."

She threw the ball, hitting me in the chest. "Hey, I wasn't ready."

Eleanor laughed. "Then, get yourself ready." She ran after the ball as it rolled into the driveway.

Grandma drove the matron's sedan, stopping short of hitting the ball. She frowned at me, rolled the window down, and motioned with her finger. "Annie Grace. Look at you. You are filthy. Get inside, and get yourself a bath. I don't want to know what you've been up to."

I turned to Eleanor who held the basketball. "I'm sorry. I'm in trouble."

Eleanor whispered in my ear. "Meet me after lights out, and I'll show you the secret passage."

"I will. I'll be there."

Grandma ordered. "Inside. Now. Take a bath. It's nearly time for supper."

Eleanor ran up to me, cupping her hand to my ear. "After we eat, some of us are having an ear-piercing party on the stairs. Meet me there first."

"I don't want my ears pierced, but I'll watch."

Eleanor raced to the court, tossing the basketball to a teammate. She called to me as the ball swooshed through the net. "See you in a little while."

**

Grandma and Mahlee were downstairs talking with the staff in the dining hall. Taddy was curled up asleep in a featherbed downstairs, tuckered out from a long two days.

The orphans were doing their nighttime school work. Some copied each other's papers. A few whined while doing their math. A couple of girls giggled.

I sat on my cot and slipped on a pair of clean socks. The smell-good shirt felt soft on my skin, and my leg had stopped bleeding. I ran my hand over my overalls, one of several pair that I have. Grandma has tried to get me to wear dresses. So far, I'm not. She's not too happy with my engineer's cap, either. But I don't wear it so much these days.

I sauntered across the floor to the stairs, sliding along the wooden slats.

Eleanor put her finger to her mouth. "Shhh! We have to be quiet, and we must hurry before the matron comes and turns out the light."

Three Indian girls stared at me. Their chocolate eyes looked like marbles, shiny like copper. One of them spoke. "You sure have pretty blonde hair. Can I touch it?"

"Sure. It's just hair. It's still kind of wet. I just washed it."

The other one put her arm next to mine. "You are pale. You need to get outside more. Is that a scar?"

"Yes. I broke my arm, and the bone poked through my skin. I was saving my cat from a chicken hawk."

The girl touched my scar. "Did you save your cat?"

"Yes. His name is White Beard. He's waiting for me at home."

Eleanor held up her fingers, and pressed her thumb and first finger together on one of the girl's ears. "It's time for the numbing."

I leaned in. "What? You pinch someone's earlobe?"

"Yes. I have magic fingers. I love piercing everyone's ears. The new girls ask me to do it. I've got this down to an exact three-minute cycle."

I rubbed my ear. "It sounds like it hurts."

The girl who had touched my arm spoke. "Not as much as breaking your arm."

Eleanor explained. "I pinch the skin until it's numb. Then I take a threaded needle, and poke the skin."

The girl who had touched my hair, whimpered. "I don't like to get hurt. My daddy used to hit me, and my mama would decide how many licks I got. She would count them off, one through seven every time."

I reached for her hand. "My friend, Mahlee, grabs my ears when she's mad at me. She'd love to paddle me if she thought she'd get away with it."

The whimpering girl smiled. "I'm still afraid."

I moved closer to her. "I'll do it first. If it doesn't hurt, then you can do it." I volunteered to show how tough I was to a group of girls on a staircase. Mostly, I was doing it for the girl whose daddy used to hit her.

Next, Eleanor pinched my earlobe, squeezing hard. "Count to sixty two times."

Another girl, whose hand twitched, got close to my ear. "Can you feel her pinching you?"

"Yes, but it doesn't hurt."

"When she sticks you with that needle it will. I'm not so sure I'll get mine pierced."

I felt myself getting lightheaded, but I wasn't letting them know. Needles don't make me brave, they make me flinch.

The twitching girl took my hand. "Your face is whiter than white and getting paler."

"I'm fine. I can do this."

The girl who played with my hair wrapped her fingers in a strand. "Do you have a daddy?"

"Not anymore. He died last year."

"Do you have a mama?"

"No, she died when I was born, but I look like her."

"So they never hurt you?"

"Well, my daddy was a hobo and he stole me from my grandma when I was five. I know that hurt my grandma. On the nights he left me alone, that hurt me. But I never let him know."

"So, you're like us. You're an orphan, too."

"I was, but my grandma is raising me now. And Mahlee is, too."

Eleanor took her fingers from my earlobe. "I'm going to pull the needle through, cut the thread, and tie it off. We're going to put Vicks on your ear lobe so it won't get infected. You'll need to keep pulling the thread through until it heals."

"I'm ready."

"Here I go." Eleanor shoved the needle through, and the other girls gasped. I felt no pain. Then she did my other ear, squeezing and squeezing until it was time to run the needle through. Minutes later, it was over.

I touched both my ears. "Oh, my gosh. I have pierced ears."

The girl whose daddy had hurt her sat down in my place. "I'm ready. I want my ears pierced like hers. She's brave."

I played with the thread on each ear. "I'm not so brave. But my friend, Taddy, thinks I am. Hey, this Vicks goo smells and burns my nose."

Eleanor laughed. "Stop rubbing your nose after touching your ears. Vicks will burn your nose."

I tapped the arm of the girl who took my place. "How did you get away from your mean daddy?"

"One day, Mama sent me to my aunt's house to live, because she didn't have enough money to feed me. My aunt brought me here three years ago, when I was six."

I smelled the Vicks on my fingers. "I'm sorry. Why did she do that?"

"She ran out of food. Before I came here, my aunt said my mama was braver than anyone. Daddy believed in too many licks when he paddled me, and my mama would take most of them. I never knew that."

I wiped tears from my eyes. "Your mama is brave. She's the best."

"She was the best. She died right after I got here. One night, my daddy hurt her for the last time. And now, he's in jail. I hope I get adopted someday."

Eleanor interrupted us. "We are having an ear-piercing party. Imogene, your first ear is already done."

Imogene rubbed her ear and smiled. "My mama had pierced ears."

I smiled. "When you touch your ears, you'll think of her."

"I will. I'll never forget this."

Eleanor gave out instructions. "Shoelace, change sides with me. I need to pinch her other ear lobe."

I moved out of the way. "Who's crying?" Sobs like a sad bell losing its tune came from behind me. I glanced up and down the hall and Bright Eyes wept. She wiped tears from her face with the back of her hand.

I slid to her in my socks. "Bright Eyes, what's wrong?"

She shook her head, and put her fingers to her ears.

"Do you want pierced ears?"

She twisted her head fast and hard.

"What then? What do you want?"

She cried and ran back to the bedroom.

I looked at Eleanor. "Why is she crying?"

Eleanor held her fingers on Imogene's ear. "She cries over everything. Maybe she's wishing for a mama, too."

We all exhaled together like a dozen balloons losing air. I realized I wasn't the only little girl in the world who wished for perfect parents or for the perfect home. These girls want what I want. I sighed, rubbed my nose, and smelled Vicks. Getting my ears pierced made the night perfect.

Plop. Plop. Plop.

We all stood to attention like five statues.

I whispered, "It's my grandma."

Eleanor nudged me. "But look who's right behind her."

The matron towered over the five of us. "What do we have here? Who is responsible for this?"

I stepped forward. "I am. This was my idea."

Grandma frowned and moved closer. "When did you learn how to pierce ears?"

Eleanor pushed me aside. "It's me. Take me to the gallows." She put her hand to her face, giggling under her breath.

The matron didn't smile.

Nor Grandma.

Day Two Never Ends

Secrets of the Heart

GRANDMA SAVED ME FROM THE wrath of the matron by taking me to her room downstairs. I peeked in on Taddy, who slept in the room across the hall. "He's snoring. He must be tired."

Grandma nodded. "The last two days have been the hardest on him." She tugged on my arm. "Come to my room. We need to talk. Let him sleep."

I scooted in my sock feet to the bed in Grandma's room, falling across the mattress. "I like your bed. We have little cots upstairs."

"You can sleep in here with Mahlee and me if you want."

"No. I have new friends. Eleanor, Bright Eyes, and Imogene. I'll sleep with them."

"Shoelace, if I let you sleep upstairs, you need to behave. Many of these girls need homes and they are being educated in American ways. We don't want to interfere with their structure."

I rolled over on the bed, sinking into the soft quilt. There's the word "structure," again. Margo needs structure. The Choctaw girls need structure. I don't like structure. I smiled at Grandma. "Interfere? I don't do it on purpose."

"But you lied upstairs. I don't think highly of someone who lies."

"But I was covering for Eleanor. She pierced my ears and Imogene's ears. The matron would have gotten her, but I knew you would let me slide."

"Let you slide? I'm too easy on you."

"No. I like it. Easy is good."

"Of course you like it."

I kicked my feet in the air. "Did you know Eleanor thinks I'm fun?"

"Oh my, we've got two peas in a pod. You two must be alike." Grandma rubbed her tummy, trying to hold in her laugh. "Just behave while we're here. We will be staying a little longer. Mahlee and I will help out in the kitchen to earn our keep."

"Yes, ma'am. I'll stay away from the matron."

"Make sure you do."

I rolled onto my back. "Grandma, do you think Margo will come home with us?"

She moved around the bed post, holding onto the wood. "I'm not sure how this is going to work out. Margo isn't keen on our being here."

"I don't think she likes us. Maybe we could take Priscilla to the hospital in Texarkana, and go home without her."

She sat down on the bed, bent down and slipped off her leather shoes. "I'm not sure what's next. A day at a time. A day at a time."

I got on my knees, leaning over her shoulder while bouncing on the bed. "I'm sorry, Grandma. I don't mean to get in trouble. Trouble follows me."

"Or you follow it. " She hugged me. "Get upstairs and get your nightclothes on. The bell rings early in the morning."

"Yes, ma'am." *Smack.* I walked into the door. "Night."

Grandma sang out her goodnight. "See you in the morning. I love you Annie Grace Kree. You're my girl, always."

"I love you, too."

I passed Mahlee in the hallway as I hurried to the stairs. "Shoelace, stop running or you will ..."

Bam. Splat.

"Fall."

I rolled like a ball across the floor. "Too late, I already did."

Mahlee shook her head and joined Grandma in the bedroom. She stuck her head back out. "See you in the morning."

I looked over the staircase railing. "Not if I see you first."

**

The matron placed her hand on the light switch, towering like a tree at the entrance to the room. "Goodnight, girls. Let's keep the talking down tonight."

She looked right at me, and then at Eleanor.

The matron turned the second floor into a room of shadows. A moonbeam of light shone through the windows in streaks of blue.

Bright Eyes faced the wall with her back to me. Her sadness and tears tonight made me want to know more, but she didn't move. Her breathing took on a constant rhythm. She must be asleep.

I slipped under my covers waiting for the moment when Eleanor and I would make our move. I whispered in the dark to her. "Are you awake? Are we going to go on our adventure?"

"Yes. We need to make sure the matron locks up downstairs. Then we can … head to the passage."

Swish. Swish. Swish.

I looked at the shadow. "Who's there?"

A voice called to me. "It's me, Taddy."

"My Taddy?"

"Yes, I'm sneaking up here to talk to you. I have to tell you something. If I don't, I'm going to burst. This secret is causing me nightmares."

I crawled onto the floor and sat cross-legged with him. "You have a secret? We don't keep secrets from each other." I lied to Taddy, knowing I had a secret, too. One I wasn't sharing with him now, or anytime soon.

"I do have a secret, so don't get mad."

"Mad? Me, get mad?"

"Yes. You know how you overreact." Taddy pulled out an envelope from his pocket.

I touched his shirt. "Why are you dressed?"

"I can't let girls see me in my nightshirt."

I giggled. "They don't care. What's in your hand?"

He yanked his hand back. "In a minute." Taddy placed the envelope on his lap.

"Hurry up, the matron might catch us."

Eleanor called to me. "Who are you talking to?"

I whispered, "It's Taddy. He has something to tell me. It won't take long."

Eleanor's voice rose. "You better hurry if we're going to … if we're going to … you know …"

Taddy tapped my shoulder. "What are you two up to?"

"Nothing. Just girl talk."

"Never mind." Taddy stood and put the envelope in his pocket. "I'll tell you later."

"No. Sit down. Tell me. You're already here."

Taddy sighed, sitting down. "I'm afraid you'll be mad."

"I'm going to be mad if you keep this up."

"Fine. I'll tell you."

I leaned back on the side of the cot. "Then tell me."

"I did something you would do. I acted like a 'vestigator, viewing something before we left home. It belongs to my mama."

"Tell me." I reached around his back and yanked the envelope from his pocket. "Does it have something to do with this?"

"Give me the envelope. It's not yours."

I read the name on the front. "Well, it's addressed to Priscilla Day. It's not yours, either."

"I know. I've read it. It's the letter telling Mama to come for Margo. But inside … inside … there's something no one knows. I'm sure Mama didn't tell your grandma or Mahlee or they would have said something by now."

"So, you read your mama's mail. You broke the law. It happens. No big deal." I giggled, making fun of him.

Taddy rattled words in one breath. "You don't understand. Margo has a baby. Her name is Isabella. The letter says Margo's keeping the baby secret from folks. I don't think Margo wrote to Mama. After all, look at how crazy she's acting."

I rose to my feet and plopped down on my cot. Taddy moved next to me, his fingers crumpling the letter.

I shoved him. "We rode all those hours on the train from Texarkana to Millerton. You didn't think for one second, one tiny moment, you should tell me, your best friend, about this?"

"I was afraid. I shouldn't have read the letter. And I'm right. See, you're mad."

"I'm not real mad at you." I touched the string on my ear. "Margo is freaking out. She did hit Mahlee with a shovel today. What you're saying kind of makes sense. We don't know what Margo's capable of doing."

Taddy nodded. "Margo acted ugly at the doctor's office. I'm scared of her. All of this is causing me to have nightmares. I need your help. You're brave. And I'm not."

I rocked back and forth, remembering the pregnant ladies at the log house on the hill. I also saw Margo holding a baby. Was it Isabella?

Taddy tapped my arm. "What's rolling around in your head?"

"I'm trying to figure out what we should do."

"I'm going downstairs. I'm telling your grandma."

"No, wait. Take this envelope and put it up. Let me think. Let me think. We need to find out who sent the letter. And we need to keep Margo calm."

Taddy leaned close, whispering in a tired voice. "I'm supposed to let you figure out our next move?"

"Yes, let me do the 'vestigating."

Taddy looked around the room at the cots. "What if my mama doesn't come through this? Will I become an orphan like these girls?"

"No, you have me. You're never going to be alone. Your mama is going to get well and be good as new." I hugged him, hoping I wasn't telling another lie.

Taddy got up. "I'm going to bed. Don't be mad at me."
Swish. Swish. Swish.

I talked to his backside. "I'm not mad. I'm not. But don't keep secrets from me and I won't keep them from you." I lied to Taddy again. I was the one keeping Margo's *lasso secrets.* The ones I'm not ready to share.

Taddy slipped off to the stairs.

Eleanor ran to my cot as soon as he left, taking a seat beside me. "So what did I hear? Does Margo have a baby?"

"Oh, no. You're as nosey as me."

"I can be. I love to know what's going on."

"I'm not sure if she has a baby." I lied to Eleanor, something I keep doing in Oklahoma.

"So, are you ready to check out the secret passage?"

"Sure, let's go."

Ar roof. Ar roof.

I crept to the window. "Black Dog's after something. I'm going to let him in. It's too cold outside."

Eleanor pressed her nose on the window. "He's probably chasing a ghost. We have them, you know."

Pam Kumpe

Before Night Two Can End

Casket at Night

I TWISTED THE KNOB ON the side door of Pushmataha Hall, the exit leading to the driveway where the matron's dusty car sat. I tiptoed onto the porch, noticing the two rails on each side. I had slipped on my PF Flyers, but I was wearing my nightshirt. It looked more like a dress.

I turned back to Eleanor and whispered, "What are you waiting for?"

"I can't leave the dorm. It's forbidden after dark."

"But you were going to the passage with me."

"I know. It's inside."

I spun around and pranced to the hallway where Eleanor stood. She folded her arms across her chest, leaning on the wall. She spouted whisper-mad words. "One day, I'll have a home. I'll have a family, too. And I won't have to follow these rules."

"Come on. I'll tell them it's my idea to let the dog in."

Eleanor laughed. "You have an answer for everything, don't you?"

I pulled on her hands. "If we hurry, no one will know."

Ar roof. Ar roof.

Black Dog ran past the porch.

We dashed outside, and I closed the door behind us.

Eleanor whispered her yell. "You shouldn't have closed the door." She turned the knob. It wouldn't budge.

I came to her side. "What's wrong? Why is the door locked?"

"This door catches on the door facing. This is why your grandma couldn't get in by herself yesterday. Remember, the matron had to open the door from the inside.

I assured her. "We can get in. We'll just use another door."

Eleanor shook her head. "The matron locks up before she goes to bed. We're locked out."

I jumped on the porch like a rabbit. "Then, we might as well look for Black Dog. You go to bed too early anyway. Hey look, there's a light on in the barn. We could get Boswell to help us."

"He won't. He would tell on us."

"But I could see if he has a key."

Eleanor called to me. "I'm not going. I'm sitting right here. I'm staying. I am."

I jogged across the grounds to the open barn door, peeking inside. A wagon sat next to a stall. Two mules were in the corral to my left. Their long ears twisted toward me.

Schrzzzzz. Schrzzzzz.

Boswell pushed and pulled and rocked, cutting a piece of wood with his saw. A lantern hung on a ladder by the loft. The sawdust flittered in the orange haze, and a fog of dust swirled above him like a tiny whirlwind. He wiped his brow, pushing and pulling again.

Schrzzzzz. Schrzzzzz.

I looked back at Eleanor, flapping my arm in a wave.

A man's voice startled me. "Why are you watching me? And what are you doing out here at night?"

Boswell held his saw too close to me. I backed up. "I'm not watching. I'm coming to see you."

Boswell put his other hand on his hip next to his gun. "A visitor comes inside, saying hello. She doesn't hide in the shadows like a thief."

I stomped my feet. "I'm no thief. I just got here. I have a problem. I need your help."

"I bet you do." Boswell put his saw on the wagon. "Problem? What might it be?"

"I'm locked out of the dorm. So is Eleanor. She's sitting on the steps waiting for me. She's afraid you'll tell on us, so I'm here to make sure you won't."

"A little thing like you ... telling me how it's gonna be. I don't think so."

I swatted at the dust in the air. "Do you have a key?"

"No, I only have keys to the tractor and the barn, and to the boiler room.

Ar roof. Ar roof.

Black Dog jumped with his front paws and stirred up the mules. They kicked at the barn wall.

Ar roof. Ar roof. Ar roof.

I grabbed Black Dog by the neck. "Stop barking. I don't want to get caught by the matron, or by my grandma. Or by the meanest and grouchiest Mahlee, who hates to have her sleep interrupted."

Boswell petted Black Dog.

He stopped barking.

"How did you do that?"

"He knows I mean business. You let him get away with too much."

"So I'm too easy on him?"

"Yep. Maybe a little." Boswell rubbed his head under the brim of his hat. "You better get to the dorm and start knocking."

"Fine. I guess I'll be in trouble again."

Ar roof. Ar roof.

Black Dog bounded to the wagon and put his nose on the finished casket. He growled and sniffed at the wood.

I climbed into the wagon to pull him off. I had to go.

Ar roof. Ar roof.

Black Dog wouldn't budge. I yanked on his neck. He was in attack mode. "Black Dog, stop yapping. It's just a casket."

Bam! Bam! Creak!

The lid flew open. A dead body rose up. It dove at me.

"Yikes! It's alive. It's after me." I tumbled backwards, falling over Black Dog. I bounced off the wagon and hit the ground. The body rolled off of me, tangling into a blob. I yelled at Boswell. "Why do you have a dead body?"

Boswell didn't answer and unraveled his dead person.

I scrambled to him, hiding behind his ruffled shirt.

He pulled on my arm. "Take a look. It's not a dead body. It's .... "

Chula sprang to her feet, making howling noises. She climbed on top of the casket, holding her stomach between laughs.

Hee, Haw. Hee, Haw. The mules laughed with her.

She made fun of me. "Ha, ha. A city girl is afraid of caskets."

"I'm not a city girl. I'm a hobo girl who lives in a town."

Chula jumped to the ground. "You are a city girl. You are easy to scare."

I sprinted at her. On the sixth time around the wagon, I slipped on the hay, but yelled, "I'm gonna get you. What a mean trick to play on me."

"You were hiding outside the barn. I decided to give you a dose of your own medicine."

I caught up with Chula by climbing over the wagon. I dove at her, my fists slamming into her jaw. "You're mean. I wouldn't hide in a casket."

"Haksobish falaia chia." Chula mouthed, rubbing her face. The dust wrapped around us like a small tornado, and she pushed me aside, pulling her arm back, ready to swing.

Boswell grabbed Chula. "Stop the fighting."

I brushed the hay from my knees, wiping a tear from my eye. "You're horrible. What did you call me? We are not friends."

Chula sat in the sawdust, pulling out her flute. "We are friends. You'll see. I called you a long-eared mule. You are stubborn." She blew into the bamboo.

Wooolllooo. Sooollllooo.

I yanked the flute from her mouth. "Stop playing. You're bothering me." I touched my ears. "I'm not a mule, and my ears are small."

Chula shook her head. "You might listen to me then. I have clues. I know things. I have answers."

"Whatever. There you go talking in riddles."

"But I have to. You are here for a purpose. I'm here to help."

"You don't help. You play your flute. You pull a knife. You push me in a grave. You jump at me from a casket. How are you helping?"

Chula dusted herself off, took her flute back, dancing toward the barn door. She chanted at me. "Time will tell. Remember what we have seen and learn from it. It will come in handy."

"I don't think so. I don't care. I need to find a way into the dorm without getting in trouble. And now, my nightshirt is torn."

Chula moved from the lantern's light to the moon's shadows. She disappeared into the night. A gust of wind wrapped itself in whistles around me. The barn turned chilly like ice.

Boswell walked to the open barn door. "Chula lives in the trees. She rides in the wind, and she soars with the eagles."

"And she sleeps in a casket?"

Boswell chuckled. "Not usually."

"Well, you need to get onto her. I've got to go. I need to tell Eleanor to be ready to see the matron's ugly eyes. We're going to have to wake everyone up." I ran from the barn. "Eleanor, I'm coming. Boswell doesn't have a key."

Eleanor stood on the bottom step, pointed to the woods by the basketball court, screaming. "Shoelace, run! Run as fast as you can! Get out of there!"

A muscled horse stormed across the grass, cutting the wind into slices of fear. A ghost clutched the horse's mane. A rope snapped in the ghost's hand.

Tadabak. Tadabak. Tadabak.

I froze.

The Night of Day Two Ends

Best Fun Ever

I TUMBLED TO THE GROUND. My legs were tangled up with something. I wobbled like a boxcar, tumbling over, rolling to my side and back. My body slithered across the grass like an unwilling lizard. "Let go of me."

Eleanor hollered. "Help us. Someone help us."

Tadabak. Tadabak.

A horse hauled me along, my head bouncing like a basketball. I wrapped my arms over my ears, protecting my head from the jabs. The winter grass poked at my arms like needles. "Ouch! Stop!"

Tadabak. Tadabak.

The rope sawed at my ankles, burning my skin through the socks. "Grand ... ma. Mah ... lee."

I flopped to my side like a tumbleweed, rolling to a stop. The horse pawed at the ground, snorting. His breath appeared like a mist, puffing in my face like smoke. He raised his head, bouncing it up and down. His black eyes glared like the moon.

The rider kicked the side of the horse, whispering a deep casket-sound, leaning toward me. "You aren't listening to my warnings. After today, your friend Mahlee has put you in more danger. Go home. Stay away. Go home."

I reached for my legs, trying to get loose, trying to get the rope off my ankles. The horse galloped and jerked. My feet were yanked out from under me. I bounced so hard I lost my breath. "Margo, please let me go. Please."

The grass burned my legs and my nightshirt shredded into pieces. It barely stayed on my shoulders. My legs hit a patch of gravel. The gouging pain ripped at my legs. I skidded across the driveway to the grass on the other side. My back stung like bee stings. "You have to stop. I never did anything to you." The rest of my words became shouts in my mind.

An evil laugh came from Margo.

Bahahaha. Bahahaha.

Eleanor's voice came closer. "Whoa. Whoa."

I lifted my head. "Stay away, Eleanor."

She raised her hands up like a tower, one too small, one too weak for this runaway horse.

I lost sight of Eleanor and tumbled to my side. I could hear her voice. "Leave Shoelace alone. She's my friend. You won't get away with this."

I bounced like a dead rabbit, catching another glimpse of Eleanor. She darted into the path of the horse. Her hands shot up again. But this time, the horse didn't turn.

Aheeee... Aheeee... Oweeee...

Eleanor dove to the side, flying like a bird with no wings. She fell flat on her back like a deer shot by a hunter.

I bowled to a stop in the grass, propping myself up.

Margo stopped her horse inches from Eleanor and leaned over. "Margo is sorry. Margo is not herself. Enough pain. No more tonight. No more. Never hurt the children. Never. I never meant to."

Silence.

Eleanor did not answer.

Margo kicked her horse and rode away. "No more. Not tonight. Enough."

I unraveled the rope from my ankles, got on my knees, crawling to Eleanor like a baby. It felt like I'd never reach her. My tears mixed with the blood running down my head. "Eleanor. Eleanor. Talk to me."

She coughed and pointed at the stump. "I tripped where the old cedar died last year. Those old roots keep coming up. One poked me in my back. It's stuck in my shoulder."

"You'll be fine. You'll see. I'm sure it's a small scratch."

"No, I'm … my throat is thick. My back hurts …"

I held Eleanor's head, touching the blood trickling from her mouth. She whispered, "I always wanted a family. I would have liked being your sister."

"Don't talk like you're not … like you're not going to be fine. We'll get the doctor over here."

Eleanor pointed to her shoulder. "See if you can pull it out."

"Pull what out?"

"It's in my back."

"I'll try." I tipped her to one side. A stick big enough to be an axe handle poked out from her back, right between her shoulder blades.

Boswell trampled over. "What's with the commotion? You two better get inside."

"Boswell, Eleanor's hurt."

He bent down, touching Eleanor's head. "Don't move. Stay right here. Lie on your side." He charged to the dorm. He was met by Grandma and Mahlee, along with the matron and several of the girls.

Grandma called to me. "Shoelace, are you …?"

Mahlee got to me first. "What happened to you? You have scratches on your face. Is that blood on your legs?"

I nodded. "You wouldn't understand."

104

"You're right. You were supposed to be in bed."

Eleanor coughed and opened her eyes.

Mahlee knelt down, gazing at Eleanor. "What did you do?"

"My back. It's aching. And throbbing."

"Let me take a look." Mahlee gasped. "Oh, we need a doctor. And we need him now."

The matron ran up, crumbling to the ground. She cradled Eleanor's head. "Baby girl, you're my brightest and funniest. You'll be fine. We'll get you fixed up."

Several girls huddled nearby, crying.

Mrs. Motes showed up in an orange robe, along with a tall man whose arms were long like a monkey. His face was kind. He knelt on the other side of Eleanor, talking to her, using soft words. "Eleanor, it's me, Pastor Motes. I'd like to pray for you."

I sat next to the pastor and repeated his words like an echo. "Dear Lord, Eleanor is one of yours. She gave her heart to you six months ago. She's your child. Hold her tonight. Don't let go of her. Whisper love to her sweet soul, right now. In Jesus' name. Amen."

Eleanor whispered something to the pastor.

Grandma patted my arm. "You're hurt, too. What did you say happened?"

"Eleanor and I fell." I pointed to the stump, the one where a girl sat, crying. "The sticks in that stump got us."

Grandma shook her head.

Eleanor coughed and spit blood. "Shoelace, where are you?"

"I'm here. I'm right here."

A pickup truck barreled down the driveway, screeching to a stop. Dr. Rigghazel jumped from the driver's seat, rushing to

Eleanor. "Little Eleanor. I'm going to take a look at you." He motioned with his hands. "Pastor, please help me."

Eleanor took my hand, whispering. "I will miss you."

I squeezed her hand. "You're not going anywhere. Just to the doctor's office."

The doctor turned to me. "Let me take a look at you."

"No, fix Eleanor. Fix her. Please."

Eleanor pulled my arm closer. "I had the most fun in my whole life with you, and it happened in two days."

Before I could speak … she collapsed.

"No, wake up! Wake up!" I tugged on the doctor's sleeve. "She's not dead. Is she?" I turned back to Eleanor. "Don't you dare die on me. Wake up!" I patted her face. I kissed her cheek. I listened to her chest. "Eleanor. Get up! Get up now! Don't do this!" I held her hand. She didn't hold mine.

I ran to Grandma, burying my face into her tummy. "Fix this, Grandma. Fix this."

"Shoelace, I can't. I can't."

I pushed her away and ran to Mahlee. "You can do it. You help her. Do something."

Mahlee reached for me, her eyes telling me death had already taken Eleanor.

I ran to the missionary man. "You prayed for her. You prayed. Why did God take her? Why does God take the people I love? I want her back! Bring her back!" I beat on his chest, crying. The pastor embraced me with warm arms, like a daddy. I melted into his hold, lost in the sadness.

Boswell chanted Indian sounds as he knelt next to Eleanor. He touched her face with his gruff hand. It was the kindest touch. He said goodbye.

Taddy hovered nearby, standing by the girl who sat on the stump. His body shook, his eyes shut. He toppled to the ground, clutching his head with his arms.

Someone picked me up. I didn't have the strength to fight. I felt myself going limp. The throbbing in my legs felt like heartbeats without rhythm, pounding and hurting.

Mahlee whispered to me. "I've got you. You're going to be fine." She put me in Grandma's lap in the front seat of the doctor's truck, closing the heavy door.

The pastor climbed into the driver's seat. He touched my arm. "Hold on. We'll get you stitched up. The doc's in the bed of the truck with Eleanor. We're headed to his office now."

I whimpered, closing my eyes. "Eleanor. I'm so sorry. We should have gone to the passage."

Pam Kumpe

Day Three

Eleanor's Hope

I RUBBED MY EYES, AND sat up. This is the room where Margo held the bloody bucket. I touched my legs. They were wrapped in gauze at the ankles. I reached for my shoulder, something tugged on my back. It must be another bandage.

Ar roof. Ar roof.

Black Dog jumped with his paws onto the bed.

"Hey, boy." I ran my fingers through his black fur. Holding him closer today didn't make my heart feel any better.

Mahlee rushed in and waved her arms. "Get down. Off the bed. No dogs on the bed."

Ar roof. Ar roof.

Grandma rushed into the room, smiling. "You're awake. Look at your hair. You're a tangled mess." She pushed my hair back, kissing my forehead.

"Grandma, I had a nightmare. I dreamed … I dreamed … Eleanor died."

"Oh, sweet girl. Eleanor is gone. Last night was real. It was a horrible night."

I wiped my nose. "No, she can't die. I love her. She's the sister I've always wanted." I played with the string on my ear lobe. "She pierced my ears. She liked me."

Grandma hugged me. "Hold onto the fun, and hold onto her memory." She stepped to the window facing the pond, sniffling.

Mahlee hugged me tighter than tight. "You're the prettiest thing this side of the cemetery." She cocked her head to the side, making a funny face.

I pushed her away. "Ouch. Your hugs hurt."

"Sorry. But you are pretty."

"I am not. I'm ugly. Look at my hair."

She rustled her fingers through my tangles. "The hair we can fix. The rest of you will take some work."

"Stop trying to make me laugh." I dug my head into the pillow and rolled to the wall.

Mahlee patted my shoulder. "We've been sitting all night with you and Priscilla. We're having her moved to Michael Meager Hospital. She'll ride the train with a nurse. This way she'll be closer to home."

I socked my pillow. "Is Taddy going with her? Does he know she's going on the train?"

"Yes, he knows. We're all leaving together after Eleanor's funeral."

"Can I go to the funeral? I don't have to stay in this bed, do I?"

Grandma turned from the window. "You will be there. I'll be with you, too. Pastor Motes said they'll bury Eleanor by the lake on the sacred grounds."

Neigh. Neigh. Neigh.

I slid from the mattress, peeking out the window. Some men riding horses were coming up the road. "Hey, who are they?"

Mahlee shook her head. "I have no idea."

Two more men on horses rode by the window.

Ar roof. Ar roof.

Grandma pulled my hair. She pretended to put it in a ponytail. "We're going home. This isn't going as planned."

Taddy rushed up to me. "You're awake." He ran his finger over my cheek. "You have scratches on your face. They are not pretty."

I touched my forehead and felt a bumpy place above my eyebrow. "What's this?"

Taddy laughed. "Stitches. You are one big stitch."

"That stump really got me last night."

He leaned in and whispered, "Why are you lying? You didn't tear up your legs and back and your nightshirt from hitting a stump and a bunch of sticks."

I slugged him. "It was a big stump, and I'm not lying."

Grandma turned to me. "Lying? Who is lying?"

I smiled. "Not me. Taddy is just picking on me, right, Taddy?"

Mahlee and Grandma shook their heads as they left the room.

Taddy continued the interrogation. "So you have stitches on your back. On both legs. On your head. Tell me how that happened."

"Stop acting like a cop. You don't have a badge."

"I don't need a badge. I know you. You don't always tell the truth and you know it."

"I do tell the truth, sometimes."

"You were next to a horse last night. Who did it belong to?"

"A ghost. Wheelock Academy has ghosts, didn't you know?"

"That's not true. You were up to something."

"I was not. I was just playing."

Taddy grilled me. "After dark? After everyone went to bed?'

"Yes, it's fun to play at night, usually. Remember your birthday party last year? We had it at midnight."

"And remember how it ended?"

"Oh yeah, not so good."

Taddy got back to his questions. "Are you going to tell me the truth?"

"Leave me alone. I'm done talking to you."

Taddy yanked my hair. "Last night you said we shouldn't keep secrets from each other."

"But I don't have a secret. That's the truth."

"I know what I saw. It was a horse, and someone was riding it. Who was it?"

I huffed. I pushed him away. I stepped in a circle around him. "Fine. It was Margo. She went crazy."

"Did she hurt Eleanor?"

"No, she didn't touch her. Eleanor tried to stop the horse and she fell." I wiped a tear from my cheek. "It was my fault. Eleanor tried to save me from Margo."

"Why would she need to save you?"

I held up a leg. "See these stitches? Margo roped me like a cow, and dragged me on the ground."

"Why?"

"Because she's crazy."

Taddy tapped his face. "You need to tell your grandma and Mahlee all of this."

I blurted out my words faster than a whistle letting off steam on a train. "I'm not telling anyone, except you."

"Why? Are you protecting Margo?"

"I'm … I'm not protecting her. I'm protecting you."

"Me? Why me?"

We sat down on the mattress side by side. The truth unfolded. "I need to tell you what happened the first night we got here. I need to tell you about last night when ..."

A half an hour later, Taddy argued with me. He didn't think I was smart or brave. "Secrets only get people hurt. You can't keep stuff like this to yourself. And you have to stop sneaking off."

"You're the one who had the secret letter that belonged to your mama."

"That was different. You could have died last night."

"But, I didn't."

"I'm going to tell them, if you don't."

I begged. "You have to keep this a secret."

Taddy jumped from the bed. "I can't. We have to tell. We're leaving tomorrow anyway. It's nearly four. You've slept a long time."

I jumped in front of him. "Wait, don't tell. I've changed my mind. Secrets can be good between best friends."

"I told you, I'm telling your grandma. I'm telling Mahlee. I'm also going to tell them I read Mama's letter. And about the baby, Isabella."

**

Grandma held my shoulders. "You are my sunshine. You have to trust me. You can't keep grown-up things to yourself in your little-girl body. To be brave and to have courage is doing what's right, not hiding things from me."

The pacing of the boots in the waiting room told me Mahlee was getting ready to give me more than a piece of her mind. She stormed up to my bed. "I would have walloped Margo and tied her up myself if I'd known she lassoed you.

How dare she drag you around by your feet. When I find Margo, I hope to use that rope on her."

"You can't be like her. She's mixed up in the head and gets confused. I don't think she wants to hurt us. She's afraid of something from her past. It's speaking louder than the present."

Taddy spoke up. "What about Isabella? Would Margo hurt her own child?'

I wiggled on the bed and put my legs up; the tightness of the stitches grabbed at my skin. "I don't think so. But if she's not in danger, why would someone send a letter?"

Kabam.

The front door of the doctor's office slammed against the wall. Grandma and Mahlee went to take a look. Grandma called back to me. "You've got company. We'll let you two visit."

Shalop. Shalop.

The sound of Cowboy boots scooting across the floor came closer. Boswell peeked into my room, taking off his black-brimmed hat. "Well, it looks like you're up and around. I brought you a poem to help you smile. I would have written it in Choctaw, but you wouldn't be able to read it."

Taddy ran up to Boswell. "I'll read it to her. I like to read." Taddy took the poem, unfolding it. He stared at the words. "Boswell, is this your handwriting?"

Boswell nodded. "Well, yes. It's called 'Eleanor's Hope.' I wrote it last night."

Taddy reached into his back pocket. "My mama's letter has the same handwriting as the poem. Boswell, did you ... did you write my mama a letter to come get Margo?"

Boswell frowned, his eyelids tightened. He fiddled with his hat, sighing. He paced, scooted in his boots, and sat down at the bottom of the bed. He took his hat in his hands, twirling it in circles, sideways. "Yes. I wrote Priscilla a letter—I had to."

Taddy stepped up to Boswell. "Why? It's not like Margo wants us here."

"I had hoped it might help. Margo's the talk of the town. Folks were saying she was pregnant, and she disappeared for a bit. Then I ran into her in the woods one day. She was leaning on a post rocking a baby. That day she was *soft* with the bundle. But I know how Margo's days can change without warning. I became afraid for Isabella."

I got up and stood next to Taddy, taking in every word.

Boswell spilled the rest of the story. "I've watched Margo for a few years. She can be rough. She accidently held a kitten too hard last month. I had to do something to protect the baby."

Grandma and Mahlee must have been listening outside the door and Grandma got into the middle of the talk. "Boswell, how did you ever find Priscilla?"

Boswell popped to his feet, inching to the corner. "I found something. I wasn't sure, but …"

I yelled at him. "Tell us. How did you find Priscilla?"

He sighed. "I am trying to tell you. When Margo first came to Millerton, she stayed in the barn. She had nowhere to live. She talked to the mules. She played with the girls. I just wanted to check her out."

Taddy wiped his brow. "She talked to the animals?"

Boswell smiled. "Yes, but that's not the problem. It was her mood swings. Happy one second. Scary the next. One day, while she was in town, I dug through her belongings. I found a picture with Priscilla's name on the back. She looked just like Margo. It read Texarkana, Union Station."

I marched up to Boswell. "Why would you send a letter without your name? It would have made things easier."

"I didn't want to take a chance that Priscilla might not come. You know, I'm afraid of Margo, too. I never meant for any of this to happen. I had hoped that if Margo saw her twin sister, things might change."

Kabam. Kabam.

"Who's in charge here?"

Doctor Rigghazel passed by my room, coming from his office in the back. "Can I help you?"

The voice called out. "I'm with the Tribal Police. Two men are loose in town. They got in a fight while getting haircuts and shaves. They took the barber's gun. They're wanted in the next county and they're dangerous. One is small and round with red hair. The other has a scar on his face and has black hair. They are on the run."

Doctor Rigghazel assured the man. "We'll keep watch. We'll be fine."

I ran to the window. "Who are they? There are five men watering their horses at the pond."

Boswell stepped next to me. "Those are Lighthorsemen and they keep the peace for the Choctaw."

I frowned. "Do you have to be skinny to be a Lighthorsemen?"

Taddy peeked between us, slugging my arm.

"Ouch."

"You are going to have to start listening in history."

"We have never studied this."

The Lighthorsemen waddled to the water's edge. They didn't look so light to me.

Doctor Rigghazel came into my room. "I guess you heard? We've had some trouble in town. I'll make sure Priscilla is safe. Until those men are caught, everyone needs to stay close together."

Grandma put a hand on my shoulder, then one on Taddy's arm. "Shoelace. Taddy. No wandering off."

We both nodded.

Boswell shuffled to the door. Taddy ran up to him, tugging on his ruffles. "Hey, wait. Tell the doctor how you know Margo has a baby. He might be able to help us."

Doctor Rigghazel squinted. "What? Margo has a baby?"

I interrupted. "Yes. She's at the log house up the road."

Grandma looked at me. Taddy came up and touched my arm. Boswell stepped toward me. Then Mahlee lifted me by my shoulders. "You saw the baby? And you're just now telling us?"

"Put me down. Grandma, tell Mahlee to stop treating me like I'm a sack of potatoes."

I fell to the floor, and Taddy reached for my hand. "Tell them everything. You keep leaving parts out."

"Sorry ... I didn't think it was important."

Unknown Soul

Thursday's Pain

Dress for Two

NOW THURSDAYS ARE ABOUT FUNERALS, and saying goodbye. Eleanor's casket sat on a table under the branches of the cedar tree at the crest of the hill. Dozens of white paper roses decorated the top of her casket.

The girls filed into the rows of chairs. Each held a homemade white paper rose. They melted into their seats like petals of sadness on a stem of lost memories. The girls waited to say goodbye to their friend.

Boswell handed white roses to a group of girls. "Place your flower in the casket at the end of the service." He patted a girl on the shoulder. "Don't cry, Imogene. Eleanor's blooming in heaven."

I tried to wave to Imogene, but she didn't see me.

The girls wore their Sunday clothes. I glanced down at my overalls that hid the bandages on my legs. Charging into the dining hall, I crashed into the matron. "I don't want to sit out there. I hate funerals."

"I know. I never thought this is how I'd say goodbye to Eleanor. It breaks my heart." The matron pulled me close. "I was coming for you. I thought you might want to wear a dress today."

"I don't wear dresses. Grandma bought me some last year, but we took them back to the store. I came home with a bunch of overalls and shirts. They go with my PF Flyers." I ran my hand over the bib of my overalls.

"Today might be a good reason to wear one." She wiped both her eyes. "You and Eleanor are about the same size. In sewing class this winter, she made a new dress. She was waiting to wear it for her birthday this spring. It's a shame to leave it in the wardrobe closet. Maybe you could wear it."

I kicked the side of my shoe with my toe. "Dresses are itchy."

Bright Eyes showed up in the doorway, sobbing. She held onto Mrs. Motes' hand, who wiped her own tears. "I made double portions of blackberry cobbler for everyone. Eleanor loved my cobbler." She wiped her nose with a hanky.

They left the dining hall, joining the others for the funeral.

The matron moved up behind me, spinning my body around. "What if I just show you the dress?"

"I like my overalls." I moved to the kitchen window. Black Dog lay on the steps of Wilson Hall with his paws over his nose.

She put her hand over my shoulder. "That dog is a wanderer. He kind of reminds me of you."

I looked up at her. "I have trouble sticking in one place."

She sniffled. "Eleanor was a wanderer, too. She was a friend to the lonely. She brought joy to the academy. Her sense of humor calmed the orphan girls late at night when I couldn't help those who cried. They will miss her. I will, too."

I felt my shoulders shake, and my throat ache. "I will miss her, too. This was my fault."

"No, it was an accident. Eleanor fell. I should have had those old roots chopped up. They were dangerous, but I kept forgetting to tell Boswell to cut them. It's my fault."

I reached for the matron's hand. "It's not your fault, either."

The matron kissed the top of my head. "I want to give you a gift from Eleanor. She would want you to have it. Please, come with me." The matron left me standing there, calling to me from the hallway. "Now, come on. We don't have much time."

She wasn't taking no for an answer. I hate to tell her, I have no intention of putting a dress on, but I was curious what the gift might be. "Coming ..."

I stepped into the matron's bedroom. She picked up a white dress. "Eleanor spent hours sewing this. She was careful to put extra fabric at the hem to let it out as she got taller."

I ran my hand over the cloth, weeping. It wasn't itchy. *Sniff. Sniff.*

The matron touched the sleeve. "Isn't this the prettiest little dress?"

"Yes, I do like it."

"If she had given it to anyone, it would have been you."

"I might take it home. I did love Eleanor. We could have been sisters."

The matron nodded. "You could have been, except her hair was black. Yours is blonde."

I giggled. "I have some Choctaw in me, somewhere way inside."

"Then, sisters you'll always be." The matron held the dress up to me. "This would look grand on you. Please, wear it in memory of the smartest little Indian girl who has come through this orphanage."

I pulled off my shirt, taking off my overalls. I found myself standing there wearing Eleanor's dress. "It's pretty. Eleanor pierced ears good. She sewed good, too."

"She would want you to have these, too." The matron handed me a pair of gold earrings. "Let's get rid of that thread."

I ran my finger over my ears. The matron pulled the strings out, snapping the studs in place. She moved me to the oval mirror at her dresser. "Pretty dress. Pretty ears. And a pretty girl." The matron hurried me from the bedroom. "The funeral is starting. One more thing. Eleanor made two dresses this winter. She'll be wearing the matching dress for her farewell party today."

I hugged her bony body. "Thank you. I will never take these earrings off. I'll wear this dress to church on Sundays, too." I grabbed the matron's hand. "I don't even know your real name."

She held both of my hands in hers. "It's Rebecca Brach. You can call me Becky."

"Becky? That's a nice name."

The matron hugged me. "We best hurry."

I scooted down the hallway, watching my red PF Flyers poke out from under my dress. They felt like clown shoes and the gauze on my legs didn't help. My forehead had a white bandage, but I felt prettier than a frog on a wooden log.

I joined Grandma and Mahlee in the second row behind Mrs. Motes and Bright Eyes. Grandma turned to me. "You look very nice."

I smiled.

The matron gave me a wink, hurrying to the front row. She joined Pastor Motes, sitting next to him.

Taddy hasn't left his mama's side since yesterday. He's ready to go home. He won't come to the funeral.

Mahlee leaned over in front of Grandma. "You do look beautiful, except for those shoes."

I stuck my tongue out at her.

Pastor Motes stepped to Eleanor's casket, clutching a Bible. He started to speak, but a gruff voice rose up like a

120

wave of sorrow in the cold breeze. A song of shaky words sang out. "Where is Eleanor? I can't find her. Is she alive? No. No. No. I couldn't save her."

I stood up in the chair to see. "It's Doctor Rigghazel and he's slinging a whiskey bottle like my daddy used to carry."

Grandma tugged on my dress. "Sit down. Act like a lady."

"I'm not a lady. I'm Shoelace."

Mahlee ordered. "Sit in that chair."

I plopped down, scowling at Mahlee.

The doctor stumbled to the casket. "I hate to put another picture on the wall by my piano. Little girls come. Little girls go. They are precious in God's sight. But I can't save them." He knocked Pastor Motes into the casket.

The pastor ordered. "Get off me. You're drunk. Must you act this way in front of these girls? Pull yourself together. We will all miss Eleanor. This is not how you need to handle your pain."

Doctor Rigghazel shouted. "Pain? No one knows my pain. No one knows what I feel when I lose a patient."

Boswell marched down the center aisle, grabbing the doctor by the collar. "Go on. Get out of here."

The doctor pulled away from Boswell, swinging his arms.

The younger girls wept and hugged each other, sobbing like they were watching a nightmare in the daytime.

I ran from my seat to the doctor. He leaned on the casket, taking a swig. I knocked the bottle from his hand. "You stitched me up and fixed my legs. You are taking care of Priscilla, too. We're alive. You didn't lose us."

He slobbered and spit. "This is true. I wish I was a good doctor."

Boswell yanked on the doctor's arm, pulling him out of sight behind Wilson Hall. They disappeared somewhere behind the gym on the hill.

Pastor Motes gathered himself and started the funeral. "Children are precious to Jesus. He once said, let the little children come to me, and do not hinder them, for the kingdom of heaven belongs to such as these. Today, Eleanor is with Jesus. We long to see her smile. But we can rejoice in her life."

The rest of his words got lost in my head. All I could think about was Eleanor's laugh, and her smile. I would give anything to go back and fix this. Goodness, this is the worst day of my life so far this year.

The girls marched like statues of sorrow with their roses. Bright Eyes handed me her flower and took my hand. We trooped together toward the open casket. At the front, I touched the edge of the box. "I love you, Eleanor."

Bright Eyes tugged on my arm. Her eyes told me how much she loved Eleanor, too. I felt of my not-itchy dress and then the earrings. "Thank you, Eleanor. We're twins today. We have matching dresses."

Dozens of paper roses decorated Eleanor's goodbye funeral. I placed my rose on top of the other paper flowers. The ache inside my heart would linger for a long time.

**

Smack.

I pushed Chula out of my way in the kitchen. "Where have you been? Where were you when Eleanor fell?" I didn't wait for an answer and took off to change clothes.

Chula followed me down the hall, grabbing my ponytail. "Stop. Let me do this. Everyone will be inside in a second. I need to do this."

I spun around. "Do what?"

Chula folded her arms around my neck. "You need a hug."
I shoved her. "I don't need a hug. Not from you."
Chula shuffled to the side, looking to the floor. "I'm trying to be your friend."
"It's not working. You jumped out of the casket the other night. Now Eleanor is inside of it. She's dead. Did you hear me? Dead." I stormed to Grandma's bedroom, slammed the door, tumbling to the mattress. I couldn't help but think how nice her hug actually felt. I shook my head. "What's with that Chula?"

Ar roof. Ar roof.

I cracked the door open, sticking my nose out. Black Dog jumped on me. "How did you get inside?"
The matron walked by. "I let him in. He wanted to see you."
I grinned, knelt down, and his pink tongue swiped my face. "Hey boy. I need a hug. How about you?"

Day Four Changes Everything

A Warrior is Born

GRANDMA'S WORDS TRAVELED UP THE staircase and to the dorm room. "Shoelace, don't wad up the dress and toss it into your satchel."

I scuttled to the rail at the top of the stairs. "Yes, ma'am. It's put up."

I hurried back and Bright Eyes sat on my cot, swinging her legs. She was peeking into my bag. She pulled out my new dress, shaking out the wrinkles.

I whispered to her. "Don't tell Grandma."

Bright Eyes crammed the dress back into the satchel and grabbed my engineer's hat. She slipped it onto her head.

I tilted her chin up. "Hey, do you want my hat? You can keep it for me. I don't wear it so much these days."

She nodded, jumping up. She shuffled to the window, humming a tune of notes much like those I've heard from Chula's flute. This was the first sound I've heard Bright Eyes make besides crying.

Grandma persisted in getting my attention. "Shoelace, run over to the doctor's office and get Taddy. He should have been here by now."

I touched the railing and stood in the spot where Eleanor pierced my ears. "Yes, ma'am. I'll go after him."

Grandma called in a sing-song shout. "We need to hurry. I don't like being late. Boswell should be at the doctor's office.

He's waiting for the nurse to arrive since, well, the doctor is drunk."

"I'll go get Taddy." My leap down the stairs began without pain. The third jump pulled on the stitches at the top of my shoes. "Ouch."

At the bottom of the stairs I cut through the front room and headed to the double doors. On the front porch, I swept my hand across the pillars, hopping down the three stairs leading to the long sidewalk. "Ouch. My legs hurt." I zigzagged my way across the grounds to the white iron fence running along the driveway. Two Shetland ponies, a black and a brown, grazed on crunchy grass on the other side.

I came to the sacred grounds behind the gym. Eleanor's casket was being lowered by two men into an open grave. There were only a few markers in this cemetery. The casket wobbled and crashed to its side. I charged at the men. "Don't hurt Eleanor. Don't drop my friend."

Mr. Lewis turned to me. "We're doing our job. It's not like she knows."

I yanked on his shirt, stomping my feet. "I hope when you die, no one drops your casket." I charged along the fence toward the front drive. I didn't care if my stitches ripped out or not. I rounded the gate, heading past Wheelock Cemetery. I kicked a mound of sand in the road, tripped, and sailed face first to the dirt, right near the spot where Priscilla got hurt. My hand landed on something shiny.

Soo-loo. Loo-soo. Woooo.

A flute whistled and somehow I knew Chula was probably smiling at seeing me flat on my face. I rolled over and sat in the road, unfolding my fingers. "What's this? It's Margo's ring. Priscilla must have dropped it when she fell."

Chula swung down from a limb next to the road. Her woodpecker sat on her shoulder. She knelt next to me. "What did you find?"

"Nothing." I stood up, rubbing my leg. I pulled my pant leg up to inspect the pain. A red spot came through the gauze. "I'm bleeding again. Rats."

Chula touched my arm. Her hand was soft and kind, unlike her personality. "Are you hurt? I need you healthy. You are here to find the missing."

"Riddles. You are one big riddle. You say something and mean nothing." I backed up, slipping the ring into my pocket. "I'm not hurt. I'm fine."

She mocked me. "Fine? Sure you are. You have a bandage on your head, one on your back under your shirt, and you have gauze on both legs and stitches on your ankles. And now..." She pointed to my right leg. "You are bleeding."

"Leave me alone. I have to get Taddy." I couldn't help but wonder how she knew where my stitches were.

She stepped in front of me. "Taddy's gone. Right about the time the funeral started, he was headed to the dorm."

I waved my hands like a crazy hobo girl. "What? Taddy was supposed to be here with his mama. He's not at Wheelock, so he must be here."

Chula pulled out her knife.

I jumped like a rabbit to get away. "Hey, put the knife up."

Chula pointed to my leg. "There's blood running down your shoe. I've got to fix this." She acted like an Indian who was ready to scalp me.

Shlack. Shlack.

She ripped off the bottom of her green silky shirt.

I whined. "What are you doing?"

"Fixing you." She then cut off the bottom of my overalls with her knife.

Kriipppp. Kriipppp.

"Hey, those are my good overalls."

Chula tied the fabric around my ankle. "If you lose too much blood, you're no good to me, or the missing."

"Stop with the riddles."

Chula dusted herself off, put the knife away, and reached for my hand. "Taddy is your friend. You must stay alive. He is going to need a warrior."

"Warrior? I'm no warrior. I'm Shoelace." I looked down at my right leg. A red shoe. A green ankle wrap. A short-legged overall. Now I really do look like a clown. But I wasn't bleeding anymore.

Chula danced around me singing words in Indian. "Himmithoa vhleha ak kia tikambi cha yohabli toba, mikmvt hattak himmithoa ..."

"What are you saying?"

She darted across the road past the rock church. Turning back to me, she sang words I didn't understand.

I shuffled to her. "What are you singing? What do those words mean?"

"You will soon find out. You will need strength. God will help you soar like an eagle. He'll give you confidence to be brave." Chula smiled, disappearing behind the bamboo.

I talked to the bamboo, hoping Chula heard me. "What's with you? You show up. You say your riddles, and then you leave. Thanks for nothing."

I hurried to the doctor's office, meeting a lady in white clothes with white legs, and white shoes. "Are you Priscilla's nurse?"

"Yes, I am. I'm going to make sure she is comfortable on the train."

"Have you seen Taddy? He's her son. He's my best friend." I held my hand out showing her how tall he is. "He's a couple inches shorter than me."

"No, I haven't seen him. Are you Shoelace?"

"Yes, ma'am. My grandma is Elsie Kree. She's the one who hired you."

"Taddy must have left. He isn't here. There's an Indian out back. He calls himself Boswell. He put the doctor in bed to sleep it off. It seems the doctor was drinking over the loss of a patient."

I hurried to the back porch. "Boswell, have you seen Taddy?"

Boswell pulled the pipe from his mouth. "Nope. He's not here. I came over right after the funeral with the doctor in the back of my wagon. Doc was passed out by the woods. I'm making sure he stays put."

"But Taddy's supposed to be here. He's not at Wheelock, and I didn't meet him on the road." I hurried to one end of the porch, glancing at the ducks by the pond. Not there. I ran to the other end of the porch, looking at the tombstones in the cemetery. Not there.

Boswell touched my shoulder. "Come on. Hop in the wagon. I'll take you to Wheelock, and come right back. I'm sure he's fine.

Crunch-roar-creak. Crunch-roar-creak.

Boswell held the reins and the wagon bumped on the dirt road as we headed toward the gate at Wheelock. At the driveway, the mule's ears turned to the side. "Boswell, what's that?"

"Oh, it's just the wind."

A shadow appeared behind the trees. One minute, it was short like Chula. The next, it was tall like Margo. Or maybe it was nothing.

Day Four Takes a Turn

When the Lucky Rock Drops

I RACED INTO THE DINING hall and looked at every face. Dozens of girls chatted together at the tables in the after-funeral-have-a-party time. One girl, who slept near Eleanor, dropped her fork. "It's weird to see her chair empty by the wall."

I moved to the girls. "Have any of you seen my friend, Taddy?"

Two girls answered together. "No."

Three more glanced at each other, shaking their heads.

Mrs. Motes and two ladies were washing dishes, and moving pots and pans around. I tugged on her skirt. "Mrs. Motes, have you seen Taddy?"

She turned and smiled. "I thought he was with his mama."

"He was, but not anymore."

Imogene stuck her head out of the pantry. She yelled over the talk. "Hey, Shoelace. Come help me." She carried a sack of flour, limping with each step. That was something I hadn't noticed before. The limp.

"Sure." I blasted across the floor to her, holding one end of the sack. "Have you seen Taddy?"

"Nope. Not since I passed him in the hall this morning. He has a cute grin."

I shook my head. "It's not that cute."

Imogene shuffled her feet. "Why are you looking for him?"

"We have to pack. We're leaving tonight." My eyes were glued to her uneven steps.

"You don't have to stare." She plopped the sack on the edge of the table. My end of the sack folded in half at the string. Flour poured like smoke to the floor, puffing up in our faces.

The girls scattered, screaming. "Watch out. You're making a mess."

"Sorry." I pinched the opening, propped the sack up, stopping the white, dancing cloud.

The matron called to Imogene. "Get a broom. Get the dust pan. Clean this mess up. We don't need to waste our supplies, so be more careful." She talked to Imogene, but her eyes were on me.

I apologized. "Sorry. It was an accident." I stepped back, seeing my footprints on the floor. "Sorry."

Mrs. Motes moved in to rescue us. "Accidents do happen. The other day, I spilled five pounds of sugar on the pantry floor."

The frown on the matron's face held words she wanted to spew. Maybe she resisted since we'd just had a funeral.

A stomping noise came up behind me. "Shoelace, where have you been? And where is Taddy? I sent you after him and you're in here playing."

I spun around, bumping into Grandma. "I'm not playing. I was helping Imogene. The flour on the floor was an accident."

"What happened to your overalls? And what is that on your leg?"

"My ankle started bleeding. It's a patch."

Pam Kumpe

Grandma shook her head. "I really don't have time for this. Never mind." She stepped closer to me. "So did you find Taddy?" Her hands were on her rounded hips.

"No. He wasn't at the doctor's office. He must be here somewhere. Chula told me she saw him walking toward Wheelock earlier, so Boswell brought me back in his wagon. Taddy must be here."

Grandma rubbed her hands together. "Who's Chula? It doesn't matter right now. Let's go check his room."

I skated down the hall and barreled inside.

Grandma marched up behind me. "Is he here?"

"No. He's not ..."

She pushed past me, opening the door wider. I scooted around her, moving to the suitcase on the bed. It sat open. "Hey, Grandma, he put his shirts in here and two pair of pants."

Grandma pointed at the dresser. "But his socks are in the drawer. It's open, too. Where is he? It's not like Taddy to be late or to hide out. You're the one who does the hiding and the disappearing."

I grinned. "Maybe he's upstairs talking to some of the girls. I'll go see."

"I'll see if Mahlee has seen him. She's walking out by the lake." Grandma disappeared from the room.

I jogged up the stairs. "Taddy? Where are you? Hello. Taddy?" I stuck my head into the giant bedroom. No Taddy.

I rushed downstairs and bumped into Mahlee when I rounded the bottom step.

Mahlee scolded me. "Slow down, girl. Did you find Taddy?"

"No. Did you?"

She shook her head.

Grandma showed up at the end of the hall, muttering. "Where is Taddy? When I find him, he's going to deal with me." She opened the door to his room again. "He's simply not here."

Mahlee plopped down on the step. "This isn't like him. Taddy is never the one we're looking for. Unless he's with you."

I scowled. "You act like I stay in trouble."

"You do."

I ignored her.

Grandma coughed into both hands. "The last time I saw Taddy, he was at the doctor's office."

I leaned on the rail. "Doctor Rigghazel is passed out. Boswell found him by a tree and put him in his bed. He said Taddy was already gone."

Mahlee bounced to her feet. "This isn't making sense. Taddy doesn't disappear." She hurried back to his room.

Grandma and me followed like puppies.

Mahlee moved his clothes around in the suitcase. I stood next to her. "What are you looking for?"

"I'm not sure, but he was here. He came back sometime today. He started to pack."

Grandma sat on the edge of the bed, hugging a bedpost. "So, did he come back during the funeral? Someone should have seen him. I don't understand."

Mahlee touched the bedpost, resting her hand on Grandma's fingers. "But he's not here. Why?"

Grandma got up and paced. "I don't understand. Taddy is missing. Taddy is …" She put her hands to her mouth, saying words to herself. Words I couldn't hear.

Mahlee held one of Taddy's shirts to her chest. "Taddy finishes what he starts. Something is wrong."

Grandma looked at the clock on the wall above the bed "It's after three. We need to head to Millerton soon. If we don't find him, we'll have to reschedule our trip. I may have the nurse go ahead with Priscilla though, because Pastor Cody is meeting the train in Texarkana."

Mahlee piped in. "Taddy better not be off playing somewhere. He better have a good excuse. If not, he's gonna get a whipping from me."

I protected Taddy with my words. "You aren't his mama. He has one, and she wouldn't like you touching her boy."

Mahlee smarted back. "Who are you to tell me what to do? You are a child. You get into trouble. You wander off. You get into things you shouldn't. You leave a trail wherever you go. Look at this floor. What is this?"

"It's just flour." I knelt to the floor, erasing my footprints. My hand bumped something small at the edge of the bed. It skidded out of my sight. I crawled under the bed to hunt for it.

"Girl, what are you doing now?" Mahlee's question came with a tug on my shoe.

"I'm looking for something."

Grandma called. "Shoelace, come on. We've got to get help. Maybe the matron knows something."

"I'll be right there." I ran my hand across the floor, catching dust with my fingers. Clutching my lucky rock, the one I'd given to Taddy the other day, I crawled out from under the bed, stood, and put the rock in my pocket, with Priscilla's ring. I hurried to the dining hall where everyone had gathered, and halted to a stop in the doorway.

Mahlee talked to Mrs. Motes. The matron shook her head at Boswell. Grandma sat down with Pastor Motes, and he held her hand like a preacher does to make someone feel better. It didn't seem to be working, because Grandma wiped tears from her face.

Boswell spoke. "I have no idea where he's gone. This isn't looking good. No one has seen the boy since this morning?"

Everyone glanced at Grandma, sighing. Her hand went to her neck. "No. Not since breakfast."

Pastor Motes used his scripture voice. "I'm praying Taddy is safe. Surely, he's fine."

The grownups started talking faster and interrupted each other. Grandma put her hands up like she wanted to scream. She pushed her chair back and shouted. "We're not finding Taddy by sitting here."

Chairs scooted and everyone scuttled off in different ways. Grandma down the hall. Pastor and Mrs. Motes went out the side door. The matron got on the phone. Boswell rushed to the back door by the panty.

Mahlee took my hand. "Come with me. We're going to find him."

Day Four Never Ends

Wasting Precious Time

TADDY'S BEEN MISSING FOR AT least four hours, depending on what time you start counting. Mahlee and me walked to the woods, the lake, and to the cemetery. We hollered for him. Everyone has hollered for him. Taddy wasn't at the train station to say goodbye to his mama tonight, either. I kissed her on the cheek, telling her the peck was from Taddy. Grandma couldn't wait to rush back to Wheelock for any news.

Now I'm curled up in Taddy's featherbed, with orders from Grandma to stay put. I feel like a prisoner. I should be doing something.

I jump from the bed, turning the knob. I skidded down the hallway in my sock feet. I'm listening to another grownup meeting from the other side of the wall.

Boswell offered advice. "It's time to call the Lighthorsemen. We need to get them involved in a search. It's dark now. That wind has blustered in with a force like a spring tornado. There's a storm brewing. The temperature's dropping fast, and the clouds are blowing in from the west. I hope the rain stays away."

Mahlee mouthed. "We need to be out there searching for Taddy. We can't leave him out there alone."

The matron spoke. "I called the Tribal Police earlier. They want me to call back if we need them."

I raced from behind the wall, storming into the dining hall. "Why is everyone just talking? Taddy didn't take a coat or a hat. Doesn't anyone care besides me?"

Grandma hugged me. "We do care. We've stepped off every inch of the grounds. We've retraced our steps and his steps. We don't have a clue why he's gone or where he went."

I wiggled free. "I could find him. I would know where to look. I'd go to the highest hill and pray. I'd be closer to God there. He could show me the way."

Mahlee held my arm. "Girl, stop talking nonsense. You're not going anywhere."

I pried her fingers from my skin. "Nonsense? Grandma prays. You pray scary prayers at Halloween. I've heard you. And Pastor Motes prays, too. Why can't I pray?" I ran from the dining hall and out the door to the shadows where the wind whistled. Sad notes fell from the sky, and my spine felt prickly shivers of sorrow. "Taddy must be freezing." I looked at the half-moon. "Taddy, where did you go? What has happened to you?"

A hand touched my shoulder.

I spun around. "What? What do you want?"

Chula jumped two feet in the air like she figured my swinging arms could hit her. "Shoelace, come with me to the barn."

I looked at the door. No one was coming for me. Grandma probably figured I was letting off steam, and she was right. I smarted off to Chula. "Why would I go with you? You don't even know where my Taddy went today."

"I know he was on his way to the dorm. That's all. But I want to help you find your strength, so you can find him." Chula held a bag at her side, another over her shoulder. She motioned for me to follow. "I have what you need inside these sacks."

"Sure you do. You talk in circles. I don't have time for this. Taddy is lost or hurt or ..." I stomped my feet, folding my arms.

Creak. Creak. Creak.

The door to the dining hall swung open. Grandma called to me. "Get yourself inside. It's cold out there. The police are on their way. They're going to search for Taddy."

I ran inside, turning to look back over my shoulder. I wanted to let Chula know I couldn't go if I wanted to. But she was gone.

Back in the dining hall, Mahlee dished out orders. "You need to get to bed. It could be a long night."

"I'm not leaving this room. Taddy is my best friend, not yours. I will stay here until he's found."

Vroom. Vroom.

I peeked through a window over the sink. "I see two police cars and some men, walking up to the door."

The matron turned the knob before anyone knocked. The men came inside, stomping with forceful steps. Their faces were filled with questions. The man with a mustache spoke. "I'm Officer Smoke. I'll be leading the search team."

The matron warned him. "You better not put my girls in danger."

He nodded and touched her shoulder. "We'll take every precaution. Everyone will be safe."

I marched over to him. "Hey, mister. It's been hours since anyone has seen Taddy. He's going to be eleven next month. He is smart with books, but he won't do good in this cold. You have to go find him, and you have to go now."

"You must be Shoelace."

"Who told you?"

"The matron warned me of a girl who might get in my way. She said you're a feisty one, but she did say you were harmless."

"I'm not in the way. Not yet, anyhow. Taddy is probably freezing out there. Go do your job. You think I'm feisty? I'll show you feisty." I slugged him in the stomach.

Mahlee used her man-like arms to pull me off the officer. "Leave him be. Acting this way isn't going to find Taddy any faster." She pushed me into a chair and put her hand on my shoulder.

I folded my arms.

Mahlee apologized to the officer. "I'm sorry. She's a handful when she gets upset."

I showed my teeth like Black Dog.

"I can handle her. Let's get busy."

Clop. Clop. Clop.

I pulled on Mahlee's hand. "Did you hear that?"

"Be quiet. Just sit."

"But I hear them. Listen."

Neigh. Neigh. Neigh.

Five men barreled through the door. The darkest Indian with long black braids talked first. "We're here to ride the back roads for you. We'll find your boy. We were already in these parts."

The matron shook his hand. "We're so glad to have the Lighthorsemen helping. Taddy will be back soon."

I shouted at the Indian from my chair. "How many little boys have you saved?"

The Lighthorsemen's boots clunked on the floor. He put his hands on the table across from me. "And you would be?"

I couldn't help but notice the mole on his nose. "What did you say?"

"I asked who you might be."

"I'm Annie Grace Kree, best friend to Thaddeus William Day, Jr. My friends call me Shoelace. You can call me Annie Grace until you find Taddy. Then we might be friends."

Grandma stormed over to me. "Shoelace. I've had it. You're being disrespectful. Go to bed. Don't come out unless I come for you." She pointed to the hallway. Her nose hairs waved at me.

"Fine. I'm going." I stopped in the hall, shouting at the top of my lungs. "You better find Taddy. He's the bestest friend I've ever had. I need my Taddy." I ran into the bedroom, slamming the door. I jumped into what used to be Taddy's bed.

I wondered if Chula was in the barn. Maybe I could get her to help me look for Taddy. I'm not sitting here. I hurried across the hall to Grandma's room, got my coat, and rushed to the door leading to the driveway. I pulled the door closed behind me, remembering too late it locks people outside. I ran to the barn. The flickering light told me someone was there.

Before Day Four Can End

War Paint

TADOOM-BOOM. TADOOM-BOOM.
I peeked inside the barn and stepped to the wagon. A headdress of feathers popped up behind a bale of hay. The feathers turned to me, and the booming stopped. Feather-Face spoke. "Are you ready to become a warrior?"

"Chula, what are you doing?"

"I'm dancing." Her lips moved between the yellow and red stripes on her face. Bells jingled on her ankles. Boswell's two mules kicked their hind legs in the corral. The horse neighed, his lips flapping. His nostrils flared, too. His nose reminded me of Grandma's nostrils.

"Why are you dancing?"

Chula handed me a drum stick. "Do you wanna hit the drum? It's time to make you a warrior."

I took the drum stick, waving it. "I'm not a warrior. I came to get your help. I want to find Taddy."

"Then we have to do this first."

Meow. Meow.

Chula jingled to the corner in her moccasins. She bent down in the shadows and turned around, holding an orange cat. "This is War Cat." He had yellow painted stripes like whiskers, and white painted marks for eyebrows.

"What is wrong with that cat?"

Chula sat him on the wagon. "I painted his face. He's ready for our powwow."

"Our powwow? You didn't know I was coming. Why would you think we're having a powwow?"

"I knew you'd be here. I always know where you are."

"You only know this because I'm either at the dorm or the doctor's office. I came to get your help. We can't find Taddy. I need you to take me into the woods. He's out there somewhere."

Chula's white teeth sparkled. "Me? Are you admitting you need me?"

I petted War Cat. "No, I'm not. I need a guide. You know the land. All the grownups are mad at me. I don't have anyone else to talk to."

Chula ran her fingers through the feather on her headdress. "So I'm your last choice, but I should have been your first. Hey, let's dance."

"Stop it. This isn't funny. I need to find Taddy. I'm afraid Margo took him. She tied me up two times, threatening to hurt him, and now, he's gone. This is my fault. I should have told my grandma about that part, but I can't now. She wouldn't understand. I was protecting him. Or trying to …"

Chula handed me War Cat, and I rubbed his face. "Never mind." I put the cat down. "I'm going back to the dorm. I'm going to let them know about Margo. The police need to know this."

Chula hit her drum.

Kaboom. Kaboom.

"You'll put Taddy in more danger. Margo doesn't take to the police, especially if they have guns. I'll help you find Taddy. If she took him, she's not known for hurting children."

I wrinkled my nose. "What about my stitches? She has a funny way of not-hurting. I have rope burns because of her."

Chula wrapped her green sleeve around my shoulder. "It's time for a powwow. I've got to prepare you for battle, so you can take your proper place in the tribe."

Ar roof. Ar roof. Ar roof.

Black Dog charged from beneath the wagon, bumping my legs. He jumped on me, and licked my face. I ran my hands through his fur. "What did you get into?"

Chula answered for Black Dog. "I painted warrior paint on his face, too. He got red and white stripes. We're going to need a good warrior dog on the trail."

War Cat swiped at the back of Black Dog with his paw. I shoved the cat away. "Stop it. You're asking for it."

Ar roof. Ar roof. Ar roof. Grr. Grr.

Black Dog growled with his top and bottom teeth. He tangled with the cat, chasing him through the barn. I ran to pull them apart, and the white horse with red marks on his face snorted at us. "I suppose you put war paint on this horse, too?"

Chula ignored me and started playing her flute.

Loo-woo. Woo-loo. Woo-loo.

The flute whistled a soothing sound and Black Dog nestled on Chula's feet. War Cat settled down next to a bale of hay as Chula's music hypnotized the barn animals. Even the mules quieted down. I felt sleepy, sitting on the first rung of the ladder leading to the loft, yawning.

Kabam. Kabam.

A gust of wind whipped into the barn, and one of the doors bounced back and forth. Chula dropped her flute. Black Dog hurried under the wagon. Chula grabbed her drum and stick, chanting. "Ya-ha-ha-way. Ya-ha-ha-way. Ya-ha-ha-way. Ya-ha-ha-way." She bellowed a chant like she was crying out from the past.

She moved toward me, stopped drumming, and reached into her shoulder sack. She pulled out a pair of moccasins. "Put these on." She tossed me the shoes.

I shook my head, catching them. "I have shoes. I don't need these."

"Moccasins will get you in touch with the earth, and they're soft."

"I don't need them." I shook the moccasins at Chula. The beads on top rattled with little clip-clip sounds.

"Try them on, then decide."

"Don't tell me what to do."

"I'm not. But your red shoes are going to feel heavy. Just try on the moccasins. You're wasting time."

I ran for Chula. She circled the wagon, escaping up the ladder to the loft. Pieces of hay fell through the slats, and she hollered at me. "Your shoes can't catch me."

"Don't make fun of me. I can catch you. You can't get away."

"I'm not trying to get away. I'm showing you how clumsy climbing in those shoes will be when you're in a hurry."

I tossed the moccasins in the dirt and charged up the ladder, catching my shoe on a rung, losing my grip. I tumbled backwards to the ground, squashing the moccasins. "I've hurt my leg. Darn ole stitches."

Chula peeked through a hole in the loft. A red feather drifted down from her headdress. Chula called to me. "Are you hurt?"

"I'm fine, no thanks to you."

Chula climbed halfway down the ladder then she jumped in front of me. "See, you need the moccasins. They don't get caught on ladders. The place we're going, you'll need steady feet."

I nodded, not sure how my head agreed with her, but it did. I pulled off my shoes and slipped on the softest shoes. They were snug on my toes, and tight on my heels. I jumped to my feet. "They're a little small."

"They're perfect. They were made for your feet. I should know."

"Whatever. You act like you know so much and do so little."

"And what are you doing? Taddy's out there somewhere, and the more minutes that tick away, the odds are he might not be found. He could be missing forever."

I charged at Chula, pushing her into the wagon. "I've changed my mind. You keep mocking me. I'm tired of it. I don't need you."

Chula twisted my arm behind my back, and we rolled in the dirt and hay. War Cat scatted at us from the shadows while Black Dog circled us. He danced his own powwow. The mules grunted and kicked in their stalls. I couldn't get Chula off of me because she pinned my shoulders to the ground.

Peck. Peck. Peck.

"Stupid bird. Get your bird off my foot."

"It's Biskinik. He's a messenger. He says they're coming. They're coming."

"Who's coming?"

Chula released me. We caught our breath and lay on the ground side-by-side. We were huffing and puffing like we'd run miles in the woods. She pointed at the barn door. "Someone will be here soon. We must finish our powwow. Then you should meet me after the cry of midnight by the passage. It's in the pantry."

I sat up, brushing hay from my sleeves. "You know about the passage?"

She grinned. "Of course."

Chula grabbed a brush from beside a post and dipped the bristles into a can. Before I could stop her, she splattered my face with something wet.

"What are you doing?"

"It's war paint. You will be a warrior tonight. I'm also giving you a new name."

"I have a name." I touched my face. "Did you paint my face yellow?"

She nodded, dipping the brush into a second can. "Now, I'm putting warrior-red on your eyebrows." Chula bent down and picked up the feather on the ground, sticking it into the back of my ponytail. I chanted under my breath. "Ya-ha-ha-way. Ya-ha-ha-way."

Chula beat on her drum.

Kaboom. Kaboom.

We jumped, chanted, and sang. "Ya-ha-ha-way."

Two shadows moved into the light of the lantern hanging on the nail. Boswell's deep voice broke my chant. "What are you doing in here?"

Chula pushed me forward. I stumbled into Boswell, and explained. "We're having a powwow. I'm a warrior now."

Another shadow came into focus. It was Mahlee.

She scolded me. "We came to the barn with extra blankets for the Lighthorsemen. And what do we find but Annie Grace sneaking out again. What is on your face?"

"It's paint. Chula did it."

"Who's Chula?"

I turned to look around, and Chula had evaporated like a mist of flour. A few pieces of hay drifted down from above my head. A chant whisper floated to my ears. "Your warrior name is Nakni Nita."

Mahlee came closer. "What did you say?"

"Nothing."

"You better be glad your grandma thinks you're in bed."

"So you're not gonna tell?"

Mahlee shrugged. "Not right now. I might use this against you. What's with the feather? And when did you start wearing moccasins?"

"They were a gift. Have you seen my PF Flyers?"

Boswell spoke up. "I'll look for them, but you better get yourself to the dorm."

Mahlee handed Boswell the blankets, and pulled on my arm. "Come on. It's getting cold out here."

"I'm coming."

She popped me on the backside. "When we get inside, get your pajamas on. I'll wrap some fresh gauze on your legs. And please wash your face."

I ran to the dining hall door, but stopped at the corner of the porch as four men on horses galloped by. I yelled at the men. "You better find Taddy. You better."

Mahlee bumped into me. "Get yourself inside before you get a real paddling."

I turned to her. "You are not my mama."

Mahlee took the feather from my hair. "If you say 'not my mama' one more time, I'm going to tell your grandma."

We tramped inside and Grandma asked, "So what are you going to tell me?"

Mahlee shoved me toward Grandma. "Go ahead. Tell her where you've been."

Grandma didn't wait for me to answer. "I can't believe you're playing, with Taddy missing. Get to bed. And stay there."

I snatched the feather from Mahlee's hand. "Thanks, Mahlee."

In bed, my eyes blinked heavy. Wiping them hard with my fists, I tried to stay awake. I'm meeting Chula in the pantry. She's the only person listening to me, and I don't even like her. But, she did give me soft shoes.

Between Day Four and Day Five

Missing the Midnight Cry

I SWATTED AT THE FLY diving at my head, and turned the other way. I pulled the quilt over my ears.

"Get up. Get up. You're a warrior now. Warriors can stay awake."

"What? Who's in here?"

"It's me, Chula. You've missed the midnight cry. Come on. Get up, Nakni Nita." Chula's words hovered over me like a fly in the dark, except this fly was sitting on me.

"Get off me." I wiggled from beneath the covers, stepped to the floor, and inched in the dark to the wall. "Where is the switch?" I ran my hand up and down, hitting it on a piece of furniture. "There it is."

The light came on, but I couldn't see Chula. I looked under the bed. I shook my head. "Where are you?"

Mumbled words came from on top of the bed.

I stood, and spun around. "I know you're in here."

The jumbled and bumpy quilt giggled. I pulled the covers off Chula. "Get out of my bed."

Ha. Ha. Ha.

She held her stomach, gasping for air.

"Be quiet. You're gonna wake my grandma up. She's across the hall. Mahlee's asleep there, too. She'll whip me. What are you doing in here? I'm supposed to meet you in the pantry."

Chula sat crossed-legged by the pillow. She straightened her shirt. "I waited for you in the pantry. I ate a whole jar of blackberry preserves. Mrs. Motes canned them last spring. She always freezes a bunch of berries. She makes cobbler all year long."

"What time is it?" I looked at the clock above the bed. "It's one in the morning? I must have fallen asleep. I didn't mean to. The pillow felt so soft."

Chula jumped to her feet in the middle of the bed, bouncing. "This is a great jumping bed."

I joined her. On each jump, I asked long overdue questions. "Where do you live? Why isn't anyone looking for you? Why is it you spy on folks?"

"I live in Millerton. No one looks for me because I'm not missing. I sit high in trees or on roof tops. They make great spots to keep watch." She jumped up and tried to touch the dangling light bulb. She missed.

I swatted at the light and missed, too. "I'm going to call you Riddles. That's all you give me." I plopped down on the mattress, lost my balance, and tumbled to the floor.

Thud. Thud. Crack.

"Ouch. I hit my head on the dresser."

Chula lay on her stomach, her braids dangling to the floor. "You better be quiet or you'll wake everyone up."

"Stop making fun of me."

Chula played with her hair. "I have to make fun before you make fun of me."

I rubbed my head. "I don't make fun of you."

"Yes, you do. You mock me without thinking."

"I do not, little flute girl."

"Right then, you mocked me."

"I did not. You do play the flute."

Chula pulled me to my feet. "We're wasting time. We need to go. Let me show you the passage."

Knock. Knock. Knock.

Three small taps sent Chula to the floor, and she hid under the bed.

I scooted to the door, turned the knob, and saw a small shadow in the hall. "Bright Eyes? What are you doing here? And why are you knocking on my door?"

She stepped inside the room, and Chula crawled out from under the bed. "Bright Eyes. You thought I was coming back to play my flute for you, didn't you?"

Bright Eyes nodded.

I chimed in. "Wait, you were playing the flute for Bright Eyes? She should be asleep."

"I woke her up by accident." Chula crawled across the bed and sat down. "I got bored after eating preserves. I searched upstairs for you, and fell over her cot in the dark."

I interrupted her. "I'm not up there. Grandma put me in this room. She wants me close."

"I know. Bright Eyes showed me."

Bright Eyes moved closer to Chula, leaned her head on Chula's shoulder and gazed upward.

Chula pulled her flute from her pocket. "I'll play a small tune for you. This is what you want, isn't it?"

I yanked the flute from her. "You can't be making noises."

Bright Eyes grabbed the flute, handing it back to Chula.

Chula smiled at Bright Eyes. "Thank you, Lizzy Beth. I'll play for you tomorrow night. You better get back to bed."

I tugged on Chula's braid. "What did you call her?"

"I called her Bright Eyes." Chula coughed, clearing her throat.

"No, you didn't. You called her by a different name."

"You are hearing things."

"I am not. I know what I heard."

Chula frowned. "What? What did you hear?"

Bright Eyes whimpered, waved to Chula, and darted from the room.

Creak. Creak. Creak.

I went to close the door, and it swung open with force, my hand keeping it from bouncing off the wall. Grandma stormed inside. "Shoelace, I can't believe you're disobeying me like this. Mahlee's swapping beds with you. She'll sleep in here. You'll sleep beside me. I'm keeping an eye on you. I can't trust you."

I hung onto the door, and Chula ducked under the bed.

Mahlee shuffled in her ugly gown from behind Grandma. "Girl, we should have sent you home on the train. You are worrying your grandma." She marched past me, pushed me into the hall, slamming the door.

Grandma tugged on my arm. I pulled away. "Let me trade pillows with Mahlee." I ran to Grandma's bed, picking up a pillow. I carried it with me, barging in on Mahlee. I turned the light on, jumped onto the mattress, and acted like a wild hobo girl. "Mahlee, change pillows with me."

She came up swinging like she does on Halloween when she misses … when she misses … her baby, Lizzy Beth.

Mahlee yelled, knocking me to the floor. "Shoelace, I'm going tie you up myself."

I stood, tripped on my moccasins, and landed back on the floor. I couldn't keep from saying the name Lizzy Beth in my head.

Mahlee walloped me with her pillow, and got tangled in the quilt. Chula slipped from beneath the bed into the hall.

Mahlee screamed. "Get out of here." She threw her pillow at me.

I tossed mine at her head. "Thank you."

The matron's voice rose like a drill sergeant from somewhere down the hall. "It's the middle of the night. My girls have school tomorrow."

I straightened my nightshirt, poking my head into the hall. "Sorry, ma'am." I ran across the hall and crawled into Grandma's bed, but forgot to turn out Mahlee's light. I jumped from the mattress, charging across the hall. I slammed into the locked door. "Mahlee, let me in. I need to turn off your light."

She hollered through the door. "Go away. I've had it with you."

The matron appeared at the top of the stairs. "Silence. Everyone be quiet."

I shuffled back to Grandma's bed, crawling into a warm spot next to her. She scooted to the side, turning her back to me. I tugged on the covers. I was exhausted, worried, and scared.

Sniff. Sniff. Sniff.

Grandma rolled over and wrapped her arms around me. "We'll find our boy. You'll see. You need to try and stay out of trouble, though. It's not helping my nerves."

"I'm sorry, Grandma. I am."

My eyes grew heavy. My hands rubbed my eyes, ears, and face. Sleep would come, but not any answers.

Morning of Day Five

Amazing Grace was not the Sound

I REACHED ACROSS THE COVERS to the flat spot on the bed and rubbed my tired eyes. I need to get dressed and go looking for Taddy.

My packed satchel sat on the dresser from yesterday. I pulled out a pair of overalls and a blue shirt. I slipped on some socks and knelt down looking for my PF Flyers. I ran across the hall instead, retrieving my moccasins, remembering the barn powwow. Remembering my shoes were somewhere in the barn.

I checked the pouch in my satchel for my lucky rock and Margo's ring, and decided to slip them both back inside my pocket.

I shuffled into the dining hall. No girls. Grandma held her head in her hands while Mahlee twirled a fork with her fingers.

Mrs. Motes poured coffee into cups for the Lighthorsemen sitting at the end of the room. She patted one man on the shoulder. "My coffee's good and hot. It must've been cold out there last night."

A man with long sideburns nodded. "We rode the trails down the river and circled back through Valiant. We ran across a couple of coyotes, but no boy."

I gulped. "You saw coyotes?"

The man looked over his shoulder to see who was talking to him. "We did. Sorry, kiddo. No trace of the boy, yet."

My throat ached and my screams were about to leak from my insides. Tears were building up in my eyes. "Grandma, what time is it?"

She sighed like a steam engine without steam. "Shoelace, it's nearly nine in the morning. You've slept through the bell, the girls rustling down the stairs. You've missed breakfast and the song. Before the girls left, they sang 'Amazing Grace' in Choctaw, in remembrance of Eleanor. And for Taddy." She wiped her nose, sniffling.

"I don't care if they sing or not. I'm not hungry."

Grandma moved to me. "Shoelace, we've got layers of worry and sadness on our minds. The Tribal Police and the Lighthorsemen are doing what they can to help us find Taddy. As for you, Mrs. Motes has agreed to watch you. Mahlee and I will be in Millerton and at the doctor's office. We are asking questions and doing our own search. You are to stay here."

I pulled on her arm. "I'm not staying here. Let me go with you. I need to look for Taddy, too." I put my hands on my hips. "Please, let me go?"

Grandma tugged me to a chair "Sit down. I've had it. Do you not see how serious this is? Priscilla's unconscious. And now, her only son is missing. I don't have time to chase you down. You are ten years old. Act like it. Don't give me a reason to paddle you." Her eyes bugged from their sockets, and the veins on her head turned blue under the skin.

I slid down in the seat. "I'm sorry. I'll stay put. I promise."

Mahlee came around the table, holding onto Grandma, who was now shaking and sobbing. Grandma bent down beside me, wrapping her arms around my neck. "I'm sorry. I was harsh. I am so worried. I'm not saying words I mean, and words I mean are not being said."

"Grandma, I'll be good. I'll stay out of the way. I'll listen to Mrs. Motes." I said what she wanted me to say, and not what I meant.

Ring-a-ling. Ring-a-ling.

The matron picked up the phone. "Yes, hello. Yes, this is Wheelock Academy. This is Ms. Brach." She paused. "Yes, she's right here."

I listened in, not able to figure out who the matron was talking to. She motioned to Grandma. "Ms. Elsie, it's for you. He says his name is Pastor Cody Westside."

Grandma dashed to the phone. "Oh, Pastor Cody. Is Priscilla settled in?" She listened, nodding. "Good. Good. I hate to tell you this. We have horrible news about Taddy. He hasn't been found yet. We have search teams on horseback and in cars. We're praying and hoping, but it's been a whole day. Did you hear me? A whole day." She broke down, dropping the phone from her ear.

Mrs. Motes helped Grandma to a chair, and fanned her with an apron. "You got a little faint."

Mahlee picked up the dangling receiver. "Pastor. It's me, Mahlee. We're doing what we can. I'm sure they'll find Taddy soon." She wiped her brow, gasping between those words.

I scooted up next to her, trying to listen to the pastor's words. I couldn't hear him. Mahlee listened for a long time without talking and when she did talk, her voice cracked. "Nothing new with Priscilla either, huh? Thank you for keeping watch over her. We'll keep you posted on what's happening here."

Mahlee pushed me away, frowning.

I stomped my foot. "Stop it. I'm not doing anything."

She scowled at me but used kind words with the pastor. "Yes, do pray for Taddy. And for those looking for him. We'll

156

talk soon." Mahlee hung up the receiver, moved to the table, and sipped from a cup. "This isn't my coffee. It has sugar."

Grandma stood, bumping into the chair. "Come along, Mahlee. Let's go find our boy." She wiped her hands down the front of her dress.

They headed into the hall as a man at the table called to Mrs. Motes. "More coffee, ma'am."

She smiled, hurrying with the pot. "Drink up. Then you can get some rest in the barn. There are blankets for you in the loft."

The burly man spoke. "Thank you, ma'am."

I grunted. "She didn't put them there. My friend, Mahlee did."

Grandma must have heard my mouthing. She stuck her head into the room. "Shoelace, I warned you."

"Yes, ma'am." I shuffled to the dining hall door and turned the knob. I stuck my head into the cold wind. "Black Dog? Come here, boy. Here boy."

He didn't come.

I could hear the girls in music class at Wilson Hall across the way singing, but I couldn't make out the words.

A touch on my shoulder made me jump. "Watch it, little bit." The cop man in dirty pants, and dirtier boots pounded down the steps. "You better keep out of our way."

I followed him outside, mocking his walk. My shoulders bobbed up and down. I tried to walk bowlegged. I stopped next to the front porch when he turned around. "I'm not little."

He scowled. "You're not too big or tall. You're a tiny one." He bellowed a laugh like coffee gurgling.

Ha-ha. Ha-ha.

"Don't laugh at me. I'm big for my age." I followed him, stopping in my tracks. Another man bumped into me. I mouthed. "I hope your blankets are itchy."

He didn't respond.

Meow. Meow.

"War Cat, you still have your powwow stripes." He jumped into my arms from the porch and I rubbed his ears.

Purr. Purr. Purr.

Mrs. Motes peeked out the door. "Shoelace, will you help me clean up the dishes? The girls will be breaking for lunch soon, and there's work to be done."

"Yes, ma'am." Goodness, I'm trapped now.

I followed Mrs. Motes inside, stacked plates and forks, and carried them to the giant sink.

Mrs. Motes grabbed bowls and pans, clanking and moving them to the counter. She hollered in a mama-like voice. "Here, put six cups of flour in this bowl."

"With what?"

"Take this measuring cup."

"Where's the flour?"

Mrs. Motes pointed to the door at the back of the room. "Remember, the pantry is off to your right. You'll see all kinds of supplies."

I took the measuring cup, dropping it into the bowl. "How much flour did you say?"

"Six cups."

I took the bowl, turned it over, and pounded on it with the tin cup. "Ya-ha-ha-way. Ya-ha-ha-way."

Mrs. Motes grinned. "I have me some good powwow help."

I circled the tables, pounding and singing.

Mrs. Motes called to me. "Hurry along. I need the flour today."

"Yes, ma'am." The pantry room was almost as big as a bedroom. The shelves wrapped around three walls. They were filled with preserves and each glass jar had a label. Strawberry, blackberry, and peach. In the corner of one shelf an empty jar, one with sticky spots on the glass, told me Chula must have snacked in this very spot.

Kapoooom. Kapoooom.

A bumping sound came from behind the flour sacks.

I whispered, "Who's there?"

A pair of hands pulled me over the burlap, to the floor. One hand covered my mouth. "Surprise, it's me—Chula. Don't scream."

I yanked her hand from my face. "Mrs. Motes will hear you. What are you doing in here?"

"I've been waiting. You missed our sunrise meeting."

"I was asleep."

"Now you're awake. Let's go find Taddy. It's time. You need to do your part."

"My part? I'm not supposed to leave. Mrs. Motes is babysitting me. If I go with you, I'll never be allowed outside again."

Chula pushed two sacks aside. She pointed at a little door the size of a dog house door under the bottom shelf.

"Is that the passage entrance?"

Chula pulled me to my knees. "Yes, it's an exit, or an entrance."

I opened the half-sized door. A flashlight sat on the top step. I picked it up, pushed the switch, and lit up the concrete steps. "It's dark in there. I don't like the passage. It's black. Too dark for me."

Chula touched my shoulder. "The light you look for is from above..."

I handed Chula the flashlight, standing up. "I don't have time for your riddles."

"Have it your way. But remember this could be the way in one day." Chula crawled through the passage door, peeking back at me on her knees. "When you need the passage, it will be here."

Mid-day of Day Five

White Horse of Hope

I SCOOPED FLOUR INTO THE bowl, knocking the opened flour sack into the others. I propped the sack upright, only for it to fall the other way. My measuring cup clinked to the floor. The bowl followed.

Klopp. Klopp. Klopp.

The clunking of boots on the hardwood floor in the dining hall caused the wood under my feet to rumble. I chased the cup, crawling through white clouds of flour swirling above my head. I pulled the cup from between two sacks as the dusty-white flour settled on the jars.

A voice inside the kitchen came with a request. "I'm looking for Mrs. Elsie Kree. We've found a boy's loafer. I need to identify the shoe."

I rose to my feet, peeking around the door.

Mrs. Motes answered with her scaredy-cat voice. "Mrs. Kree is in Millerton with Mahlee. Boswell took them to town. You must have passed them on the road."

Officer Smoke glanced at me, sighing. "I rode in from the other side of the lake, so I didn't see them."

I rushed to Mrs. Motes as puffs of flour jostled from the bowl. I plowed right into her backside. She grabbed the bowl from me. "Girl, careful now." She took a long look at me. "I sent you for flour. It appears you've dumped most of it on your head."

I wiped my face with my hand, and moved to the cop washing his hands in the sink. "Did you … did you find Taddy?"

Officer Smoke shook his head. "Not yet. But we think we know which way he left, if the shoe we found is his."

I tugged on his sleeve, and dust flew into my face. I coughed. "Do you have the shoe with you?"

"No, the shoe was taken to our check point by the doctor's office. We've set up a tent near his pond."

My moccasin shoes itched on my feet. I was ready to run straight to the tent. Mrs. Motes must have known this because she came up behind me and held my arm.

I pulled free. "I have to see. I have to see if it's Taddy's shoe. He got them for Christmas from his mama. I know what size, too. I'm the person who knows everything about Taddy."

I suppose my pleading made sense to Mrs. Motes, who hugged me like Grandma does when she makes up with me. "I'll take you. You can ride with me. I'll get the matron's car keys."

Officer Smoke went out the side door without saying a word.

Mrs. Motes untied her apron and moved to the long hallway. "I have to remind the matron that the older girls will have to prepare lunch. I'll be right back. Stay right here."

I circled the tables like a wild horse. I wanted Taddy found, not his shoe. I wanted to ride the train home to the tree where Taddy and me play. I wanted to go to the spot by the creek where we go to church on Saturdays with our hobo friends. I even wanted to go to school where I beat up boys and get sent to the office. I wanted Priscilla to wake up. I wanted Taddy to be alive. Time's getting away. I'm not waiting for Mrs. Motes.

I ran to the back door by the pantry, cracking open the wooden door. The little curtain on the windowpane waved goodbye to me.

I stepped outside, and water dripped from the tower. Small puddles muddied the ground. I tiptoed around the small building next to the tower. I stopped because someone was talking.

A deep voice said, "If that's his shoe, then the little boy vanished north along the river. I hope he didn't fall into those rapids."

I kicked the dirt, hoping for the right second to run toward the front of the dorm, for the right moment to run and check out the shoe.

Another man responded with his remarks. "The longer he stays lost, the less likely we'll find the boy. The wolves or coyotes, or the wild pigs will get him."

I choked on spit, and started to yell at them, but I didn't want to get caught for sneaking off. Two horses galloped by with the riders, and they rode toward the main road.

I turned and stumbled on something, slicing my moccasin. I wiggled my toes. My black sock now stuck through the leather. I picked up the pointy rock, flipped it over in my hand, and tossed it to the sand.

I ran my hand over some old horseshoe tracks. Daddy and me used to follow horse tracks on the rail. He showed me how to touch them to see if they were fresh. These were not.

Ar roof. Ar roof.

Black Dog jumped on me. I wrapped my arms around his neck. "Come on, boy. Go with me. Let's go see if it's Taddy's shoe."

Neigh. Neigh. Neigh. Pupple-fuffle.

A horse sneezed or spit, causing me to stumble. I stepped around the building where the two men rode by on their horses. I was facing a sparkling white horse the color of fresh snow. He kicked the dirt with his back hoof. He *pupple-fuffled* again. He knelt down like he wanted me to climb on his back.

"Nice horse." I ran my hand along his silky mane.

Pupple-fuffle.

He nudged my arm with his nose. His mane blew in the wind like a wave to my heart. His blue eyes shone like the blue ring in my pocket. I petted his nose, and he snorted. He knelt down again, his front leg extending as if he welcomed me to ride.

I rubbed his nose. "Can I sit on you?"

He bobbed his head up and down.

I climbed on, straddling the muscled horse. My legs felt hope rising up from his strength. He raised up, standing high enough for me to see inside the dining hall window.

Ar roof. Ar roof. Grrr. Grrr.

Black Dog hunkered behind the white horse, ready to attack something.

"What is it boy?"

Margo rode into view on her horse. "Get out of the way, dog. Go on." She held onto a rope, waved it above her head, and lassoed my body. "Girl, you're coming with me."

I wiggled, trying to get the rope off. "I'm not. Did you take Taddy? Let me go. I'm gonna scream."

"You scream, and it will be your last." Margo tugged on the rope, and her horse kicked at Black Dog.

Yelp. Arrr. Arrr.

Black Dog cowered to the steps, disappearing around the side of the dorm.

Margo came up next to me. "You'll see. Things are not as they seem. I am not who you think I am. Ride with me, and you'll save Taddy's life."

164

"What? This is crazy? I am not coming with you."

"You will, or you will find yourself being pulled on the ground." Margo loosened the rope, pulled it over my head, and put the rope around my horse's neck. "Hold on. We have a long ride ahead of us."

"I'm not going with you. You are not my mama." I slid off the horse, rolling to the ground. Margo jumped from her horse, tied my hands and feet, and tossed me on the horse.

"Stop. Let me go. The police will get you. You'll see."

I tried to see what Margo was doing, but I was looking at the side of my horse's stomach. My hands on one side. My feet on the other. Margo lifted my chin. "Be quiet. Or you'll come up missing, too."

Margo rode her horse in front of me. I found myself bouncing on the back of the white horse. We went slow, and rode into the thick bushes. Blood rushed to my ears. I slobbered from my mouth, unable to swallow at this angle. We rode long enough for the sun to change places in the sky. Long enough for me to cry all of my tears.

"Whoa. Whoa." Margo climbed down from her horse, coming to me. "I'm untying your feet so you can sit upright. Don't scream. Don't kick the horse. Don't try to outsmart me, or I'll tie you in one of these trees and leave you. You'd die before they got to you."

I nodded, feeling the blood drain into my body as I sat right side up. I held the mane with my tied hands. I need my grandma. I need my Mahlee. I don't understand why this is happening.

Margo led my horse behind hers, and we galloped down the hill on dark, shadowy trails. I have no idea how I'm getting away. If she thinks I'm helping her, Margo is wrong.

She yelled at me. "Don't let go! The road is rough. The ride is worse."

Pam Kumpe

Day Five Goes on Forever

Wind Horse Rides Away

THE WIND WHIPPED MY HAIR like a horse's mane, and I held on tight. The white horse galloped and raced, snorted and neighed. My horse kept right behind Margo's horse. He had no choice. She had him roped to her.

Not one Lighthorseman came our way. Not one tribal officer. Not one person.

Margo called to me. "Hold on, or you'll slide off. The trail is even rougher in these parts. I need you alive."

I tugged with both hands on the mane. What does she mean, she needs me alive?

We turned right on a tight trail, then back to the left. We met some leaning posts like the ones in the woods by the church at Wheelock. These posts pointed not one way, not two, but five or six directions.

We rode for miles, left the area, and made new trails. We doubled back on others, circling the same trees. We cut across a shallow pond. My moccasins were wet, and my socks soaked. "Can we slow down? I can't hold on."

She turned her horse around and rode next to me. "Keep your hands on the mane. I'm untying them so you won't fall."

I rubbed my fingers together, grabbing tighter. "Did you take Taddy? He never hurt you. He doesn't even know you."

Margo kicked the side of her horse, her dress flying like an upside down balloon. "We've got to make up for lost time. Taddy is in danger. We might be too late."

My horse took off in a pace faster than we'd ridden earlier. My hair tangled in knots. My shoulders and my arms ached like the time I hit fancy-dress Clara for making fun of hobos. My eyes burned from the cold air. I leaned forward, locking my fingers on the mane, fading in-between being awake and wondering if I was going to fall off. "Can't we stop? I can't hold on much longer."

Margo didn't answer. Her moods were keeping pace with the change in temperature. The air turned colder, but the wind let up. We came to a clearing without trees, riding up and down the hills. Each slope reminded me how a wrinkled quilt looks on a mattress with its valleys and dips. I counted each gallop of my horse. "One. Two. Three. Forty-five. Eighty-two." I stopped counting at a hundred. I couldn't feel anything. I was numb.

Margo slowed, riding her horse to the shade. The tree's branches hung like a canopy with holes. She turned to me. "We'll stop here for a minute. Not long. Just for a minute."

My horse knelt down like he wanted me to slide off. I swung my leg over and jumped down, whispering into his ear. "Thank you. You're a nice horse. Maybe you could be a getaway horse."

The horse nudged me, snorting.

Margo pulled me to the ground. "Sit here. Don't move. Whatever you do, don't scream." She handed me a tin container with a lid. "There's some water in there. Don't drink much. It's got to last."

I slapped the can to the ground. "I'm not thirsty. I'm not drinking anything you give me." I spouted off ugly words before I could stop myself.

"You'll go thirsty then." Margo picked up the can, swallowing a long, hard drink. "It's not poison. I drank some." She tossed the water can at my feet.

I pulled my knees to my chest and sat with my arms over them. I watched Margo pace in a circle around the tree. She mumbled and said words under her breath. She kicked the tree. "This is not the way it should go. I need the girl to help me find Taddy. I need her." She put her hands to her ears. "Stop the voices. Everybody be quiet."

"Are you talking to me?"

She turned to me. "I might be. I need your help."

"What is it? Don't you remember what you did with Taddy?" I struggled to my feet, ready to fight her. I didn't care if she tied me to a tree, or hit me, or killed me. I had to know. I had to find out why she took Taddy. And why she needed me.

She shoved me in the chest. "Sit down, and shut up."

I coughed. "I'm not here to help you. I'm not going to listen to you. I'm not your slave."

Margo took the rope from her horse and tied me to the tree. "You're gonna have to keep quiet. You can't draw any attention. We have to go through this part of the country like we are deer. Invisible by day. Traveling by night.

"What? We've been traveling for hours in daylight. You make no sense. You are crazy like they say." I kicked at her twice, but moccasins can't hurt anyone. If I had my PF Flyers on, then I could have gotten in a couple of good kicks.

"Crazy? I'm not crazy. I'm the one who helps. I'm the one who saves the babies. I don't kill them. I save them."

"You talk in riddles, too. What's with Oklahoma? Everyone talks, but nothing makes sense."

"I make sense. I simply want to be left alone. Priscilla came here uninvited. I left her. I left Taddy."

I wiggled. "I have to go to the bathroom. Let me loose, so I can."

Margo squinted. "It's a trick. You'll run."

"I won't. I promise." I lied. I hoped to get a few feet away from this crazy woman so I could get down the hill. I had to make a break for it. I wasn't sure what she might do next, but if she kept me tied up, I was stuck here without anyone to help me.

Margo loosened the rope on the tree, but tied my ankles together. "You can hop like a rabbit to your spot. Hurry up."

I hopped a couple of feet. "I'm hurrying. I can't do this with my feet tied."

She came over, taking the rope off my legs. One end of the rope got tangled on a bandage under my overalls. Margo pulled up my pant leg. "Did I hurt you the other night?"

"Of course you did. If you'd left me alone, Eleanor would still be alive, too." I shouted at the top of my lungs, hoping someone was near, hoping a farmer might catch a word or two.

Margo put her hands to her head. "I tried to stop. I did. I tried to stop. I told you. I told you *we were* going to hurt someone. But you insisted on tying up the girl."

I screamed at Margo. "Who are you talking to?"

Margo glanced at me, then to the right and the left, and mumbled words of hate. "You are the reason. You are the reason Eleanor died. It's not my fault. If you had gone home, and if you had stayed out of my business, I wouldn't need to have you with me now—to find Taddy."

I danced around her like a circus performer. "Do you have Taddy or not?"

Margo's hand slicing across my cheek stung. I fell to my knees. I took off running, and lost my torn moccasin. I charged between some trees, bruising the bottom of my foot with each step.

Clop. Gallop. Gallop. Clop. Neigh. Neigh.

A nudge on my back sent me rolling down the hill. The white horse caught up with me. I landed like a sack of flour at the bottom. Between his teeth, the horse held my lost shoe. "Thank you, Wind Horse."

I slipped my shoe on, realizing I'd just given the horse a name. A rope sailed over my head, and my body landed sideways in the dirt. Margo tied my hands again. She tossed me onto Wind Horse. "Stop trying to get away. You will never make it. I will leave you at the bottom of the pond, if you run again."

I rubbed my face. "Where are we going?"

Margo pulled my horse along. We rode down the ravine. I caught a glimpse of a rickety, wooden building surrounded by weeds on the hill. The sun cast a light shadow across the slanted roof.

"Is Taddy in that shack?"

"Be quiet. Just be quiet." Margo stopped and climbed down from her horse in front of the shack.

She snatched me from the back of Wind Horse, and I crumbled to the dirt. I tried to stand, but my legs cramped. I rubbed my calf. "What are we doing here?"

Margo yanked a piece of cloth from her dress pocket, wrapping it around my eyes. "You need to listen. Stop asking questions."

I quivered, wobbling with each step. "Why blindfold me? I've already seen the shack."

Margo held my arm, leading me somewhere. I stubbed my toe on something. She ordered. "Step up. Or you'll fall."

A creak told me we were going inside. A bam-slam behind me told me we had walked through a door. "Where are you taking me? At least, untie my hands."

"Shut up. Rest for now. We have a long ride tomorrow." Margo shoved me to the floor, untied my hands, and slipped the cloth from my eyes.

"I thought we rode at night? I don't understand. You cover my eyes for three feet? You are crazy."

"I'm not crazy."

A sting on my face sent me to the floor.

I whined. "Stop hitting me. I'm not your punching bag. I don't think you even know where Taddy is."

"Shut up. I do, too. We'll find Taddy when I'm ready."

I rubbed my face, squinting in the dark. The room formed a jail cell around me. A lantern sat on the desk by the door. I wiped my nose with my hand. "What is this? Why are we here?"

Margo didn't answer, lit the lantern, and pulled the door to the room closed. The door knob clicked.

I hobbled to the door, rattling it. It was locked. I screamed. "I'll burn this place down if you don't let me out." I picked up the lantern.

"You'll not be burning anything down if you're smart." Margo unlocked the door, came inside, snatching the lantern from me. "Sit in the dark. See if I care if the rats get you." She pulled the door closed, locking it again.

Alone in the room, I looked for an escape route, like a passage. But I was trapped. The walls were laced with cracks, and the light of the moon shone through like a dozen flashlights beaming toward one spot—the locked door. The window was boarded up. There was the desk. But no chair. Box springs. But no mattress. A blanket. But no pillow. What are those black dots on the blanket? Are those rat droppings?

I pounded on the door. "You better let me go. The police will be looking for Taddy and me. They'll lock you up and keep you in jail forever for taking two little kids."

Margo opened the door and came inside. "I brought you some cheese. The rats like cheese."

I mouthed. "If we're looking for Taddy, why aren't you in any hurry? Where is he? We need to find him."

Margo set the plate down on the desk, taking a pair of handcuffs from her dress pocket.

"What are those for?"

"I'm doing this for your own good. I'm chaining you to this bed post. You must decide. You have tonight to think it over. One night. If you won't help me, I'll leave you locked inside this room at sunrise, with the rats."

Morning Sunrise of Day Six

When Splinters Fly

A RAT SCURRIED ACROSS THE floor to the corner as I rubbed crust from my eyes. I'm pretty sure the rat slept with me last night.

Bam. Bam. Bam.

Margo shouted at me from the other side of the wall. "What do you have against this door?" Her words shattered the quiet, and the rat disappeared behind a rusty pot.

I yelled at her. "You can't get in."

"Why not?"

"Because I've blocked the door with the box springs and with the desk."

"Why would you block the door?"

"I'm tired of you slapping me, and I'm not going with you."

"Let me in. We've got to go now. I'll never hit you again. Besides, I don't hit."

"You do hit. You've slapped me twice. I have a bruise on my face. I can prove it."

Margo wailed. "I'm sorry. I don't mean to hurt you. I won't hit you. I can stop. I will keep my hands quiet." The knob shook. "Now, open this door."

"I can't. The door's blocked."

Margo raised her pitch. "Move the furniture. Move it, now."

"I'm not. I'm staying here."

Silence.

I leaned against the door. "Are you there?"

"I'm leaving. You can stay here. You're more trouble than I need."

Two rats peeked at me from behind that same pot. I moved the box springs and shoved the desk. The desk toppled against the door frame. I couldn't get the door open. "Please, don't leave me here to die. No one will find me in this shack."

Margo pounded on the door. "I've got an axe in the other room. I'll be right back."

I sucked in air. "An axe? What are you going to do with it?"

She yelled. "I'll cut my way into the room."

"Wait. You might hit me with the axe."

Silence.

"Are you there?" I called to her and kicked the door with my foot.

Thwack. Thwack. Thwack.

The wood splintered above my head. I yelled into the key hole. "You're going to hit me."

Thwack. Thwack. Thwack.

"Then move away. Cover your head. I'm coming in."

"Just don't cut me."

Margo made a hole the size of a big window. She piled into the room, hurling over the desk. She toppled to the floor. "Let's go. We're wasting time."

I held my hand up. "I'm handcuffed to the box springs. I can't move."

Margo dug in her skirt pocket, pulling out a key.

I laughed, climbed over the desk, and jumped through the hole in the door. "I'm not chained. The handcuffs are huge, and they slide right off. I'm not you're prisoner. I'm out of here."

"What? See, this is why I slap you."

I yelled from the porch through the screen. "The handcuffs are made for grownups. I'm just a kid." I turned to run, slamming into the belly of Margo's horse. He kicked at me, and I ran behind a tree.

Margo shouted from the porch. "You can't get away, not unless I say so. I might say so, but I'm not saying so right now. You think you can outsmart me? You think you can run? Not today. Maybe not tomorrow, either. Taddy's out there. I've got to save him."

I frowned at the mean ole horse and at Margo. She charged at me. Her hand went back like she was going to sting my face with her fingers, again. Wind Horse showed up from behind me. He *pupple-fuffled*, stepping in front of Margo, blocking her.

I gave Margo my what for. "Where is Taddy? You're the one who took him. Everybody thinks so. Locking me in this house hasn't found him, either."

She reached around the horse, pulled me by the arm, throwing me to the ground. "I never took the boy. I wouldn't take him." Margo rolled me onto my back, and pulled out a roll of gauze. "Your bandages need changing. If you're going to help me, I need you to be strong. You need your health."

"You are scaring me. I don't know what you are doing."

Margo almost sounded like Priscilla when she talked about my bandages, and almost sounded sane. She sort of sounded like Chula, too.

I winced. "Be careful."

"Sit up. Let me look at the place on your back."

I obeyed her like I was on an invisible leash. I slipped one buckle from my shoulder, and lifted my shirt.

"You're a skinny white girl."

I mouthed fighting words. "I have Choctaw in me. I'm a warrior."

"You're a tiny one."

"I am not. I can fend for myself."

"Sure you can."

Margo replaced the bandage on my shoulder blade, watching me with kind eyes. "I need you to be with me when we get Taddy. He will be afraid of me, but if he sees you, he'll know things are gonna be better."

"You don't have Taddy?"

She put her hand to her neck. "No, but they do."

I slapped her hand. "I don't know if I should trust you. You've locked me up. You've hurt me. Slapped me. Roped me. And threatened me. How do I know you're telling me the truth?"

"I told you, girl. I meant to scare you, but you didn't leave. You didn't give me a choice." Margo twisted my arm.

I yanked free. "See, there you go. You're doing it again. Stop hurting me."

"But, you argue with me. You cause me to get riled up."

I tried to figure out how Margo could act crazy and sane, in one breath.

Margo tapped me on the shoulder. "I have to tell you this. Right before Eleanor's funeral, I followed Taddy from the doctor's office to Wheelock. Scar and Red rode up on their horses behind the dining hall. They were up to no good." She stopped talking mid-sentence, looked at the sky, and dashed inside the shack.

I stood up, unable to move. I'm confused. I'm drawn to Margo like a magnet, but repelled by her meanness. I'm afraid the next slap she dishes out to my face will knock me cold.

176

Brown Horse chomped on the grass next to the tree. Wind Horse had disappeared somewhere. If I hurry down the hill and through the bushes, I could get close to the river. I stepped toward the woods.

"Where are you going?" Margo's voice cut through the wind like a knife. She pressed her nose on the screen. "We haven't finished our talk. I'm not going to hit you. I promise." I hollered at her. "You're crazy. I'm not helping you. I will not. I need my Taddy. I'm leaving right now. I'm going for help. If those men have Taddy, we need the Lighthorsemen."

Margo slammed the screen against the wall, marching outside. In her hand she held the axe. She jumped to the porch, screaming at me. But then, she collapsed on the steps, covered her face, and dropped the axe.

She rocked like a baby. In her hand, she held a piece of paper close to her chest. She bellowed. "I miss him. I left him. I want him. I need to find him. I love him. I can't keep him. He won't understand."

Margo ran to the top of the hill, wailing like I did when my daddy died. It's like she couldn't control her sad thoughts anymore. They exploded in a rage.

Wind Horse showed up, and nudged me. He latched his lips onto my wrist, tugging me to the kneeling Margo. He placed my arm onto Margo's shoulder.

Wind Horse knelt down beside Margo, rested his head on her other shoulder. It's like he gave her a horse-hug. Margo's sobs quieted. She waved the paper in front of Wind Horse. "I have to show Taddy this photograph. He needs to know. He needs to know everything."

Before Noon of Day Six

The Crazy Lady Saved the Baby

I MOVED MY ARM FROM Margo's shoulder. "What's with the picture? Why does it make you cry?"

Margo mumbled and rocked, then bolted to her feet. "It's my picture. I want to show Taddy. Not you."

A gust of wind sent a chill through my clothes. With each mumble from Margo, a chill of sadness fell from the clouds. A storm brewed over our heads like the one thundering inside of her.

Swoosh. Swoosh.

"My picture." Margo flew down the hill, tracking her photo in the whirlwind of sand and leaves.

I caught up with her, taking in the path to my right, which might be a possible escape.

Margo grabbed my arm. "There it is. Get the photo for me."

"That looks like poison ivy. Get it yourself."

"It's winter. Those are just weeds. Get my photo."

"I thought you didn't want me to see it."

Margo pushed me out of the way, stomped to her photo, and picked it up. She glanced at it, turning to me. "Get your eyes off of that trail. We're going another way. We have to go. We must go."

I shook my head, more confused than ever. I inched a few feet away, shuffling in my moccasins.

Margo shoved me and screamed. "Never mind. Go home. Go on. I'll get Taddy. I'll save him. I don't need you."

I moved down the path, and her sobs grew faint. I kept stomping and running until my heart pounded like a powwow drum. The clouds thundered and rumbled with my heart, and the crumpling leaves told me—I'm not alone.

Margo lunged at me from behind a tree. "I've changed my mind. I need you to help me find Taddy. He won't come with me. He'll listen to you. Can you come with me? I won't hurt you."

I found myself nodding yes, because if I didn't she'd hurt me. "I'll go with you. Where do we look?"

Margo's face lit up. "He's with the brothers, Scar and Red. I'm sure of it. They take from people, but they don't usually take people. Taddy must have gotten in their way."

"Then let's get him."

Margo crumpled the photo in her right hand, yelling in her crazy voice again. "I can't! I can. I should. I will. No, I won't! Wait, I gave him away once. I don't know how to get him back. They will want something in return. I have nothing to swap, unless ..." She looked at me. "I give them you."

"You are trading me for Taddy?" I ran like a deer, but my sleeve snagged on a bush, causing me to fall.

Margo's hand pulled my hair, and she stood me to my feet. "You can't go. I need you. I've got something to swap."

I yelled at her. "We need help from the police or the horse cops."

"No, we don't need them. They'll spook the brothers." Margo waved the wrinkled photo at my face. "I have to show Taddy this."

"Why?" I snatched the photo away. "It's just Priscilla. She's a whole bunch younger, and she's holding Taddy. But who is the man?"

Margo took the photo from me. "That is Thaddeus William Day, Sr. He's Taddy's pa. And … that's me with them."

I looked at the photo again. "No, way. That's Priscilla. I know her." I glanced at Margo's tired face, and down at the snapshot. "Well, maybe. It could be you. But I think you're lying."

"I'm not. I can prove it."

"Why does this matter? Why do I care if you're in a picture with Mr. Thaddeus? Taddy told me you used to live with them."

"But … he doesn't know this. No one does." She ambled to the wooden fence leading to the shack, and ran her fingers along the slats.

"Know what?" I talked to her like she wasn't crazy.

"Look at the picture. Look at my ring finger." She held the photo under my nose.

"So what? It's just a ring."

"Look again."

I put my nose inches from the picture. "I see an oval stone."

"It's not just any ole ring. My pa gave that ring to my sister, Margo."

I shook my head. "What? You're Margo."

"No, I'm the real Priscilla. We traded places. Our pa gave Margo the ring."

"I don't understand. Why would you two trade places? You're lying to me."

"I'm not. I'm Priscilla." She put her hand to her heart. "I'm Taddy's mama."

I paced in a circle. "No, you're not. I know his mama. She is unconscious, but I know her."

180

"No. We traded places to protect Taddy from me."

I held my ears, shaking my head. "This is too mixed up. I don't understand."

Margo marched around me muttering more words, pointing at the photo. "That is me in the picture. I was Priscilla, but now I have to be Margo."

"But why do you have to be Margo?" I put my hand inside my pocket and felt for the ring, which was still nestled next to my lucky rock.

"I left Taddy in the cold one night. I forgot him at the store four times. I forgot to feed him. I forgot who he was. So I had to leave. I had to go away. I was afraid for him."

I shouted at Margo. "People don't just leave their kids and give them new mamas."

Margo charged up the hill. "Enough. No more talk. A storm's coming. Get inside. I know who I am. You don't."

The wind burned my face and pellets of ice skipped from my hair to the ground. The shadow of confusion turned into a real ice storm. We ran to the shack. The walls let in most of the cold air, and the dark fireplace whistled.

"I've got coats in the back room." Margo rushed to get them.

I touched the window pane. "Margo, the horses. They need to get out of this weather."

She rushed by me, slipped on a coat, and tossed me a flannel jacket. She hurried out the front door, only to return with our horses.

Clop. Clop. Clop. Clop.

Wind Horse and Brown Horse followed her into the front room. I touched Wind Horse on the nose while Margo ran her fingers down the mane of Brown Horse. "I might need to get me a barn. Might not. Might build one. Might even change my name."

"There you go. Talking all weird."

Margo's eyes twitched. "Priscilla hates me. Or maybe she's forgiven me. Or maybe she loves me. I can't remember."

"Priscilla doesn't hate anyone. She can get testy, but hate isn't inside her." I thought my head might explode. "This is crazy. Who trades places for life?"

"Me and my twin. That's who."

"But you had a baby. Mamas want their babies."

"I wanted to love him. But my mind … it goes places without me."

"Maybe you've mixed this story up with your little girl. I know you have a baby."

"I'm not mixed up. Not with this story. Priscilla knows the truth. She'd tell you. I know the truth. And now, you know. As for my little girl, I do have a baby. She's with my friends at home."

"So are you gonna keep her? Or trade her off?"

Margo rubbed her hands like they were wet, like she was washing away sins from her past. She shouted so loud, the horses bumped into each other. "We need to get Taddy home to the only mama he's ever known. Storm or not, we're going now."

"It's freezing out there."

She stepped next to me. "I can't do this alone. I promise, I won't hurt you."

"You won't hurt me?"

"I'll do my best."

When Night Falls on Day Six

Shoots of Bamboo

WIND HORSE SNEEZED, AND HIS snorting reminded me of Taddy when he sneezes. I hope Taddy's not hurt. I hope we find him. Margo bounced in front of me on her horse. I called to her. "Where are we going? Are you sure you know the way?"

Margo didn't answer, but her head went up and down. Did she say yes or was it because she's on a horse?

Sadness slipped through me every time Wind Horse took a step. "Margo, we've gone over this part of the trail. We're lost."

No answer.

"Margo, we need to turn around."

No answer.

"Margo …"

Nothing.

The only good thing that's happened in the past few hours is the ice from this morning didn't stick. The wind is cutting through my coat. I'm freezing from the gusts that whip between the trees. "Whoa, Wind Horse." I pulled on his mane. "Not too fast."

Gallop. Plop. Gallop. Plop.

Margo kicked her horse. He galloped faster than a deer running from a bullet fired in the woods. Wind Horse joined the race. I hung on like a kangaroo holding onto its mama's tummy.

Margo adjusted the sling-satchel on her back, and shifted her axe to the other side of her shoulder. Her rope hung from a loop on the satchel. A couple of blankets were tied to her waist. She took a glance back at me. "What are you doing, Shoelace? Keep up. The trail is rocky through here."

"I hear water trickling over there." I pointed to the right near the east, away from where the sun hid low.

"No, we don't need to go there. The brothers don't like the river."

"How do you know?" I called to her, and Wind Horse neighed.

"I told you, I know them, and they aren't the water kind."

"But it's going to be dark soon. We're lost. I know it."

She rode back to me. "We are close. I can sense it. I smell smoke. Someone has a camp." Margo turned her nose up like snotty girls do back home. "Don't you smell the wood burning?"

"I smell something. Do you really think it's them?"

"It's them. It must be."

"I'm going to check the river." I guided my horse through a web of brush, going as far as I could until the tall weeds and thorny bushes blocked the way. Then I saw a post ... like the ones leaning in the woods by the orphanage.

Margo rode up behind me. "I guess this is as good a way as any. But why do you keep stopping?"

"It's one of the leaning posts. We must be going the right way."

"What? You find your way following posts?" Margo guided her horse back to the main path. "Never mind, I'm going back to the trail. You better follow me."

"I'm going this way." I turned Wind Horse to the right, and several feet along the tight path, another three-foot leaning post pointed straight ahead.

Margo yelled for me. "Come back. We should follow the smoke."

I hollered with my brave voice, since there were trees between Margo and me. "I'm following the posts. They are taking me to the river. I see a forest of bamboo up ahead."

She screamed with her giving-up voice. "I hope you're right." Margo galloped up behind me. "It was easy to find you. Some leaning posts guided me toward your tracks. Who would put leaning posts in the woods anyway?"

I grinned. "An angel may have put them there for us."

"We have spirits, but no angels."

I twisted around, staring at Margo. "You may have an angel. You never know. I could be one."

She wrinkled her nose. "Sure you are."

"Hey, look, there's another post. It's pointing to the left."

We rode in silence for a good ways. I couldn't help but wonder why posts lean and why friends get taken. I wiped my face with my coat sleeve, and got lopsided on the bare back of Wind Horse. "Oh rats, I'm slipping off."

"You're not much of a rider, are you?"

"I've stayed up with you. I can do anything you can do." Somehow, my words sounded weak with my back on the ground.

Margo dismounted. "Let's walk the rest of the way toward the river. Look how tight the path is now. This bamboo is thick. We'll have to slip sideways in some spots to get through. I'm tying the horses on this dead tree."

The wind rustled the tops of the bamboo. They swayed like a boxcar rocking back and forth on the rail. The sounds were softer though, like the sound of rain drops splattering in the wind, but it wasn't raining.

I took a few steps forward, stubbing my moccasin on a stump from a bamboo shoot. "Ouch, these moccasins aren't good for walking out here."

Margo corrected me. "They are quiet like a mouse when sneaking up on others, though."

We forged ahead through the bamboo until we were so far inside the tube forest, I couldn't see our horses. I pushed my bangs from my eyes. "I hear someone."

Margo stopped, nodded, and whispered, "See the smoke up there?"

"Yeah. Do you think they have Taddy?"

"We're about to find out." Margo motioned for me to get behind her, but I didn't.

We tiptoed, side-by-side, and came to a spot where I could see water trickling over stones in the river. Two men dozed with their caps pulled down over their faces. Two bony horses were tied to the bamboo.

Margo whispered, "The ugly one with the brown boots is Scar. Red is the one in the gray boots."

I tugged on Margo's arm. "But, where is Taddy? I don't see him."

Cough. Cough. Cough. Achoo. Achoo.

I barreled into the clearing, standing in front of the crackling fire, with my arms waving. "Taddy's here. I know his sneeze. I have to get to him."

The men riled up from their sleep, their hats tumbled to the dirt. They pulled pistols from their sides, pointing them at me. Red shouted. "Who are you? And how did you get here?"

Scar echoed him. "Yeah, who are you?"

"I'm no one you care about. I'm here to get Taddy. Where is he?'

"We don't have no Taddy."

Cough. Cough. Achoo. Achoo.

"Then who is coughing and sneezing? I know his sneeze. He's my best friend." I put my hands up like I was going to punch them. Glancing behind me, I hoped to see Margo. But she wasn't showing herself.

Red moved closer and took my arm, twisting it. "Who are you looking for in the bamboo? Who is with you? You didn't come here by yourself."

"I did. No one is with me. I'm alone."

"Sure you are."

I swung with my free arm, kicking with both feet. Red tossed me to the ground, and I found myself tangled in the arms of the brother with the scar. "Put me down. I'm taking Taddy home with me."

Scar laughed. "Sure, you are."

Red snatched me from Scar's grasp and carried me across the camp, screaming at his brother. "You are letting this girl get the upper hand. Come on. Get some rope and tie her up."

"No, don't. Let me go."

A fist plowed into my face, sending me to darkness.

**

I wiggled on my side, facing the shoots of bamboo. My hands were tied behind my back, and I inched to my knees. My right eye was swollen, hurting with each blink. A few feet in the weeds, I could see a small body. It wasn't moving. I screamed in my throat, afraid to make any noise, and whispered, "Taddy, is that you?"

I didn't see the brothers, but their horses were still at the camp. The moon shone, and the cold wind shot bursts of freezing air into my face.

The brothers broke the quietness, arguing. "What are we going to do with these kids?"

I rocked in my spot, using each motion to move closer to Taddy.

Behind the tree, in the flickering fire light, Red stepped out where I could see him. "I told you to take care of the boy. Now, you'll have to take care of two little interruptions."

Scar marched to the fire. "I'm not killing them. You'll have to do it."

Red swung his brother around. "I don't mind. I'll do it at dawn before we ride out."

I leaned beside the body and toppled sideways. It was my Taddy, and he had both of his shoes. "Taddy, are you alive?" I tapped him with my foot.

He stirred, whining like he was arguing with someone. "I want my mama. Take me to her. I'm not afraid of you. You'll see. They're coming for me."

I whispered, "Taddy, roll over. It's me, Shoelace. Be quiet, so they don't hear us."

He moved his head, worked his hands under him, rolled over, and faced me. The tears ran from his eyes, making a puddle on the ground under his face. His jaw had dried blood on it. His chin had a bruise. He voice shook. "Shoelace?"

"Yes, I'm here. I'm here to rescue you." I sighed, not sure how I planned on keeping my word.

"I'm hungry. They hit me. I was packing my clothes when I heard noises in the kitchen. They were taking food from the pantry. I ran to my room, but the one with the red hair grabbed me. He carried me outside, and threw me on his horse."

188

"We'll get away. You'll see." I leaned forward, kissing his head. "I'm so glad to see you. I thought you were dead." I cried puddles, too.

Taddy shook. "I thought I was going to die, to be ... gone forever. I want my mama."

"We'll figure something out. You'll see." I sat up and leaned on the bamboo shoots. Taddy crawled up next to me, whimpering. We both swayed, having trouble staying right-side up with our hands tied behind our backs.

Taddy put his head on my shoulder. "How did you find me?"

"I came with Margo. She saw the bad men take you. She knew you'd listen to me if I came with her. She's out there somewhere, probably getting us help."

He shook his head. "I'm not sure she's the helping kind."

I nodded. "She's got thinking problems. Her brain hears stuff we don't, but she wants to be normal. It's hard for her."

Taddy had fallen asleep on me. I wasn't too sure he heard all of what I'd said.

A whisper from behind me took my breath. "Shoelace, don't move. It's me, Chula. I'm cutting your hands free."

Swoosh. Swoosh. Slice.

My arms bolted forward, free, untied. I rubbed my hands together. Chula's arm shot around me. She handed me her knife. "You may need this."

I took it, jostled Taddy, and whispered, "Hey, wake up. Can you stand? We need to run."

He stared off into space like he forgot I was sitting beside him. Then he turned to me. "Are we escaping?"

"Yes. I've got a knife, and I'm cutting the rope on your hands."

Taddy hugged me. "If they catch us, they'll shoot us."

"If we stay, they'll shoot us." I reached for his hand, and pulled Taddy with me into the patch of bamboo.

Through the shadows off to the side of their fire, we crawled like puppies lost in the mud. I could hear that Scar's and Red's words were turning into fighting talk. Red screamed. "We should kill them now. Let's get it over with."

Scar pushed his brother, and the two of them fell to the ground, punching and hollering.

Taddy and me scooted behind a clump of bamboo, walking backwards into the darkness. One step. Another. Then we were out of sight. I'd stuck the knife inside my back pocket hoping not to stab my backside.

I saw a leaning post. I knew which way to go. I tapped Taddy on the shoulder. "Four more steps. Five more minutes. We will escape."

I can't believe Margo came this far with me, and didn't try to save Taddy.

Middle of Night before Day Seven

There You Are

THE BAMBOO FELT LIKE A maze with too many short paths. Too many no-paths. It shot to the sky with wispy branches, like arms reaching for help. I could only see inches in front me. I reached for Taddy. "Taddy, take my hand. Stop letting go." His fingers were cold, lifeless. He pulled from my grip. "Taddy, take my hand. We have to stay together, and keep moving."

"But, where are we going? It's black. I can't see a thing. Have you seen my mama? Can I go home? Can I …"

Sniffle. Sniffle.

In Taddy's mind, he was still being held prisoner back at the camp. His words were lost letters and mumbled sentences.

Flick a flack fleck. Flick a flack fleck.

I looked at the dark sky. "Wonderful. Now it's raining. We need to find a dry spot." My heart pounded in beats faster than I could count. My squeeze on Taddy's hand took on a death grip.

We inched around the bamboo and my damp clothes were sticking to my skin. "Taddy, take my coat." I peeled the coat from my arms, giving it to him. My shoe got caught on a stump, causing me to fall flat on my tummy. I yanked him to the ground with me. "Sorry, Taddy."

I reached for my best friend who sobbed, who swung at me. "Leave me alone." He slugged me in the chest, giving a whispered yell. "No, don't hit me. Not again. No more. Let me go home."

I wrapped my arms around Taddy as we sloshed like wet rags. "It's me. Shoelace."

"Annie Grace? Annie Grace Kree? If it's you let me touch your PF Flyers."

"I'm wearing moccasins. It's a long story, but it's me."

Taddy ran his fingers across my nose, over my forehead, touching my skin like a blind person. "Annie Grace, there you are. It's you. Can we go home? I'm scared. Don't leave me."

"I will never leave you. Right now we have to find a dry place to sleep. I'm freezing. I'm sure you are, too. If this bamboo wasn't here, we'd be soaked to the bone."

"I want my bed."

"I know. We'll be home soon."

Thubalup. Thubalup. Gallop. Gallop. Shawick. Shawick. Snap.

Taddy cried. "I hear horses. They're running. What's popping? It sounds like a rope."

I felt my heart race. "Scar and Red must know we're gone."

The ground shifted under us, sending our wobbly legs into the brush. Sticks cut at our skin. "Taddy, don't let go. I don't know what's happening, but we are getting away."

We thudded in the wet dirt, piling on top of each other near the river, next to a cliff of rocks. "Taddy, are you hurt?"

"No. But they're coming for us. They'll kill us if they find us." He whispered, his words broken by sobs.

"If we go along the river, we'll end up at Wheelock. Stay with me."

We stood and moved two steps, then froze when the screams deep in the bamboo rattled our ears. Someone was losing a battle with each shrill noise. The yells came through the bamboo. "Stop. Untie me."

Another man's voice hollered. "Leave now, or I'll shoot."

Taddy and me huddled together near some rocks. The rain had stopped, leaving leftover water drops to run down the bamboo. The wind rushed at us like a night-tornado, and my skin ached from the cold.

I scooted on my knees, calling to Taddy. "Over here. By the bluff. It'll block the wind."

The screams coming from toward the camp tore through the darkness. "You can't hang us in the tree by our feet."

Kaboom. Kaboom.

Taddy reached for me. "That was a gun."

"Be quiet. They don't know where we are. It's too windy and dark to track us."

Kaboom. Kaboom.

I grabbed Taddy, and we rocked like babies by the river, shaking in our wet clothes. My heart boomed with fear. "Listen. I don't hear anything now."

Thubalup. Thubalup.

I squeezed Taddy's hand, whispering. "Don't move."

He curled up tighter with his hands around his knees. Little whimpers snuck out from his mouth like a kitten crying in the night. We sat together for a long time. The night went silent.

"Geronimo." The woman's voice called into the night with words I once used on the rail. A horse stomped, and the nose of the rider's horse snorted at us. The rider hollered. "It's me. Margo."

I sat up. "No, way. Are they following you?"

"No. Not tonight. Not tomorrow. Not ever."

"Why? What happened back there?"

Margo climbed down from her horse, and the clouds parted. She dropped her sling to the ground and her axe clunked on a rock. Her rope was gone. She grinned. "I took care of the brothers. They won't be bothering us."

I touched the sleeve on her dress. "What's all over you?"

She pushed my hand away. "It's just a little blood."

Taddy screamed. "More blood?" He wiggled closer to the rocks, whimpering. "Don't hit me."

Margo stepped to him. "It's not my blood. No one is going to hurt you."

I tugged on her arm. "I wouldn't talk to him. He's talking like you do when you get riled up." I spoke those words into the wind, wishing to grab them back.

Margo grabbed the blankets from her horse. She tossed one at me. "Here, give Taddy one."

I shook my head. "But, the blanket is wet."

"Wet? Why would it be wet?"

"Because it rained."

Margo shook her head. "It didn't rain on me. Sometimes the rain dumps water on certain parts of the land. You must have caught a wet cloud." She tossed the other blanket to me. "See. They're dry."

I unfolded the blanket, put it around Taddy's shoulder, and wrapped it around him. He leaned to his side, turning his back to me. He hugged the rocks, shaking.

Margo sat down, wiping her axe handle with the hem of her dress. "Got to clean this. Don't need the blood to stain it. Need to be clean for the next time."

I grimaced. "Could you put that up? You're scaring Taddy."

"Taddy? I think it's you who is scared of me."

"I'm not, either." I lied to her, choking on the fear stuck in my throat.

Margo ran her fingers over the sharp part of the blade. "Self-defense, I'd say. Them brothers would have killed you both before morning. Or me, if I hadn't taken care of them."

I took a closer look at her clothes. "What have you done?"

"This is not your worry. These men were not playing outlaws. They were aiming to take Taddy's life. And then you walked into their camp without a gun, without rope. You are a stupid girl."

"You told me they don't hurt people. I thought you were with me. You let me jump out there, and yell at them. I was alone, right when I needed you."

"You act before thinking. You should think more."

"You should talk. You're the one who ..." I felt ugly words slipping out, sharp like an axe. "I looked for you, and you were nowhere. You let that man sock me." I rubbed my eye. "When I woke up, I was tied up. Why did you even come?"

Margo stood, running her hand up and down her horse's nose. "I came to save Taddy. Ended up having to save you, too. You are both safe now. The bad men are gone."

My stomach rumbled, gurgling. I threw up on Margo's axe.

Arrgh. Arrgh.

I wiped my mouth. "This is not supposed to happen. Oklahoma is horrible. I want to go home."

Taddy rocked. "Me, too. Take me home. I want to go now."

Margo gave me a frown. The bloody axe was not her biggest problem. Or mine. We were still stuck in the dark, and a long way from Wheelock.

She inched over to Taddy, knelt down, lifted his chin, and kissed his forehead.

Taddy didn't resist. He was caught in a dark place inside his own thoughts, and letters and words snuck out like a broken alphabet.

Margo touched his head. "Hi, little one. You are perfection. Simple perfection." Her gentle touch looked like love to even me. It's like the love only a mother could give to her son.

I paced around Brown Horse, shaking my head. Could Margo be Priscilla? Could Margo be Taddy's mama? I didn't know. I couldn't think. I am so confused. I walked up behind Margo and watched her soothe Taddy's tears.

He peered into her face, glancing at Margo's hand on his chin. He propped himself up. "You look like my mama. I miss her. I can't wait to see her. Can we go home?" His voice sounded like a wounded coyote. His hands reached for her neck.

Margo jerked away. "I hurt. I leave. I mess up. Your mama wouldn't do that to you."

I ran between them. "Taddy, wrap up. You're gonna freeze." I slid my hand into my pocket. "Here, Taddy. I found your lucky rock. Take it."

He opened his hand and cupped the rock. "I want my mama."

I covered Taddy's shoulders with his blanket. Margo moved to his other side and snuggled close. He leaned his head on her arm. "I want my mama."

Unknown Soul

Day Seven Begins

The Road Leads the Other Way

I USED A ROCK TO lean on, and soaked up the not-so-quiet night noises. Taddy and Margo slept, while the river trickled like a sideways glass of spilled milk. The bubbles reflected light from the sky, which now sparkled with stars.

I trembled, folded my arms, and listened to the wind. I wished for Grandma and Mahlee, hoping Margo took care of Scar and Red like she said. The long necks of the bamboo rubbed together like sandpaper on a piece of rough wood. I worried with each crack and bend in the thicket that something was going to jump out at me. I pulled Margo's axe close to my side.

I rubbed my eyes, feeling of my clothes. Damp. But the blanket was dry. My stitches itched under my clinging overalls, and my eyes were heavy. Taddy's curled up under a blanket. I'm waiting for the sun to rise. I dozed, only to jerk awake every few minutes.

Margo's head just fell onto the belly of her sleeping horse. She's snoring like a rooster not ready to get up. The mud on her shoes made me look at my moccasins. I sure wish I had my PF Flyers back.

Margo popped up like a squirrel. "What? Where are we?"

"We're by the river. We saved Taddy. Remember? He's alive."

She glanced over at him. "Taddy is here." She smiled. "He's small, isn't he?"

"He's not too big. He loves to read. He has the best memory. He never forgets anything."

Taddy sat up, wiping his face with both hands, stretching. "Mama is gonna get me for getting my pants this dirty." He wiped his hand over the dingy spots.

I stepped to him. "Margo will help us find our way. We can wash your clothes before you see your mama."

Taddy looked over his shoulder at the bamboo forest. "But, the bad men." He pointed. "Will they bother us?"

Margo rolled up the blankets, answering. "Not today. Not ever."

Taddy moved near the river, squatting, splashing water on his face. The orange sun snuck up behind the bamboo, and Taddy talked to the wind. "They had me tied up. Those brothers talked to me like I wasn't there. They kicked me with their boots like I was rotten wood."

I crept closer to Taddy. "I'm sorry you were hurt. You're safe now."

Taddy fell down like a limp doll next to the water. "I feel sorry for them. If they had a mama like mine, they'd be nicer. A mama will teach you how to treat folks."

"You're right. You have the best mama." I hugged him from behind, my sobs matching his.

Taddy sat up. "I need … I need to get home to my apartment in Texarkana. Mama will make biscuits. I can sleep in my own bed. I need a clean shirt and fresh pants. I need dry socks, too. I need to go home."

Margo nudged me. "We best be going. You two, ride my horse. I'll walk for now. We'll cut through the bamboo back to the trail. It's not far from here."

Margo lifted Taddy to the horse. She put me behind him, and I held onto his waist. I looked around. "Did you see Wind Horse last night?"

"No, he's gone, I guess. He'll show up when we need him."

"We kind of need him now."

Brown Horse dodged branches, ducking around the tube trees. I pointed to the sky. "Taddy, look at the clouds. They're showing us the way home."

Taddy tilted his head, but didn't answer. He started crying again. He wept with a wheezing sound wrapped in fear. "Are we almost there? Is my mama any better?"

"She's at the hospital in Texarkana. Grandma sent her ahead on the train with the nurse. Pastor Cody is taking care of her."

Taddy sighed a long breath. His arms dropped to his side. He fell backwards against me, and I held onto his shirt.

"Taddy, grab the mane. Hold on. We're going to fall if you don't."

Margo stomped on the weeds, and looked back at us. "Is everybody all right?"

I peeked around Taddy. "We're good."

"Just checking. We'll be at the trail in no time." Margo smacked through the thicket. "Darn ole weeds."

I hollered. "We've been riding this way too long. We should have followed the river."

Margo spun around. "Wait here."

I called to her. "Where are you going?"

"I love tree climbing. I can see the whole world in a tree."

Taddy sighed. "Me, too."

On the highest limb, Margo called to us. "From up here you can see everywhere you want to go, and everywhere you wish you could go. Guess what I see? I see the road. It's to our left, not far from here."

She climbed down the tree, jumping beside us. She led Brown Horse, and we rode long enough for the sun to shine right on top of our heads. I wasn't so sure she saw the road, or if she wanted us to think she knew the way.

Crunch-roar-creak. Crunch-roar-creak.

I called to Margo. "Did you hear that? It's a wagon. We have to be close to the road."

Margo pulled on the rope around Brown Horse. "Hang on. It's up ahead. I hear the wheels crunching on the rocks."

Branches slapped at us, and the narrow road tightened around us. If we turned right, we would go back to the shack, to the camp, and to the escape spot by the bamboo. Going left would take us to Wheelock, hours away.

The winding crook in the road brought a mule into view. He was pulling a wagon. The man with the reins favored someone, and when he grinned, the biggest smile stretched across the entire width of the road. He stood, and nearly fell from the wagon. He yelled with a squeal. "Taddy? Shoelace? Margo? You're safe. You're alive."

I waved, bouncing on the horse. My heart smiled with hope. "Boswell, you came for us."

Ar roof. Ar roof. Ar roof.

I called to not-my-dog. "Black Dog. Hey there, boy."

Boswell pulled the wagon up next to us. "I was taking this casket to the next town. I cut through these back roads. I can't believe I've found all three of you." Boswell put his hand to his face. "Margo, you know they think you took Taddy?"

Margo danced in a circle, clapping her hands like a child. She stomped in the loose dirt. "Not me. I didn't take him. I came for him. I came for the boy. Tell him, Shoelace. Tell him."

I started to answer, but Boswell climbed down from the wagon. He put his hand on Margo's shoulder. She pulled her axe from the sling, and Boswell jumped back.

She wailed. "I never took Taddy. I never did hurt him. Red and Scar took him."

I wanted to tell Boswell that she did take me, but I trapped the words inside my mouth.

Boswell grabbed the axe, slinging it to the ground. "Stop this crazy talk. Margo, stop."

"I am. I am. I can. I am."

Boswell sat Margo down on a stump by the road. "Quiet. Just sit. Think. Don't talk."

I slid down from the horse, and Black Dog jumped from the back of the wagon. He ran around me until he'd licked my arms clean. I rubbed his head, and explained to Boswell what happened. "At Wheelock, Taddy stumbled onto the bad men in the kitchen, and they snatched him. And … and Margo, she … she … was only…" I stopped talking because Margo looked at me with both eyes squinted, like she thought I was going to tell how she roped me and kidnapped me. But I wasn't telling, at least, not yet.

I inched closer to Margo, and she folded her arms. I waved my hand like a teacher holding a ruler in class. "Margo knows the trails. She helped me find Taddy. And then, she had to defend herself last night. You'll see. Just ask Taddy."

Taddy whined. "I don't know anything. I just want to go home."

Boswell stepped up to me. "Are you sure Margo helped you?"

"Yes, Margo and me. We were warriors together."

Taddy tumbled from the horse to the ground, shaking and trembling. "I want my mama. I need her. She needs me."

Black Dog cuddled up next to Taddy, licking his nose.

Boswell bent down, cradled Taddy, and carried him to the seat on the wagon. "Are you hurt, boy?"

Taddy didn't answer and tears dropped from his eyes again.

I moved to Boswell, bumping his gun by accident. "Sorry, I didn't mean to touch it."

"Guns aren't toys. Don't play around them. You'll get hurt."

"I know." I felt a shiver run through me just thinking about guns. I felt dizzy and joined Taddy on the wagon. I wrapped my arms around him, and Black Dog jumped in behind me. "Boswell, I'm so glad you found us. I can't wait to see my grandma and Mahlee."

Boswell stood by the mule. "Your grandma is sick with worry, and your Mahlee friend hasn't stopped mumbling. Mrs. Motes is blaming herself for letting you get out of her sight."

Taddy whispered, "Can we go now? Can we?"

"Yes, this casket can wait. Margo, tie your horse to the wagon. Let's go." Boswell got on the seat next to Taddy. "Son, it's gonna be fine. You're safe now."

Margo picked up her axe, putting it in the sling. She climbed onto her horse. She moved to our side of the wagon, muttering. "I've got something to do. Got to do it. Can't stop myself. I may never get this chance again."

I looked into her eyes. They burned with fire. I challenged her. "What are you saying?"

"I have to explain to Taddy the reason behind the reason. My reason. Not his. Mine." Margo grabbed Taddy by the waist, pulling him to her horse. She rode off, yelling. "I've got to do it. It's today. Or not at all. One day. I only need one day."

Taddy screamed. "Stop. I need my mama."

Boswell bailed from the wagon, charging down the road. "Margo, come back with the boy. This isn't making you look innocent."

She stopped her horse, calling back with a deep voice. "I have to save the baby. I have to hold the baby. Give him up. And save him."

I perched myself on the top of the seat. "Margo, stop. Bring Taddy back."

Taddy slumped down, his arm reached back, his fingers stretched, and he sobbed with each gallop.

I jumped down from the wagon with Black Dog. "You can't take Taddy. I just got him back."

Boswell held his gun out in front of him. "Margo, don't make me use this."

Black Dog growled, leaping from the wagon.

Margo pulled on the mane, turned the horse sideways in the road. The horse reared his front legs, galloping away.

Boswell ran back to the wagon, his boots puffing in the sand, his Indian braids bouncing under his hat. He climbed into the seat. "Shoelace, get up here. We're going after Margo."

A shadow stepped in front of Boswell's mule. It was Chula, and her words sounded like a tune on her flute. "No, Boswell. Shoelace must follow her."

I climbed up next to Boswell, shaking my head. "Not me. I'm not going after her."

Wind Horse galloped in from the side of the trail, snorting. Chula pointed at him. "Shoelace, ride him. Follow Margo. Be sure to keep watch. That which you think is, and that which is not, could be."

I swallowed hard. "Why me? Why not Boswell? He's a grownup."

Chula spoke, waving her arm. "Because you are the one. God never picks the wrong person to be a warrior."

"Me? Are you sure?" I found myself standing next to Boswell with my head held high. I felt braver when my eyes met with the sparkle in Wind Horse's eyes.

Chula chanted in her powwow voice. "Nakni Nita. Warrior Bear. Go save Taddy."

Boswell shouted at Chula. "What are you doing? Margo's getting away. I'll go for the Lighthorsemen. I saw a couple of them riding behind me, up the road. I'll go for help."

Chula argued. "She will need them. But let her see. Let her see why Margo weeps. Why Margo frets. Why Margo cares."

Boswell nodded, put his gun away, and took the reins. "Shoelace, I'll be with you soon. Follow Margo. Keep up with her, but don't let her see you."

"You two are doing too much talking, and Margo's long gone. I'll have to hurry." I looked at Chula and then Boswell, and slapped Boswell's arm. "You better be right behind me."

Boswell held my chin up. "Be strong. You are Taddy's wind of strength. Ride into the sun. Listen for the chimes."

I dove from the wagon, rolling in the dirt. I brushed myself off, strutting up to Wind Horse. He knelt down, and I climbed onto his back.

Boswell tossed me a sack. "Here's my lunch. It's blackberry cobbler and biscuits."

"Thank you. I'll save it for Taddy." I kicked Wind Horse and we rode like the wind. I bounced between being afraid and being brave, but I had to save Taddy.

Ar roof. Ar roof.

Black Dog ran up beside Wind Horse, and Boswell's words whistled in the branches. "Ya-ha-ha-way."

I felt a surge of strength pushing out the fear, and I whispered, "Ya-ha ha-way."

Day Seven Ends

Wind Chime Forest

WIND HORSE DODGED THE BRANCHES, and I ducked my head. The arms of the trees pointed at me like swords ready to knock me off the horse. Black Dog sniffed the dirt, keeping pace with the gallops.

"Black Dog, want a bite?" I tossed him a crumb, and he smashed it with his nose into the sandy road, gobbling up dirt and bread.

Ar roof. Ar roof.

He ran in a circle around Wind Horse, his ears flapping, and his head bobbed up and down like he was begging for more food.

I tossed the last piece of biscuit to Black Dog, and he caught the bread in the air. He munched it down like he'd caught a plateful of table scraps.

I had planned to share this food with Taddy. Too late, I was starving. I peeked in the sack, at the cobbler wrapped in wax paper that begged to be eaten. I folded the top of the sack down, sliding it inside the top of my overalls. I'll save Taddy the dessert.

The road turned into a narrow path to the right and also to the left. I could go straight ahead on the road, but Margo wouldn't go that way. It's out in the open. I bet the trail to my right leads to her shack. I'm going that way.

Unknown Soul

The trees tangled with the tall weeds. I couldn't see around the trunks without seeing more clumps of trees. I hope I'm going the right way. Margo may have taken a side trail. The pastures falling over the hills are somewhere behind those trees, but I'm not sure how long I'll have to ride or how far. Margo and Taddy are out there. I'm bringing Taddy home.

The streaks of sun moved from my right shoulder to my left. Maybe I should turn back and get Boswell. If I beg him, maybe he'll come with me.

I pulled on Wind Horse. "Whoa, buddy. Let's get some help. I'm not sure this is such a great idea."

Wind Horse stomped, rearing back. His front legs kicked in the air, over and over again.

I clutched his mane. "Stop. You're gonna knock me off."

Snort. Snort. Neigh. Neigh.

Tightening my grip on his mane, I pressed my legs against his side. "Wind Horse, you're not listening to me. Stop it."

He kicked at the dirt with his right leg, raising his head up and down. Wind Horse picked up his pace, running ahead to the fork in the trail. He cut to the right. I fell forward, hugging his neck. I shouted at him. "Why are you running? What's got you spooked?"

Wind Horse took another path to the left, and I hung on for dear life. He slid through the thicket like we were being chased. At the end of the trail, he jolted to a stop and tossed me to the bushes. "Yikes. Ouch. What are you ..."

Pupple-fuffle.

Wind Horse snorted in my face.

"You better hope I didn't break anything. My grandma will get you. She's tired of me getting stitches."

I felt of my legs and arms. Two arms. Two feet. I rubbed my head, wiping blood from my hair. "Wind Horse, you've gone and hurt me."

He bumped my face with a gentle nudge of his nose.

I pushed him away. "Move. I'm mad at you." I stood up, and saw the purple oozing through my bib on my overalls. "Darn. I've smashed Taddy's cobbler."

Black Dog licked my clothes, and I swatted at his ear. "Stop. That's Taddy's dessert."

Ar roof. Ar roof.

Black Dog stuck his nose under a bush beside me, taking off after something.

Wind Horse galloped ahead of me on the path. The shadows lurking behind each tree made it hard to see. Jogging after him, I found my horse near a patch of grass at the edge of the woods. "Sorry for yelling at you. It's not your fault. You're just a horse."

Neigh. Neigh. Neigh. Pupple-fuffle.

I moved in front of him. The neighing wasn't coming from Wind Horse. It came from somewhere past the meadow up the hill where a group of trees circled a giant cedar tree.

I pointed to the cluster. "I've never seen a tree that tall. It twists and turns, and reaches and climbs. What a great climbing tree."

I touched Wind Horse, and he nudged me with his nose. I stepped into the sun. "There's Margo's horse. He's alone. I bet Taddy is with Margo in there."

Running, I called to Wind Horse. "Come on, boy. Let's go."

Wind Horse *pupple-fuffled*, and galloped to Brown Horse where they ate dry grass together. He chomped on the crunchy weeds, looking at me. If I didn't know better, I would think this horse does things to me on purpose.

I yelled at him. "Come on, boy. Let's find Taddy."

Wind Horse didn't move, but Black Dog darted from the woods, knocking me down.

Ar roof. Ar roof.

I petted Black Dog on the head. "All right then, you can come with me." I got to my feet, moving to the outer edge of the circle-trees.

A hand wrapped around my arm from inside the thicket, forcing me to the ground. The voice screamed in my ear. "Why are you following us? I warned you."

I twisted my head to see Margo, and yelled at her. "You took my Taddy. Not the first time, but this time. No one is gonna believe you're innocent if you keep this up."

Margo assured me. "He's not hurt. Taddy's asleep by the bald cypress. He hasn't spoken a word since I rode off with him."

"Why would he talk to you? You scare him. You scare me." I smarted off to her, wishing I'd wake up from this terrible, awful week. "What's a baldyeeecypress?"

"It's the tallest tree around here. It reaches over a hundred feet toward heaven. I climb that tree so God can hear my prayers."

I pushed Margo off, standing up. I pointed toward the towering trunk. "You pray in that tree? I didn't figure you were the praying kind."

Margo shoved me to the ground. "You are too big for your britches. Your grandma needs to take a switch to you."

I rolled my eyes, shaking my head.

Margo explained her praying ways. "You come from a world where folks pray inside churches. I come from a world where folks pray when they can, and where they want."

"Whatever. I don't care where you pray. Where's my Taddy?" I got to my feet, hurrying toward the baldyeeecypress tree. In the hollow of the giant trunk, Taddy was curled up in a

209

ball. I fell to his side, putting my hand by his nose, feeling for air. He was breathing.

Margo rushed up behind me, twisting my arm. She whispered, "Don't ruin this. I have to make *known the unknown*. It's been too long coming."

"Stop hurting me. Let go." I yanked my arm free, rubbing it.

Margo snarled. "Do you promise?"

"Why should I?"

"A piece of Taddy's life is missing. I have the part he needs. I must make this right, now that he's finally here. After today, I will leave it be."

"What are you saying? You talk like I know, but tell me nothing. I don't understand."

"Just promise. I won't hurt Taddy. Not one hair."

I marched in a big circle, running my hand on the bark of the tree. "Why are there pieces of glass and rock hanging on the branches of those other trees?"

"Those are my forest-clinkers."

I moved to one of the shiny ones, jingling it.

Clank. Clank. Clank. Clank.

The shadow of lights bounced from the stone and glass forest-clinkers, causing a tune to rise up from the walls of the forest. I turned to Margo. "How did these get here?"

Margo smiled. "I put them in the trees. They're my wind chimes. I make them from broken soda bottles, rocks, and arrowheads. I make one every year in February."

"February? Why then?"

"For Taddy's birthday."

"What? I don't understand. You don't even know him."

"I know him better than you think, remember?"

I rubbed my face. "Oh yeah, I forgot. How is bringing Taddy to a tree going to help him?"

"I miss him. I pray for him in this tree." Margo tapped the giant trunk with her hand. "I keep him with me by coming here. Now, he's been here for real."

"Then come home to Texarkana. You'll see him all the time."

"I can't. I have so many confusing thoughts. I get mixed up. I do mixed-up things. Undoing my mixings can be too hard. My ways include too much confusion."

I felt sorry for Margo. She reminded me how lonely I feel not having my mama, and how I wish for my daddy to come back to me. I love Mahlee and Grandma. They love me, but the wishing still comes, especially when I see others who are sad like me.

Margo danced. "Do you see the rainbows? The sun shines through the branches at sunset. Look at them. The glass reflects different colors. This is my Wind Chime Forest where no one cries, and babies don't leave or have to die." She looked at Taddy. "Little ones come home, and God forgives."

I followed Margo as her hand brushed across each chime. She stopped by a bare branch. "I'm putting the next wind chime right here for Taddy. He'll be eleven next month. I'll sing to him. I'll weep for him. And I'll wish for him."

Clank. Clank. Clank. Clank.

Margo hurried to the hollow of the giant tree, crawling inside next to Taddy. He stirred, wiped his face, glancing at her. "Margo, I heard your words. I'm confused. I know my mama wants you to come home with us. You can still come, if you want. Please say yes, so I can go to her. So I can go home, too."

Margo wiped a lone tear from her cheek. She reached into the hollow part of the tree, picking up a tin box, opening it.

She pulled out a stack of envelopes, handing them to Taddy. "It's time to let you know."

Taddy squinted. "Let me know what?"

Margo sat next to Taddy, running her fingers through his hair. He sat up, letting the envelopes fall from his fingers. He scooted over. "Stop touching me. My mama is the only one who can touch my hair."

Margo sighed, and her rattling words took off. "I wanted to tell you. I thought it was right. I wanted to fix things. I didn't know what else to do. I wanted to save you. I hope I have. I wish it could be different, but somehow it can't. But these … they … they are for you."

Taddy stood to his feet, wobbling and leaning on the inside of the tree. "I want my mama. Take me to her."

Margo moved to him on her knees, holding the tied batch of envelopes. "Take these. Please. There are six letters written to you. Keep them for now. When you are ready, read them. I'll take you back to Wheelock. My trying to fix this has only made it worse."

I scaled the giant tree, wishing to climb all the way to heaven myself. Wishing we were home. Wishing God was listening.

Taddy shuffled to the wind chimes and wept.

Margo ambled up to him. "Can I have one hug before we go?"

Taddy turned to her without answering. His hand slipped into hers like it fit her grasp. He talked to her with words that made him sound older than ten, more like thirteen. "You have a little girl, and she needs you. I have my mama. She needs me. You can take me back. I'll tell everyone that I left with you on my own. You won't be in trouble. I don't need a hug. I need my mama."

212

I leaned back on the branch, my heart beating so fast I could feel thumping in my ears.

Margo cried. Taddy cried. And I prayed. "God, please fix this." I'm sure my prayer floated up the tree to heaven because with all these tears they had to go somewhere.

Taddy picked up the envelopes, holding them out. "Take me home. Take me home. I want to go home."

Margo hugged Taddy before he could say no, and then stepped on Black Dog's paw.

Yelp. Yelp.

Margo cried. "I've hurt your dog. I hurt whatever I'm near. I hurt too many things. I can't stop the hurting." Margo took off running down the path toward the clearing, where Wind Horse had stopped to eat.

I climbed down the tree, moving next to Taddy. He crumpled to the ground. The batch of envelopes fell on my moccasins. I flipped through the stack. They had stamps on them with Taddy's address, but they were never mailed. I stuck them inside my shirt with the squashed cobbler, hoping to read them, wishing to see what they said. I prayed the letters would be the answer to why Boswell and Chula would let me come out here all alone.

Behind a group of wind chimes, Margo screamed. "I'm not guilty. I didn't take Taddy. I saved him. I can tell you who did. Taddy's safe."

A Lighthorseman rode up on his horse. Boswell stomped up the path behind him, calling to me. "Shoelace, it's me. We're going home."

The Lighthorseman got down, hurrying to Taddy, cradling him. I rushed to Boswell, and he gathered me up. "You're gonna be fine. Taddy will be, too. We're going to Wheelock."

Morning of Day Eight

Letter Number Six

I HUNG MY HEAD BACKWARDS over the edge of the bed, letting my hair dangle to the floor. Most everyone's at the chapel praying. They're thanking God for Taddy and me coming home alive. Many of the girls peeked into my room to smile or wave before they left.

Mrs. Motes keeps checking on me every few minutes. I wish she'd just go pray with the others. She's fretting over the cut on my head, and the handprint bruise on my face from Margo. She thinks I look too thin. I was gone for less than two days. I was skinny before I left.

Grandma's banished me inside this room. Taddy's hiding out across the hall in his bedroom. He's not talking to anyone about the kidnapping. The first one. Or the second. He did get to see Pastor Cody, who came in from Texarkana, but Taddy only gave him a smile. Pastor Cody sat with him during the questions from Officer Smoke. Taddy cried, eventually falling asleep at the table. Now, he's probably asleep across the hall from me.

During Officer Smoke's interrogation, I tried to answer for Taddy, but the mean cop slapped the table whenever I spoke. That's how the banish-to-Grandma's room came about for me.

Margo's stuck in the bedroom next to me, too. There's a door connecting our room. It's locked on her side. I keep squatting down to listen, but she only mutters.

Unknown Soul

The Lighthorsemen and the police are comparing stories. They've requested Margo stay put until they figure out if she's guilty or not, or if they think she did illegal stuff. Mahlee's parked a chair in the hallway, acting like a guard. She's watching Taddy's door, my door, and Margo's door. When I peek into the hall, she snaps her fingers at me. I feel like I'm trapped. There's no window in this room. It's like being in Margo's shack without rats.

I'm jumping in the middle of the mushy bed, watching it sag in the center. Up and down. I'm bored of sitting, bored of lying down. Tired of trying to sneak into the hall. So I'm jumping.

We're taking the train tomorrow afternoon. I can't wait to see the front porch, to see my cat, and to sit in my tree. Pastor Cody told us Priscilla moved her arm. She shifted around in her bed at the hospital. She hasn't opened her eyes, yet.

I'm free-falling like a tree cut down in the woods. I plop down to my hind side, swinging my legs over the edge of the bed. My clean overalls feel good. My shirt with the blackberry stain got tossed. Grandma said it was beyond fixing. I tossed Taddy's letters under the bed before she took my dirty clothes. The envelopes are hidden for now. Maybe I should read one.

I got on my knees, fishing for the envelopes with my hand, pulling the letters out from under the frame. I better not read them. Someone might come in my room. It's been a few minutes since Mrs. Motes has checked on me. I'll put the envelopes inside my satchel for a better time.

I put my legs straight out, tossing the satchel beside the dresser. I rolled up my pant legs, touching the clean gauze covering my stitches, wiggling my toes inside the moccasins. They felt like skin on my feet, like they fit better than a glove, or too-tight socks.

Doctor Rigghazel doctored my legs with fresh bandages
last night. He stitched up my head, too. I wanted to smack him
when he breathed sour whiskey breath in my face. I don't like
the doctor, and I'm not good at hiding it. I'm not good at
staying in this room, either.

I turned the knob on the door, peeking out again. Mahlee
sat rocking in a wooden chair not meant for rocking. She
wiped her hands together, put them on her lap, and then wiped
them again. She's the self-appointed guard, but the officer
standing with his eyes closed and arms folded could care less.
He's the real guard. He's there to keep Margo in Pushmataha
Hall until they decide to arrest her or not.

Bright Eyes poked her head out from the big room. She's
wearing my engineer hat. She must not have joined the others
to pray. She shuffled up to Mahlee, tugging her sleeve.

Mahlee quizzed Bright Eyes. "What are you up to, little
one? Did you stay here to help Mrs. Motes get the noon meal
going?"

Bright Eyes nodded.

I knew their talk wouldn't take long, since Bright Eyes
doesn't have much to say. I took this as my signal to dart
across the hall to Taddy's room while Mahlee visited with
Bright Eyes.

Creak. Creak.

The floor felt my steps and told me so. Moccasins don't
sneak on hardwood floors, just in the woods. Bright Eyes saw
me, her eyes bugging wide open. She hopped around in the
hall, hugging Mahlee with a great big swing of both arms.

Mahlee reacted. "Well, someone sure needs some attention
around here." Mahlee placed Bright Eyes in her lap, stroking
her hair.

I scuttled to Taddy's door, opened it, and slipped inside.

Taddy whispered a yell. "What are you doing in here? No more questions. No more. I want my mama. I want to go home."

I crawled into the bed next to Taddy. He turned to his side, putting his back to me. I tapped his shoulder. "If you would just talk to Officer Smoke, he would release you from bedroom-jail. You have to help Margo. She protected us, even though she stole you, again. She did try to help. You need to tell him. You promised her."

Taddy sighed. "We were leaving with Boswell, and then she snatched me. I didn't want to go with her. I wanted to go home. I only told her stuff so she'd leave me alone."

I patted his back. "The Taddy I know doesn't break promises." I jumped off the bed, flying over him. "Hey, I'll be right back. I want to show you something."

Taddy called to me. "I don't want to see anything. I want to be alone."

I made a face at him, turned to the door, and opened it. I looked up and down the hallway. Bright Eyes no longer talked to Mahlee, as the not-rocking chair by Margo's door sat empty.

Mahlee's voice rang out from the kitchen. "Yes, Mrs. Motes. Bright Eyes and me will help you set the table."

I darted to my room, running past the sleeping guard, and pulled the strap of envelopes from inside the satchel. I peeked back into the hall, darting back to Taddy's room. Mr. Guard gave me no mind when I ran by the second time. He simply lifted his head, and snorted.

Taddy sat cross-legged on the quilt. "What's that in your hands?"

I tossed the letters at him. "These are for you from your aunt. She wanted you to have them. You left them behind. I figured you'd want to read them."

I said *aunt* to Taddy, and wondered if Margo might really be his mama. Could her words be true? Could part of them speak of secrets that made sense?

Taddy shoved the letters away. "I don't want to read what she wrote. Since we got here, she's caused nothing but problems for my mama and me. I hate her."

In one swoop, I snatched the letters and walloped him. "How can you hate someone who saved your life?"

"She only sort of saved my life. She talked strange, mumbling words when we were riding the horse, saying Priscilla is Margo, and Margo is Priscilla. She would whisper in my ear, and say it's time I knew the reason for the reason. She's lost most of her mind and what is left, gets stuck on the same words. I don't want to be around her."

"Aren't you the least bit curious what these letters might say? They're addressed to you."

Taddy touched the stack and slid the string off. "I don't know. Reading a letter may only make her sound crazier."

I sat across from him. "Come on, let's open one. We're banished to our rooms until we leave tomorrow. It'll give us something to do. You know you want to."

Taddy picked up one of the tinged envelopes, flipping it over. "There's a number written on here. This one has number three."

I glanced at the others. "Here's number five, and number two. Oh wait, this one has number one." I counted the envelopes and stacked them in order. Margo said there were six envelopes. Number six was missing.

Taddy fidgeted with the envelope, crying. "I used to sit in my tree by myself in Texarkana. I made straight A's, attended school one block from my apartment, and walked to the hobo church. Nothing bad happened until I met you, Shoelace. I want to go home."

I hugged his neck, feeling a tinge of hurt from his words. "But, look how exciting your life is now. You're not bored anymore, are you?"

He coughed. "You're right, you are never boring." He held the envelope to his nose. "Smells like dirt."

"Some of them look old. Come on, open the first one."

"Fine. I'll read one."

I slid from the bed. "Wait a second. Let me check for the missing envelope. It might have fallen under my bed. I'll be right back."

"What do you mean?"

"Margo said there were six letters. We only have five. She told you in the Wind Chime Forest."

"Do you really think I was listening to her?"

"Whatever." I peeked outside the door and heard new voices. This time Grandma and Pastor Cody were talking in the kitchen.

Grandma spoke. "The children need to get home and get back to their regular routine. I'm going to keep Annie Grace out of school for a week to rest. I expect Taddy will stay with us until Priscilla gets well."

Pastor Cody gave his preacher talk. "Well, I'll do anything to help. I'm praying they can bounce back and put this behind them."

I slipped across the hall, sneaking into my room. I knelt down, opened my satchel, and dug inside. The noise coming from under the connecting door leading to Margo's room made me stop. I stuck the envelope in my pocket.

Margo argued with someone. "I'm not staying here another minute. If they don't believe me, then let them arrest me. If they don't arrest me, then they believe me. I didn't kidnap the boy."

A man talked. "Margo, stop shouting."

Margo popped off mean words. "Who are you to tell me what to do? You drink too much whiskey, and work too much. You haven't held our daughter since I came back with her."

"She might not be mine. You hid your pregnancy from me. You could be lying about who the father is."

"You know she's your baby. I hid the pregnancy because I was afraid you'd ask me to ... to not have the baby."

I knew the man's voice. It's the doctor, and his yells at Margo are meaner than Mahlee's screams in the dark.

Doctor Rigghazel defended himself. "I only perform surgery for the women who ask. It's their decision not to have a baby. I'm helping them. If I don't do it, someone else will."

"You're helping them? By not letting a baby have life?"

"Stop talking like that. It's not my fault. I'm a doctor. They pay me for services rendered."

"You are making money on them. You are not a healing doctor, you're a killing doctor."

"I'm not a killer."

"You are. Why do you think I hold funeral services for each one? It's not because they're alive."

"I'm not as evil as you think."

"Then why don't you want our baby?"

"I can't have one right now. Works got my time. Besides, it's my choice."

"You should have thought about such matters before you got me pregnant."

"Like I said, Isabella may not be mine."

"Get out of here. Leave me alone. I will take her and you'll never see either one of us again."

"You are not mentally capable of keeping a baby, and you know it."

Bumping, shuffling, and arguing bounced around in the other room. I better knock on the door to check on Margo. "Hey, Margo, lunch will be ready soon. Are you in there?"

Margo answered with a squeal. "Yes, I'm here. Doctor Rigghazel was just leaving."

A door slammed, followed by Margo yelling. "Good riddance."

Tap. Tap. Tap.

Margo called to me from the other side of the door. "Shoelace, thank you. He scares me."

"You're welcome." I sat against the wall, pulled the envelope from my pocket, and held it. I couldn't help but think about how much she scares me. I took a deep breath, got to my feet, barreled into Taddy's room, and saw tears pouring from his eyes. "What's wrong?"

He held up a letter. "What does this mean? What ..." He held up another one. "They say the same thing."

I stood at the foot of the bed looking at the opened letters that were strewn on the quilt. I picked one up, then another. My breaths grew shallow. My chest hurt. "They do say the same thing. 'Dear Taddy, your mama loves you. Happy birthday.' "

Taddy grabbed the letters, wadding them up. He tossed them to the floor, jumped from the bed, pacing. "Why is Margo saying she's my mama? I don't understand. Each of the letters has a date written on it, too. She did this each year? Did she write me letters and never mail them?"

I tucked letter number six inside my bib.

Knock. Knock. Knock.

A girl's voice called through the door. "Are you in there? Are you?"

"Who's there?"

"It's me. Imogene."

I opened the door, seeing Imogene's glowing face.

"Look, what I'm wearing. These are the fastest sneakers—ever."

Taddy jumped from the bed. "Those are not yours. Give them to Shoelace. She needs them, so we can go home."

Day Eight before the Storm

When Shoes Fit

I PULLED IMOGENE INTO THE bedroom. "Where did you get my shoes?'

"I found them in the loft in the barn. Mrs. Motes and the matron had some of us girls collect up the dirty blankets them horse-cops slept on during the search. I put them on and wanted to show you."

I smiled, hugging her. "Thank you for bringing them to me." I kicked the letters out of the way, sat down, and knocked the moccasins from my feet. "I love my red shoes. These moccasins were starting to feel good, but they aren't the same."

Imogene limped to me, squatting down beside me. "You don't want the moccasins? I would love them. I would wear them. Every time I put them on, I could remember my friend with the yellow hair and pierced ears."

I pointed at the shoes. "Do you see how dirty they are? And the right shoe has a hole by the little toe."

"I don't mind. Thank you." She hugged them to her chest. "I can't believe it. I've had two good things happen in one day. This is the best day of my life."

Knock. Knock. Knock. Tap. Tap.

Taddy sat up on the edge of the bed. He shook his head. "Are we having a party? I'm not in the mood for playing."

I laughed, slugging Taddy. He almost sounded like my old buddy.

Tap. Tap. Tap.

I cracked open the door. "Bright Eyes."

She scooted through the slit in the door, crawling up on the bed next to Taddy, smiling. She held something small in her fingers.

I moved to her. "What do you have there?"

Bright Eyes unfolded her fingers. She held the dream catcher from upstairs, and shoved it toward me.

"What? Do you want me to take it?"

She sighed, opening her mouth wide open. New unheard words spilled into the room. "I brought this ... this ... for you."

I jumped up and down, and put my hands on her shoulders.

Bright Eyes stepped back from me. "I ... I want to gi ... gi ... ve ... give you good dreams. You are ... my friend."

Tears flooded from my eyes, getting trapped in my eyelids. I blinked, unable to stop crying. "Bright Eyes! You talked. You talked." I picked her up like she could be my little sister. "You found your voice."

Bright Eyes hugged me, giggling. "I have words."

Taddy jumped up. "What's the big deal?"

I pushed him. "The big deal? Since Bright Eyes was sent here, no one has heard her say a word. And now, she's talking. She's talking!"

Imogene hugged Bright Eyes and me. "This is great. She talked. I've seen three good things in one day."

I turned to Imogene. "Three good things? I know what two of them are, moccasins and this. But what's the other one?"

"This is why I came in here. I came to bring you the shoes and to tell you."

Bright Eyes wiggled from my arms. "Tell me, too."

Imogene reached for my hand. "I'm leaving Wheelock Academy. I have a new family. I'm being adopted. My new parents came four times to pick out a girl, and they picked me."

I choked on the party unfolding in Taddy's room. "You have a family now? When do you leave?"

"Tomorrow at noon. I'll have my own room and a horse, and my new parents have yellow hair like you. Can you believe it? They love me." Imogene's smile shot a moonbeam of hope in the room.

I ran my fingers through her short hair. "This is the best news ever."

Taddy pushed by me, slipped his loafers on, and picked up the letters from the floor. "Everyone is having good news but me. My mama is still unconscious. I want to be alone. I have to study my math in my head, so I won't get behind in school. Everybody out."

I picked up a letter, placing it on the bed. Taddy scrunched the paper, tossing it in the trash can. I tried to make nice with him. "You have good news. Pastor Cody said your mama moved her arm. She's mending. It takes time."

Taddy backed himself into the corner. "I hope you're right. You tend to be wrong more times than not."

Imogene interrupted us. "The both of you fight like brother and sister."

Taddy and me spoke at the same time. "We're not."

Bright Eyes giggled. I laughed. Taddy snickered. And Imogene grabbed her belly. "Taddy, your mama will pull through. I prayed for her at chapel this morning."

Taddy wiped his eyes. "That's mighty kind of you."

I felt my toes tapping. My PF Flyers getting ready to dance. "Hey, everybody on the bed. We're dancing on the mattress so we'll remember this moment for the rest of our lives."

Taddy yanked on my arm. "I'm not jumping with you. You need to let me do my work."

Bright Eyes wrapped her fingers around Taddy's hand. "The matron will get us."

I smiled. "Not if she doesn't see us."

I pulled Taddy to the mattress, and the four of us jumped, laughed, and giggled, knocking each other around like wind chimes.

Voices oozed from beneath the door, and I stopped bouncing. "Wait, stop. Don't you hear it? There's laughing and giggling in the hall, too. Let's go see."

> **Snow Cream**
>
> *In a quart jar, combine well:*
> 1. *½ cup of half-n-half*
> 2. *1 can sweetened, condensed milk*
> 3. *2-3 teaspoons real vanilla*
> 4. *Evaporated, canned milk, enough to fill to one-quart (15 ounce can)*
> 5. *Drizzle combined mixture into a big bowl of snow.*
> 6. *Use pure white snow, never yellow snow.*

We tumbled from the bed, hurrying into the hallway. A sea of girls ran into the front room. We chased them. They pointed out the windows. I peeked over a shoulder. "What is it? What are we looking at?"

The matron clapped her hands. "It's snow. We have flurries. Beautiful snow. I love snow." She opened the double doors. "Everyone get your jackets, and let's have a party. We'll make snow ice cream later, if we get enough snow."

Bright Eyes tugged on the matron's skirt. "I like snow."

The matron stopped mid-step, did a double-take, and bent down. "My sweet little Lizzy Beth."

My eyes grew bigger than a full moon. "What did you call her?" No one listened, or cared what she said, but me. The girls were playing and laughing. Taddy and Imogene were, too.

I yanked on the matron's arm. "What did you call her?"

She turned to me, rattling on with happy words. "This is glorious. Just glorious. We hoped Bright Eyes would love it here. And finally speak. Now, she has spoken, and it's on the day it snows."

I interrupted her. "Did you call her Lizzy Beth?"

She scratched her chin. "I … I may have. Lizzy Beth is her real name. She's one lucky girl. We're having several adoptions, and she's one of them. Her new parents will be thrilled to hear her speak. They will be here any second." The matron pointed. "Her tote bag is ready."

I moved to the window. "Who's in that car?"

"It's them. They've come all the way from Jefferson, Texas. It's a glorious day. They won't believe she's talking."

I had to talk to Mahlee. I ran to the dining hall, rushing to Mrs. Motes across the room. "Where's Mahlee? Where'd she go?"

"She didn't tell you? She and Pastor Cody are headed to Millerton to catch the train to Texarkana. They're going early to check on Priscilla. You, Taddy, and your grandma are still going tomorrow." She looked at the clock hanging on the wall by the phone. "They're probably pulling out of the station right now."

I ran out the side door of the dining hall, wishing Mahlee had said goodbye. She's probably mad at me since I argued with her about Margo and how things happened. She kept telling me to come clean and to tell the truth. I yelled at her. Actually, I yelled at everyone.

I thought about Mahlee's gone-crazy night in front of the hospital last year. Her Lizzy Beth would be about the same age. Three or four. I shook my head when the dates ran together. I'll just have to talk to Mahlee when I get home. "Burr. It's freezing out here."

I opened the door to go inside when Black Dog tugged on my pant leg with his teeth. "Hey boy, where have you been? Is your paw better?"

Ar roof. Ar roof.

"Good boy." I rubbed his ear. He lapped up snowflakes before they floated to the ground. "Come inside. It's cold."

I shut the door behind me, running to the front room where I opened the double doors. I stood on the porch, listening to the giggles coming from the girls running in the snow. I joined them, forgetting about not having a coat. I kicked at a pile of snow on the ground, and put my hands on my hips, but I couldn't stop thinking about Bright Eyes and Mahlee.

I wiped the snow from a porch step, sat down, catching flakes in my hands. A man and woman rushed past me. The man ruffled my hair. Their smiles stretched as long as the bridge on the lake out back. Black Dog pranced around their feet and followed them inside.

I watched a snowflake land on my shoe, cupping it in my hand, eating it. I caught four more flakes with my tongue. I talked to a snowflake coming toward my nose. "Could Bright Eyes be Mahlee's little girl? Her baby? The one she gave away in Memphis?" I jumped up and stomped in the snow, making PF Flyer marks in the powder.

I answered myself. "Naw, she can't be. Mahlee's not Indian. The two girls happen to have the same name. That's all."

The smiling man and bouncy woman scurried outside.

Bright Eyes skated over to me. "Bye. Eat ice cream for me. I love you."

I hugged her like my grandma does when she's scared I might not come home. Like she did yesterday when we were rescued. "Bye. I will never forget you."

Mrs. Motes called to me. "Get a coat on those bony arms. I let you get away from me the other day. It's not happening again. Your grandma wouldn't be happy if you got sick."

"Where is my grandma?"

"She rode to town with Boswell to say goodbye to Mahlee and the pastor. She left me in charge of keeping watch over you and Taddy. You know how well I do with babysitting. I've never had my own children. Sometimes I forget to check on you youngins."

"Then where is Taddy?"

"He didn't want to get snow on his clean clothes. He's helping me in the kitchen."

"Why couldn't Taddy and me leave today?"

"Officer Smoke is finishing his investigation tonight. Says he needs to talk to you and Taddy one more time. Says he'll decide what to do with Margo after that."

I followed Mrs. Motes inside, shutting the door. I shuffled down the hall past the officer watching Margo's door. I went into Grandma's room, reaching for my coat beside my satchel, when something grabbed me by the leg. "What? Who's under my bed?"

The voice under the box springs answered. "It's me, Chula." She slid out and stood to her feet. "I brought you a going away gift. I want to give you my flute. But you have something you need to do first. Your time is short, and you still have to save the future-missing children. And you only have tonight."

"I don't understand. Who is missing?"

"It's time. You are here to do this. You must, you are the one. The storm's coming. The healing is ahead."

"Whatever …"

Night of Day Eight

When it Snows it Pours

THE WHISPERS IN THE DINING hall were going strong. Grandma's not talking about going home. She's wearing her favorite slippers tonight while chatting with Mrs. Motes and the matron. This snow has us stuck at Wheelock. So much for driving to the train station. The roads are iced and packed with snow. The flakes keep dropping like soap-powder, and the breeze is worse than a spring tornado. I'll never get home.

The matron called to me from across the table. "This should be our last winter storm before the roses bloom. I'm glad Bright Eyes was able to leave with Gladys and Boyd Winston. They probably drove out of the storm."

I twirled a fork on the table, thinking about my last talk with Bright Eyes before she left. She had asked, "Why does everyone call you Shoelace?"

I told her how my daddy gave me the name. She begged Mr. Winston for a hobo name, too. He ran his hand down his long beard. "You came here from Memphis. We'll have to call you Blue Memphis."

I will forever remember Bright Eyes wearing my engineer cap, and turning to Mr. Winston as they walked to the car. "What's a hobo?"

Now, it's after ten, and the matron has the girls bedded down. I'd come into the kitchen to sit with my grandma, and she didn't send me away.

Taddy's pouting because we had hominy at supper, saying it was gummy. He wanted his mama's cooking. He left the table without eating. He hasn't come out of his room since.

Margo's still down the hall with a guard by her door. The snowstorm kept Officer Smoke away, so Mrs. Motes moved a cot into the hall for the guard to sleep on.

I jumped from my chair. "Where's Black Dog? We haven't brought him inside." I ran to the door, cracked it open, and the gust sent a blanket of snow onto the floor. I hung onto the door knob, but only for a second before Mrs. Motes shoved me aside.

"Girl, please close the door."

Black Dog darted in-between us with icicles hanging from his coat. "There you are. You're freezing."

Mrs. Motes brought a rag over, wiping him down. I watched how gentle she was with him. If she ever did have children, she'd be a nice mama. "Hey, Mrs. Motes, how come we never see Mr. Motes?"

She laughed. "He works here at the orphanage, but he also helps at the boys' school in the next county. Mr. Motes spends his time going back and forth, preaching and teaching. He got caught at the Jones Academy tonight. Winter storms put everyone on edge."

I jetted over to Grandma. She was sipping her coffee. I sat down, snuggling up next to her to get warm. Black Dog crawled up under the table, while Mrs. Motes poured the matron some more coffee.

Grandma touched my arm. "Shoelace, get some sleep. It's late. You've had a rough few days. I'm so proud you're fine. I'm worried about Taddy. He's going to have a few nightmares from being kidnapped."

I nodded, calling to not-my-dog. "Black Dog, come on. You can sleep with me."

Grandma grunted like she was going to say no, but she didn't.

**

"Black Dog. You need to quit wallowing on my feet. I can't sleep with you on my legs."

I rolled over, punching my pillow, trying to sleep. I dozed off, jerking awake every time I closed my eyes. The two brothers, Red and Scar kept popping in my mind. I would see the wind chimes in the woods, too. I'd see Taddy tied up by the tree, curled up in a ball.

I jumped from the bed, digging around in my satchel, looking for the dream catcher. "There it is. If Grandma's right, Taddy's going to need this. He might have worse nightmares than me."

I ran across the hall, opening Taddy's door, switching on the light. I climbed onto the mattress, trying to balance myself. I reached for the clock so I could hang the dream catcher in its place. "Watch out, Taddy."

Thud. Cla-plunk.

"Mama. I want my mama." Taddy bolted from the bed, rubbing his head. "Shoelace? Why are you standing on my bed?"

"Hi, I was hanging this for you. It's a dream catcher. You'll have good dreams with this over your head. These things catch nightmares." I swung it in the air, reaching for the hook. "There. I've got it on the nail."

Taddy swatted at me with his hand. "Get off my bed. I'm tired. I'm ready to leave this place. I want my bed. Now it's snowing. I'm so tired." He crawled up in the bed, and got under the quilt.

I stepped to the bottom of the mattress, jumping. "Hey, since you're up, let's have a party. Just you and me."

Taddy sat up. "Get down. And stop jumping."

"Nope. I'm gonna jump, until you say yes."

Taddy dove at me, punching me in the jaw. His fists pounded my face. "Get off my bed. Get out of this room. We could have died this week. My mama could have, too."

"Stop hitting me. We're not dead. So stop acting like you are." I shoved him back, pinned him down, and sat on his chest. "Your mama would paddle you for treating me this way. Just so you know, I'm not gonna tell her."

Taddy started crying. "I'm sorry. I'm sorry. I'm sorry."

I reached for him, hugging Taddy's neck. "We're best friends. I'll take a black eye from you any day. It's a sign you're alive."

Taddy whined. "But I don't hit people. I'm sorry."

"It's fine. We'll be home soon, and I'll be knocking you out of the tree."

We both wiped our eyes, sitting there without saying a word. I had to break the silence. "Hey, Taddy. Let's have a midnight party. We can have fun. We're stuck here. Let's make the most of it."

Taddy sighed. "I suppose you're not leaving until I say yes."

"So, are we having a party?"

"I suppose."

"Get dressed. I'll be right back. Don't forget your coat."

I hurried to my room. Black Dog was on my pillow sound asleep. Grandma was still talking with the matron and Mrs. Motes in the dining hall. The snoring guard sent a whistle through his nose. He didn't see me. Margo could escape and he wouldn't know it.

I stuck my head into Taddy's room. "Follow me. We're sneaking out the side door by the matron's car. We're going to Wilson Hall. At the bottom of the hill is a door that leads into a basement. That's the gym. We can shovel snow down the stairs, into that room, and build us a snowman."

"You're crazy, you know. We're gonna get in trouble."

"It's party time. When did you ever get to build a snowman inside?"

"I haven't ever built one outside."

"Then come on."

**

On the basketball floor of the gym we pushed piles of powdery snow into stacks. "Isn't this a great idea? We can make a snowman and not freeze to death." I rolled and rolled and packed and packed the snow. This ball was bigger than Black Dog's wash tub.

Taddy worked on the second ball. "This is the softest snow, and not too mushy."

We placed the middle ball onto the bottom one, and made a third ball a little smaller. We stood back and looked at our masterpiece. I hugged Taddy around the neck. "Look. He's a little crooked, and fatter in the middle. But he's grand."

Taddy stepped back, laughing. "He kind of reminds me of Doctor Rigghazel. He's a little round like him."

We both gave out belly laughs, using our deep fun voices.

I pointed to the snowman's blank face. "We need something for the eyes. He can't see."

Taddy pulled on the buttons on his coat. "I'll snap these off. They'll work great."

I looked by the bleacher seats for something to use for a nose. "Here's a crayon. It's orange. This will make a great nose."

Taddy yanked on my arm. "We need some sticks for his arms, and he needs a hat."

"Hey, the stairs lead up to the classrooms. We could go up there and find some rulers. We could use them for his arms."

"Do you think maybe someone left a hat in the coatroom?"

I nodded. "I'll race you up the stairs."

Taddy didn't come.

I stood at the top of the crooked staircase without windows. "Taddy, where are you?"

"It's dark up there. I don't like the dark anymore."

"I'll find the switch. Wait a second." I ran my hand along the wall at the top of the stairs. "I found it. The lights came on up here."

"I'm coming. Let's see what we can find."

Taddy's voice wasn't whimpering or quivering, and he acted like he was having fun, though he knew we'd be in trouble for sneaking out in the snow.

In the hallway, we charged to the first classroom. "Hey, I found two rulers on the teacher's desk."

Taddy moved past me, heading into the coatroom. He stuck his head out the door. "I found a scarf. We can wrap it around our snowman. I don't see any hats or caps."

We bumped into each other as we moved back to the hallway. Taddy ran off, hurrying down the stairs. "I'm finishing the snowman."

I started to follow him, but a bumping noise coming from the end of the hall in the room above the gym made me stop. I stared at the swinging doors. On the other side, someone or

236

something was making noises. No one should be inside this building.

Ding. Ting. Clank. Bump.

I pushed open the door, seeing a shadow.

Before Day Breaks

A Daddy's Hug Feels like Hope

CHULA'S FINGER SHUSHED ME, AND the door swung, swatting my backside, causing me to jump. Photos littered the hardwood floor in the aisle between the chairs, and Chula sat cross-legged on top of the upright piano in the corner by the stage.

I took a step.

Shh ... Shh ...

I bent down and picked up a photo. It was a little girl with black hair and dark eyes. She had one of those Wheelock haircuts. I grabbed another one. Same hair. The face had the same chocolate eyes.

Chula slipped off the piano, circling the windows to my right, slicing the new moonlight with each step. She shuffled up behind me. "I told you to hush. Sit down. We wait. You are here to listen, so your heart will hear."

I obeyed, something I do with her, but not sure why. I sat in the aisle seat to my left, taking in the room. This must be where the girls have plays and put on shows.

Ping. Ding. Dong.

I sat up taller.

Chula put her hand on my shoulder. "Stay here. Listen. For now, listen."

At the piano, someone hunkered down on the keys like a snowman with a larger middle. The snow clouds drifting by the window allowed the moon's glow to light the shadowy room. I could tell that it was Doctor Rigghazel, and he mumbled words of sorrow, words of pain.

Clank. Clank. Clank.

"My bottle. I need my drink." The doctor swayed on the bench, pounding the piano keys with one arm as he reached to the floor.

Ding. Ping. Dong. Dong.

He toppled to the floor like a snowman melting. "It's empty. The bottle is ... empty."

I stood on my seat, pushing Chula's hand from my shoulder. I used my shush voice. "What's he doing? He's drunk again?"

Chula jumped into the chair next to me. "There's more going on here than ..."

Creak. Creak.

I glanced behind me. Taddy's nose poked in-between the swinging door. He stepped inside, calling to me in a low, I'm-scared-of-the-dark voice. "Shoelace, are you in here? You've been gone forever. The snowman is perfect, but he sort of toppled over. The gym's too hot for snow to live."

I bounced from the chair, ran to him, and pulled Taddy into the room. I put my hand over his mouth. "Be quiet. We're listening."

Ummmm...

Taddy yanked my fingers backward, freeing himself. "We? Who is we?"

"Me ... and ..." I looked down the aisle, at the chairs, and across the room. I glanced to my right and to my left. "Well, it was Chula and me. Now, she's gone. You must have scared her."

"Who is Chula? Is she one of the girls from the orphanage? And why would she be afraid of me?"

"She's not afraid. She's … she's sort of … well, I do know she is an Indian girl for sure, but she doesn't live here at Wheelock."

"You're talking crazy. You must be seeing ghosts. We've made a lake in the gym, and we better get back before we get in so much trouble your grandma whips both of us."

Clunk. Clunk. Boom.

Taddy backed up against the door, his eyes like buttons on a snowman. "What is that noise?"

I pulled on his arm. "Be quiet. It's the doctor. He's drunk."

Taddy slid from my grasp. "I'm going to the dorm. I'm done with this snowman party. Your parties are not parties, you know." He darted through the swinging doors, disappearing from the auditorium.

I moved to the left side of the room, glancing out the window. I caught a glimpse of Taddy running through the snow.

I sat down on the floor like a leaning post, wondering if I should help the doctor, or if I should run. Doctor Rigghazel reminds me of my daddy when he drank. Daddy spent too many nights in jail, sleeping it off. I wish I could have helped him. But I never knew how. Never got the chance. Now Daddy's dead. And it's too late.

Chula appeared in the corner. "Do this for your daddy, and let God show you how to help the doctor."

I turned to her. "How did you know what I was thinking? And where were you when Taddy came in?"

"I was here. But he can't see me. The doctor can't, either."

I stood, touching the cold window pane. "What are you saying? You aren't making sense. Of course, I can see you."

"That's what I said. You can see me. But others might not."

I squinted at her, my sleepy eyes heavy. I thought of the times I've seen her. "Hey, Boswell saw you. He's talked to you. Are you crazy like Margo?" I rubbed my eyes. "What about Bright Eyes? She saw you, too."

Chula grabbed my shoulders. "She needed to see me. Just like you do. What I am telling you will change you forever, and forever change how you feel about angels and God."

I shook free. "Now you sound like a preacher girl."

"I'm not a preacher girl ... I'm an angel."

I tumbled to the floor, tripping on my own feet. "But why would I need an angel? I'm not the one who is drunk or crazy like Margo. I'm just visiting."

"You need an angel because, I'm here. I go where God sends me."

I jumped to my feet, shoving Chula. "An angel? You? You're an angel? If that's true, where were you when my daddy fell from the train? Not one angel helped him that day. I don't believe in angels."

"Well, they believe in you. I'm an angel in training. You'll need to ask God about your daddy."

I shook my fist at her. "I have asked God. He doesn't answer me."

"Oh, but he has. He has sent me."

I shook both my fists at her. "And you're the best God can do?"

"God is always doing what's best for us. He loves us."

"I'm not so sure he thinks of me too much."

Chula reached for my hand. "He thinks of you more than you know. The reason Boswell sees me is because he's Wheelock's angel. He came with the first Choctaw girls. He's here for those who feel they are missing and forgotten. Everyone can see Boswell."

"No way. You are not telling me the truth. Boswell's an angel? And you? No way."

I started to run from the auditorium when the drunk-snowman on the floor hollered. "Who's there? Is that you, Rose? Sweet girl, is that you? We need to get home. The snow's a-coming, and we'll get trapped in a ditch somewhere if we don't leave now." The doctor stood, staggering across the front, leaning on the edge of the stage.

Chula stepped away. "This is still listening time. Speak only when the doctor's finished." Chula pushed the swinging door. "I'll be close by."

"You're leaving me alone with him?"

"You are not alone. God is here. I'm near."

Doctor Rigghazel pointed at me. "There you are. Come sit with me. Your mama's gonna be worried. She didn't want you to go with me today. She said six was too young for such a long trip on the wagon to Hugo."

I started to run, but the doctor ran instead. He rushed toward me. He picked me up, and held me like … like my daddy used to. He carried me to the piano bench, slobbering on my face with sour kisses. I wiggled, trying to get free, but somehow this felt like a hug from my past. The doctor sat me down, and he took his place on the bench. "Rose, this is your song. Let me play it for you."

Ding. Ping. Ding. Ding. Pong.

I choked on his whiskey breath, hearing him sing, "Rock-a-bye baby in the tree top. When the wind blows the cradle will rock. When the bough breaks, the cradle will fall. And down will come baby … cradle and all."

I slipped from the bench, tripping on the whiskey bottle on the floor. The doctor hit the keys with his fingers. "Death. Death. The ditch brought death. You fell. You fell. I couldn't tell. But then … I saw the blood, and your eyes saying goodbye."

I crawled to the front row of chairs, hoping to make a dash from the room. "Leave me alone. I'm not Rose."

He ran for me. "But you are. You're my baby. No one wanted me as a child. I grew up an orphan boy. But when I had you, I had everything. I had you."

I mouthed. "You can't have me. I'm not Rose. I'm Annie Grace Kree. Remember?"

The doctor jerked me by the arm. "Who are you? What did you do with my Rose?"

"I never had your Rose."

He reached for my other arm, shaking me. "Where is she?"

"I don't know. I don't know her."

The doctor gasped, his hands sliding down me like snow falling to the ground. He crumpled to his knees, whimpering like a baby. He yelled. "She is dead. She is…she is gone. A long time ago. A long time ago." He curled into a ball on the floor, weeping like I do when I miss my daddy.

Chula stood behind the doctor, whispering. "So much for listening."

"I tried to listen. He kept singing to me. And then he screamed about someone named Rose."

Chula sat on the floor, rubbing the doctor's head like my grandma does when I have nightmares. She motioned to me. "Shoelace, come sit with him. He needs to heal. He needs to cry. He needs to talk to God. He needs to find his peace."

"I'm not sitting with him. He's drunk."

"You should. He needs you."

"He doesn't need me. He'll slobber on me."

"He doesn't know what he needs."

I treaded over to the broken snowman. His crumpled body looked sad. I sat on the floor, and my knees bumped the whiskey bottle.

Chula took my hand, helping me run my fingers through his scratchy hair. She whispered, "He's going to talk to God. Just sit with him."

The doctor's sobs filled up the entire auditorium. He sat up and I jerked away, scooting a few feet from him. He threw his arms up toward the ceiling, screaming. His first words were lost in the haze of the moonlight. I couldn't understand them. I got to my feet, ready to run.

The doctor knocked over chairs, kicked some, and stomped so hard he crushed the whiskey bottle in his last frenzy. His fit turned into a fire of questions to God. "Why? Why did you take her? I hope she's happy with you. Why? She was my life. I did everything for her. I lived for each moment we had together. That's why she went with me that day. How could you do that to me?"

Doctor Rigghazel collapsed, like a puddle of melting snow, his arms twisted, his face weeping. He'd exhausted all the words that were bottled up inside of him. It's as if his hate couldn't live inside any longer.

I puddled to the floor next to the wall and held my knees.

Chula touched my leg. "Tell him. Tell him God loves him."

"You tell him. You're the angel." I knocked her hand from my pants.

"I will. I'll whisper hope into his ear."

"No, go tell him out loud. I want to hear your angel-talk."

"This is not the way it's supposed to go."

"Sorry. I'm not doing your work for you. You're just a little orphan girl like me."

"I'm not. I'm an angel. I can prove it."

I got nose-to-nose to Chula. "Then prove it."

"If I show you, will you tell him?"

"Sure. It's not like I'm going to have to."

Chula bent down to put her arms around the doctor. The moonlight shifted like a spotlight, focusing on them. I wiped my eyes, backing up, blinking. Four beings stood like statues. One glistened. He looked like my hobo friend, White Beard. Another was clear. I could see through him. He looked like the man who gave us bacon at the mission in Memphis. The other two looked just like Slow Tom and Fast Tim from Hobo Church. All four held out their arms like swords.

I ran to them. "White Beard? Slow Tom? Is that you, Fast Tim? And the cook? How ... how did you get here?"

In one voice, like four snowmen, they answered, "Sometimes you have angels around you and you don't even know it. But tonight, you know."

I lost my breath, falling into a pile of photos. I looked over my shoulder, and only saw ... only saw Doctor Rigghazel and Chula.

She moved to me. "I've shown you who I am. Now, you are to show the doctor who God is."

"I have no idea how to do that."

"I'll tell you what to say. Remember, he can't see me."

I sat down with the doctor.

Chula whispered, "Tell him, God so loved the world that he gave his one and only son, that whoever believes in him shall not perish but have eternal life."

I turned to her. "That's kind of long."

"Say it, just tell him."

I leaned over and repeated her words, not sure what most of it meant.

The doctor mumbled, curling up tighter. He hugged a chair leg. "What? What did you say?"

Chula spoke more God words. "For God did not send his son into the world to condemn the world, but to save the world through him."

I got in her face. "Are you sure this is what I'm supposed to be saying?"

She turned my head. "Tell him the rest. He needs to hear this. And so do you."

I finished telling the doctor the God words, and he popped up like a brand new snowman. "Where did you learn those verses? Did your grandma teach them to you?'

I sat cross-legged opposite him. "Nope. Never heard them until tonight."

"What? You must have learned them in Sunday school. My Rose used to say that first part to me after church on Sundays."

I looked around the room, hoping to see where Chula was, but once again, I'd lost her.

The doctor reached for my hand. "I'm tired and worn down. I'm lost. I'm so sorry for what I've done. I want to change. God, I need your help."

Chula appeared, placing her hand on his chest. She raised her eyebrows. "He needs a new heart. This one is breaking."

I looked at the doctor's eyes. His sorrow leaked out with more cries.

I whispered, "Is he going to be all right?"

Chula put her other hand on the bib of my overalls. "You also need a new heart. Those verses aren't just for the doctor. They're for you, too."

I looked down at Rigghazel, who didn't respond to Chula's words. He wept, shaking and sobbing. He acted like he didn't sense her. Could Chula really be an angel? She talks funny. Acts weird. She shows up at the strangest times.

The crying snowman sobbed. "God, help me. Help me fix this. Help me do something with my life. I've become something I can't live with."

Chula pulled her flute out, playing dancing notes. The doctor stopped crying, but I was weeping now. The next words I shared with him would forever change the snowman on the floor. It would forever change me, too. We would both learn how God can put ears in your heart.

A Late Rescue

Worth Saving

THE BLUE BEAM WAS COMING in from the four windows on each side of the auditorium. The notes danced with the music coming from Chula's flute. Questions for the doctor rose up inside me. I wanted to know more about Rose, quizzing the doctor. "When did your little girl die?"

He snorted, taking a deep breath. "Eight years. This June."

I sat with my back against a chair. "My daddy died last year. But my mama died when I was born." I wiped a tear from my cheek.

The doctor straightened up, leaned on one arm, and tucked both of his feet behind him. "You never knew your ma?"

"Nope. Pastor Cody says I look like her."

"Then ... then ..." He hiccupped. "Then she must have been pretty."

"She was. I've seen her picture." I shuffled some of the photos in my hands. They lined the floor like a trail of tears. "What's with all of these pictures?"

"Those are from my wall at the office. They are other girls I couldn't save." A blue streak of moonlight shot across his face. "They are the faces of Choctaw girls from Wheelock. Many died from the fever. I lost fourteen girls the winter after Rose died, and three teachers. I can't save anyone." He pulled a photo from his pocket. "Now, I've got Eleanor's photo. It never ends."

"But you can save people. You can. You saved me."

"How can a drunken ole doctor save anyone?"

"I know how. I know what you could do."

"Sure you do. A little city girl telling me what to do. Now, that's great."

"I'm not a city girl. I'm a hobo girl with a grandma."

Ha. Ha. Ha.

"Why would I listen to a hobo girl?"

"Because an angel thinks you're worth saving, even if I don't." I turned to look at Chula.

The doctor touched my chin. "Who are you looking for?"

"You don't see her?"

"See who? Maybe you're the one who drank the rest of my whiskey." He laughed a horrid laugh from somewhere deep inside his gut.

"I'm not drunk. I'm a kid. I don't drink. Don't you see her?" I picked up more pictures and pointed at Chula, who wiggled her legs. "She's sitting on the stage. She's playing a flute."

Doctor Rigghazel crawled to a seat in the front row, pulling himself up like a lizard having dizzy spells. "Show me where she is. I don't see anyone." He mocked me, pointed his long arm, wobbling like a flag caught in the wind.

"She's right there." I stepped up to Chula, and she grinned, her smile saying, see I told you, he can't see me.

Doctor Rigghazel continued with his tone. "So what's your invisible angel telling you?"

"She's not talking right now, she's playing her flute."

The doctor spit into his hands, like sneezing and coughing and choking. His eye lids blinked faster than I could figure out what to say next. He slid from the chair to the floor, his head not too steady, his body not ready for a chair. "Tell me, what's she saying? Can she see me on the floor?"

I moved in front of him, dropping the photos. I planned to give him the lecture I'd always wanted to give my daddy. I'd rehearsed it, and now it's about to spew out. "Maybe the angel would tell you to stop drinking. Maybe the angel would tell you to do better. To stop thinking of only yourself. "

The doctor's eyes bugged wider, spitting leftover saliva to the floor.

I dug up some more words. Words that I hoped would cut him in half. I shouted. "You send babies to heaven too soon. You make Margo cry about it, too. And then, you cry like a baby over losing Rose. What about those babies? You shouldn't take babies away before they laugh or cry. Or before they can take a breath. They are … they are little humans."

"Stop judging me. Their mothers pay me to help. I'm helping the women." He wiped his mouth with his hand.

"But who is helping the babies? What would Rose say about her daddy doing this?"

Doctor Rigghazel grabbed my arm. "I've had enough of your attitude, little girl."

I mouthed off, not finished with my scolding. "You don't have to drink. You hide behind your bottle. My pa drank every day. He missed seeing me. Missed being with me. And now, he's gone. He spent too many nights in jail, and you are in jail, too. You are stuck in the lost nights and sad days."

"Girl, you whine and talk of not having your pa. You are no different than me. I don't have my Rose. And you don't have your pa. We are the same. We are both alone."

Chula spoke to me. "Tell him, he's not alone. He has Margo and Isabella."

I took her cue, yanking my arm free. "You are not alone. You have Isabella. And crazy Margo." I put my hand to my face, wishing I'd not said the word crazy. "And I'm … I'm not alone. My grandma loves me. My Mahlee loves me. Taddy loves me. Eleanor loved me, too. And Bright Eyes. Imogene's my friend. I'm not alone. I'm not. I'm not." I stomped my feet on the broken glass, crunching slivers of it into the floor.

Doctor Rigghazel wobbled to the piano and hit a few keys. *Ding. Ping. Dong. Ding. Ding.*

He cocked his head, tossing me a squinted look like he wanted to shout ugly words at me.

Chula whispered, "Let him speak. Listen."

The doctor gurgled. "I hate to admit this. I hate to. I won't. But I might." He turned around. "You, my little friend, could be right. I have a three month-old baby girl who needs her pa. I would want my ... my ... Rose to know her pa isn't a bad man."

He moved to the window, placed both hands on the window pane, and pressed his head on the glass. He wept, letting some more trapped sounds leak from his guts.

I crumpled to the floor, letting my past leak out, too. I whispered to Chula. "My daddy wasn't a bad man, even though he left me alone on the rail. I was scared without him. I missed him so much."

Chula slid from the edge of the stage, hugging me. "You need to go to the doctor. He's ready. He's ready to change. He's ready to forgive."

"Ready to forgive?"

"Yes, he's mad at God for taking Rose."

I gathered myself, shuffling to the window next to the doctor. I whispered, "My daddy was worth saving. So I suppose ... suppose ... you are, too. I was angry that God let my daddy die. It hurt more than falling from a boxcar."

I slipped my fingers into his palm. The doctor wrapped his hand around mine, looking down at me. I gazed into his red eyes. His scruffy beard and hair needed a good trim. I spoke into the cold. "I hope God's not mad at me for being so mad at him."

The doctor slithered to the floor, sticking his feet out in front of him. "I've been pretty mad at God about Rose, too."

I sat next to him. "Maybe we should tell God that we're sorry. Grandma's always making me say I'm sorry."

"Your grandma's right. But I think God knows what's happening here. I used to be close to him, and it's time I talked to him again, instead of using the bottle for my answers. That's not working so good for me."

I nodded. "I get in a lot of fights at home. I think it's because I'm mad at God, too. I want to stop hitting everyone. But, it's hard."

"Change is hard. We both need to make some changes."

"My grandma says Jesus loves everyone. I hope she's right. She says he forgives us, too."

Doctor Rigghazel squeezed my fingers, giving me a half-grin. "I'm going to need God's help. I'm not taking the lives of any more babies, either. And no more whiskey."

"I need God to help me, too. But he doesn't really talk to me. He just takes the people I love."

"Losing our loved ones is one of the hardest things. I expect God knows all about that, since his son, Jesus, died for us."

"I heard he had scars on his feet and hands, and someone stuck him with a sword."

"Yes, Jesus went through a lot of suffering. Just because he loved us."

I looked at my arms. "I have a lot of scars. But nothing like that."

Doctor Rigghazel got on his knees by a chair. "Come join me. I haven't prayed in a while, but I think I need to."

I scrunched up beside him, folded my hands, and kept my eyes wide open.

The doctor sighed. "God, I don't know how it got this bad. But God, I'd like to come back. Please save me from my choices. Save me from myself. Give me a reason to live."

I glanced at the doctor's face, and his scruffiness didn't look so scruffy anymore. "Are we done praying?"

"Not yet. You might want to close your eyes."

"Who said we have to close our eyes?"

"It helps you pay attention."

"Fine." I closed only one eye, and kept the other one on the doctor.

He reached for my hand. "God, I know your Son died for me. Please forgive me, and change my heart. I want to obey you and follow you." He coughed, spitting into his hands, sobbing like a baby that had new life.

I finished his prayer with both eyes open. "Hey God, while you're saving folks, can you count me in? Save me, too. I'm tired of being angry at my daddy. Tired of fighting. Tired of feeling so lost."

**

Bam. Bam. Bam.

The double doors bounced off the wall. Taddy's screams disrupted the sobs coming from the doctor, and me. "Shoelace, my hands are turning blue. All the doors are locked at the dorm. I can't get inside ..." Taddy stopped rambling, pointing at the doctor. "What are you doing with him?"

I shouted back at Taddy. "We're praying."

"That's funny. You don't pray. What's really going on in here? He's drunk. Listen to him. He's slurring."

"Nope, he's praying. He's almost not-drunk. The doctor is having a sorry-party with God."

"Sure he is."

I let go of the doctor's hand, spun around, and scratched my head.

Taddy spun around, too. "What are you looking for?"

"I'm wondering where Chula is."

"The little girl that only you seem to see?"

I bit my lip before I spoke. "You wouldn't believe me if I told ya what's happened here tonight."

From somewhere in the night air, Chula whispered to my heart. "Nakni Nita. Annie Grace Kree. The Shoelace girl. She is now a true warrior. She is alive."

I touched my heart, not sure if warrior fit, but glad my heart felt new. I got lost in the memory of my daddy's smile, and thought of how this must be the look on God's face. He must smile like my daddy when brokenhearted people pray to him.

Taddy waved his hand in front of my face. "Hello, are you in there? We have to get inside. And get to bed. Look at my fingers. They're frozen. If your grandma finds out we're not in our rooms, there's no telling what she'll do to us."

I hugged the doctor. "I've got to go." I ran with Taddy through the swinging doors into the hallway. "I'll race you down the stairs to the gym."

He bumped into me. "I thought we were already racing."

At the bottom of the staircase, I jumped to the gym floor. My feet swam ahead of me, sending me flat on my back in a puddle of water. "Our snowman's melted. He's left a swimming pool in the gym."

Taddy swooshed behind me, sliding into me like a rock falling from a mountain. "Sorry. I lost my balance."

We skidded across the floor, landing near a basketball post. Taddy whined. "Look at this. The gym is flooded. We'll get licks for this, too."

We stood to our feet, and headed toward the exit door. Taddy wrung water from his pant legs while I squeezed water from my overalls. We hurried into the night, a gust of wind slapping at us. Our feet sunk into the snow. Our clothes became icicles, and our legs dragged with each step.

I stuttered. "Hurry, we'll sneak in through the dining hall. They always leave the side door open."

"I bet it's locked. The matron always locks up at night. She's the rule maker and she doesn't break them."

"The gym door was unlocked. Maybe this one is, too." At the dining hall steps, I reached for the knob.

Taddy yelled. "Hurry up. I'm freezing."

I shoved him back. "Stop pushing."

"But, I'm so cold. I can't feel my hands."

I turned the frozen knob. "You're right. The door is locked. We'll have to knock." I raised my fist, ready to pound on the door when it swung open. Grandma stuck her head out, and the face of someone who is worn down from my disobeying her, frowned at me.

She ordered. "Inside, now. I don't know what in the dickens I'm going to do with two children who can't mind me. Not one second have you listened to me, Shoelace. Not one. And Taddy, you are starting to listen to her too much."

We stepped inside like snapped icicles from a roof. Neither of us said a word.

Ring-a-ling. Ring-a-ling.

I tapped on Grandma's arm. "The phone's ringing."

She pushed me. "Never you mind."

Ring-a-ling. Ring-a-ling.

Taddy looked at me. "The phone's ringing."

I mouthed. "She doesn't care."

Grandma tugged on my sleeve, keeping a hand on Taddy's shoulder." The phone isn't any of your business. Someone will get it. Right now, you both need dry clothes, and you need to warm yourselves. I'll decide your punishment tomorrow."

The door beside my room creaked. Margo stuck her head into the hall. "The phone's ringing. Isn't anyone going to answer it?"

Grandma sighed. "Everyone's asleep, or should be. I'll get it in a minute."

The guard grumbled but slept away on his cot. I bent down, whispering. "Officer Smoke wouldn't like you sleeping on the job. I might have to tell him."

The guard's nose rattled out another snore.

Ring-a-ling. Ring-a-ling.

Margo stomped past us. "I'll get the phone."

I shook free from Grandma, peeking into the kitchen. Margo's face went white as she talked into the receiver. She screamed, slamming down the phone. "That was Pauline. Part of the roof has caved in at my house. She's there with Eliza and Isabella. Pauline and Eliza are due any day with their babies. We have to get Boswell, and go for them."

Grandma pushed me out of the way, rushing to Margo. "What? Who needs help?'

Margo waved her arms. "We have to save the babies. We have to save the babies."

Day Nine Begins

When the Letter Is Read

I ROLLED TO THE CENTER of the bed, pulled on the quilt, and wrapped it around my face, leaving my nose uncovered on the pillow. I slid my toes under the warm, fat legs of my grandma.

"Girl, I've been in this bed ten minutes and you've gone and jabbed me with those long toenails. The morning's coming in two hours. I've spent most the night holding the cutest baby this side of the Red River, but I'm worn to a thread."

"This side of the Red River? What about me? Aren't I cute?" I moved my feet, curling up close to Grandma's back, hoping she forgave me for sneaking out to make a snowman. I'm glad she didn't know about the melting part yet. I'd be getting a whipping with a switch.

She rolled over to face me. "You're the cutest granddaughter on the Arkansas side of the Red River." Grandma moved a strand of my hair behind my ear. "Little Isabella, with her button nose and cocoa eyes, will melt an old heart like mine anytime."

I smiled. "Can I go see her?"

"No, she's asleep in a room with Eliza and Pauline. After Boswell found the doctor, and they retrieved them, the time got late. I was afraid they would get stuck in the snow. But finally, in the wee hours, a crying baby woke me up. I was bent in half with my head on the kitchen table."

Grandma's eyes shut. I tapped her nose with one finger. "Stop playing in bed. I'm going to sleep."

"You can't sleep. We need to catch a train."

She yawned. "We'll catch it tomorrow once the snow melts."

I lifted one of her eyelids. "Are you awake?"

She slapped my arm. "Stop bothering me."

"Where's Margo? What's she doing?"

Grandma rolled away from me. "Never you mind."

I tossed the covers off, putting my feet to the floor. "Cold. Cold. Cold." I jumped onto the mattress, toppling over Grandma.

"Get off me, Shoelace. Get yourself back in this bed. Two hours. Give me two hours."

I rolled off. "Is Margo in the room next to us? Is the guard keeping watch? Where's the doctor? Is the snow melting? Grandma, have you ever seen an angel? Like four, all at the same time?" I asked question after question. Grandma wheezed, snoring through each one. I tugged on her ear. "Are you awake?"

Grandma's arms flew every which way, and the quilt folded over her feet at the bottom of the bed. "Enough. I've had enough. If there's an angel in this room, would you please sit on my granddaughter?" She sat up, rocked like a toddler, and pulled me to her chest. "Shoelace, this has been the longest week of my life. The longest ever. I have to get some rest. Please. I'm so grateful you and Taddy are alive, but I'm worn out like a dirty apron. I'm exhausted."

Her tears fell onto my blonde hair. I held my breath until I thought I'd pop. "I'm sorry. I am. I'll be still. I'll lie down and rest. I promise. Do you want me to turn off the lantern?"

"No. Leave it. It gets too dark in here."

A few minutes later, Grandma's snoring rattled my ears with a snort like Wind Horse makes when he sneezes. I sighed, listening to the creaking walls. I wished for the sun to come up, so I could get out of this room.

I held my fingers in front of my face, counting the days since we arrived. Too many for one hand. If the snowstorm had waited, I'd be home. If Boswell hadn't written that blasted letter, I'd be home. If Margo wasn't coming with us, we should just go home.

But wait, Margo talks like she's Taddy's mama. And the picture of her with Taddy's pa has me wondering. Where did I put letter number six? I inched to the side of my bed, reaching to the floor for my satchel, hoping the letter was in the pouch. Fumbling, I found the envelope. I dug for a pair of socks, since I'd lost the other ones under Grandma.

I sat on the cold floor, slipped the socks on, and crawled to the door. I reached for the knob, listening for a deep breath from Grandma. Yep. She's out.

I cracked open the door, enough to crawl into the hallway. A light from the kitchen cast a shadow of orange my way. I sat on the floor to read the letter. I opened the envelope and unfolded the paper. Should I open Taddy's door and give him the letter? Naw. He's just going to yell at me. He's tired of all of this.

I didn't want to hurt Taddy or make this worse, which is something I'm good at doing. I'm good at causing trouble without trying. So for now, I'm reading the letter by myself.

Dear Taddy,
I stood outside your apartment in Texarkana on your birthday in February, when you turned ten. I wanted to knock on the door, but I could only stand there and cry.
I saw you come to the window, looking through the glass. I have to tell you, I almost died. I love you, and here's why. I am Priscilla. I am your birth mama.
Now, the one you call mama, she is really Margo. Your pa loved her more, and my not-so-calm days kept me from loving you the right way. So we, the twins, the ones so many call crazy, swapped places to save you and to protect you from me. Everyone thought Margo was the crazier twin, but it was me, Priscilla. One good trade made you safe.
Every time I think of you, it's like a thousand hugs to my heart, and it's like a thousand broken memories, too. No matter what, I will always love you.

Love,
Mama

I leaned on the wall, sobbing sad tears for Taddy, and sad tears for myself. Black Dog showed up from the end of the hall. He put his snout on my leg, licking the letter. I petted his ears, hugging him. "I have a cat at home. You would like him. He's nice like you."

Black Dog panted, swiping my nose with his tongue.

I'd give anything to have two mamas fighting over me, and thought about the fluffy old grandma snoring in the bedroom behind me. She'd fight for me. She actually did when I was five. The time Daddy took me. And there's Mahlee. She gets mad at me, but she would knock someone out if they hurt me. I do have two mamas fighting over me.

My mamas just didn't come from the regular mama-mold. They love me the same, though.

I tucked the letter inside the envelope, crawling back into the bedroom on my knees. I shoved the letter into my satchel. Maybe I won't ever tell Taddy about this letter. I'll just have to wait and see if he needs to know.

The ding-dong of the bell on the second story roof sent a chime through the dorm. The girls would be getting up for school, breakfast would be served, and Imogene would go home with her new family today, if the roads are clear.

I put on my overalls and clean shirt, closing the door to the bedroom without waking up my grandma. I hurried to the heater in the kitchen to get my shoes. Mrs. Motes shuffled like she'd not been to sleep. "Mrs. Motes, where's Margo. Is she sleeping?"

Mrs. Motes shook her head. "Last night she slipped out when Boswell and the doctor rode up the hill. We haven't seen her since the middle of the night. If Officer Smoke makes it here, he won't be happy." She sighed, wiped her hands on her apron, and handed me a glass of milk. "You, my dear, have no idea how quiet the academy was before you arrived."

I nodded, wishing for breakfast at home.

The dining hall door slammed against the wall. The wind rushed inside like a wolf on attack, along with Margo, who barged into the kitchen. "Are they here? Is Isabella alive? Where's my baby?"

New Morning

To Hug or To Hide

MRS. MOTES TOOK MARGO BY the arm, guiding her down the hallway past the room where Taddy slept, past the bedroom with my grandma. I crept behind them, hoping for a chance to see the baby.

I tugged on Mrs. Motes' dress. "Can I see Isabella, too?"

Margo snapped at me. "No, she's mine. No one sees her."

I ran in front of Margo. "What do you mean? You don't hold her or stay home much. She might like to be held." My words tumbled from my lips like a knife slicing bread. My words not only hurt Margo, they hurt my heart, too.

Mrs. Motes moved me aside. "You're in the way more than you show the way. Maybe you should go to the kitchen."

"I'm sorry. I only wanted to see Taddy's little ..." I gulped, catching myself before spouting off another set of words. If I keep smarting off to Margo, she might hit me, or worse, knock me to the other end of the hall.

Margo stepped backwards, her fists flying in the air. "Shoelace, you know more than you should. You should know when to keep quiet."

"I'm sorry. I am. Can I please look at Isabella? We're leaving tomorrow. I may never see her again."

Margo gave me her sad look, and she hugged me. Her moods change. They come and go. I can't get used to how she reacts to me. I suppose this is how my grandma must feel when I obey one minute, and then I don't.

Mrs. Motes stopped at the door across from the matron's bedroom. She gave Margo a side hug. "You have a few minutes before the guard comes back. He's searching for you, and he's afraid of losing his job. You best hurry and get back to your room. Go see your baby girl. I've placed her in a metal tub with some blankets. Pauline and Eliza are asleep in the bed next to it."

Margo turned the knob, stuck her head inside, and yanked me by my arm. "Come with me."

The morning sun peeked in through the curtains to our left, and the pregnant ladies' bellies poked up under the covers like two giant watermelons. They took up the whole bed. One had her foot on top of the quilt. The other lady whistled through her nose.

Margo tiptoed to the tub by the dresser, kneeling down to the floor. I stepped behind her, peering over her shoulder at a sleeping round face with dark hair. "She's little. When was she born?"

"October 12. She was born in Valliant."

"What's a Valliant?"

"It's a town up Highway 70. I stayed in a room with some friends of Mrs. Motes. She and her pastor husband took care of me."

I sat down on the floor and touched the blanket. "They helped you? They knew you were pregnant?"

"Yes. Mrs. Motes saves me blackberry cobbler and sneaks me flour for baking, too. They are good people."

I smiled. "Mrs. Motes is nice. She has kind eyes."

Margo ran her fingers through the hair of her baby girl. She whispered, "Want to know a secret?"

"Yes, sure."

"This is not the doctor's baby."

"What? But you said she is."

"He needs someone to love. I told him she was his. If he loves her, he might save the others. He might stop the ..." Margo's voice trailed off.

The ladies in the bed moaned. Their bellies hit each other as they tugged on the covers, snuggling into the mattress. Margo and me sat next to the tub, simply staring at Isabella.

"But if the doctor finds out he's not the pa, he'll get mad. He misses his daughter, Rose. He also told me he's ready to love this baby."

Margo gave me a glare. "The doctor won't admit that Isabella is his. Like I said, she's not."

"How do you know?" I was asking grown-up questions, not sure how or why I got mixed up in this kind of talk.

Margo laughed under her breath. "I'm kidding you. She's a Rigghazel. She's his. He's the pa."

I sighed. "I don't know when to believe you, and when not to. You say you're the real Priscilla, and then you play with my mind about whose baby this is. I am so confused."

Margo didn't respond to my last words. She grabbed the bundle and held Isabella close, rocking on the floor.

I peeked at Isabella's feet. "She's pretty. She's got big toes, though. What's her middle name?"

"I never gave her one. She's simply Isabella Rigghazel on her birth certificate. I used her daddy's name."

"But she needs a middle name."

"She doesn't have one."

"I know. Give her the name Rose. Isabella Rose Rigghazel."

Margo recited the name. "Isabella Rose Rigghazel. It's a good name. In the spring, the arbor between the dorm and the classrooms blooms with the prettiest white roses. We could nickname her Spring Rose."

"I like that nickname. It's kind of like a hobo name. That will make the doctor happy, too."

"Yes. He would like that. Maybe. If he's sober."

I smiled, thinking of his talk with God last night. "I bet he's not drunk anymore."

"What makes you think he'll stop drinking?"

"I have a feeling."

Creak. Creak.

Mrs. Motes peeked inside the room. "The guard has returned. Both of you get to your rooms. Shoelace, go to your grandma's room. Margo, climb in bed. If he looks in on you, act like you've been asleep for hours. Be sure to put your nightclothes on."

Margo placed Isabella Rose into the tub, kissed her cheek, and leaned over. "I love you. No matter what happens or where I go."

Eliza and Pauline slept through our visit, and we moved to the hallway. The matron and the Wheelock girls came through the halls singing, "Wheelock, Wheelock, we love you. We long shall remember and honor you."

I jumped in with the girls, parading to the kitchen for breakfast. No time for sleep. Inside the dining hall, I searched for Imogene, finding her in the back part of the room near the pantry, sitting with her back to me. I cupped my hands around her eyes. "Guess who?"

Imogene laughed. "I know who this is. You are the pale-skinned girl who laughs hard, plays harder, and breaks most of the rules."

I giggled, sitting down with her. "Did you find out when your new family is coming?"

"Not yet. If they can get through on the highway, I'll leave today. I'm packed and ready to go. I'm going to miss you. Thanks for the moccasins." She took a bite of toast, swallowing with a loud gulp. "I left my black leather shoes in the barn the other day when I slipped on your shoes. I'm going back to get them before school starts."

I leaned on my arm. "So who's breaking the rules now?"

"There's no rule about getting my shoes."

"I'll go with you."

A hand on my shoulder sent my arms to swinging. I turned to see the guard who can't keep up with Margo. "I need to talk to you, young lady."

"Why, I'm not in trouble. I haven't done anything wrong today. It's too early for anything to be my fault."

"I know you know where Margo's been. I know you know. You can tell me. I expect Officer Smoke will make an arrest today. He's going to get her for kidnapping, I'm sure. She has caused enough havoc in this county. It's time they put her away."

"She is innocent. I've already told you. I've told Officer Smoke, too. I've told the Lighthorsemen. Margo's not guilty. She helped us."

"If she rescued you, then how did you and Taddy end up in her forest hide-out? How come? Tell me. You know something you're not saying." His hand got tighter on my arm.

I jumped up, stomping my feet, yanking free. "You are not my mama. You are not the boss of me. You are not getting me to say something bad about Margo. She's ... she's ... different than other people. But she tries to do the right thing."

"I've heard you don't know the difference between what's right and wrong yourself."

Mrs. Motes came up behind him, placing her hand on the guard's shoulder, causing him to spin like a top. Mrs. Motes smiled. "Sir, I expect your place is not in here in the dining hall scaring my girls. You should take yourself to the hallway. I'll bring your breakfast plate to you. Margo is in her room, asleep."

The guard gave me a frown, giving Mrs. Motes one, too. "I'll go for now. This isn't over. You'll see."

Mrs. Motes called to him. "Shall I let Officer Smoke know you slept through our saving two pregnant ladies and a baby last night? If it hadn't been for the doctor and for Boswell, there's no telling what would have happened to them."

The guard slithered away, and Mrs. Motes pointed to me. "As for you, sit in the chair and act like a lady, please."

I plopped down in the chair. "Yes, ma'am."

Mrs. Motes moved to the kitchen counter where the older girls helped serve the food.

Imogene gulped her milk, swallowing hard. "Are you still going with me to the barn?"

"Sure. I need to get away from that guard. I could play with the cat, too."

Imogene smiled. "I thought you liked Black Dog."

"I do. He's pretty neat, for a dog."

"I'll get my coat. Meet me on the front porch in two minutes." She limped to the hallway. Her left leg was shorter than her right, but she moved faster than many of the girls.

I took a drink of milk as a gust of cold air rushed under the table. "Who opened that door?"

Officer Smoke stomped by two of the longer tables, marching up to the matron. He put his hands on his hips, right above his two guns, calling to no one in particular. "We've found Red and Scar. Well, not them, but we found their boots. We also rode up on their horses. I had Boswell put them in the barn. It's time to take Margo to my office for some serious questioning. I need answers, and the snow's gone from the roads. I'll get her and be gone. I'll send for the horses later."

I charged him. "You can't take her. I've told you, she is not involved. Well, she's not involved in the taking Taddy part. At least, not the first part. She's not guilty. Taddy will tell you."

Officer Smoke reminded me. "Well, Taddy isn't talking. He could help clear this up, but he's got nothing to say."

A weak voice called to us from the hallway. "I have plenty to say. I'm Thaddeus William Day, Jr., and Margo's my aunt. She saved my life." Taddy stood in his nightshirt, pointing at Officer Smoke. "I want to go home. I want to go now. I'm tired, and I want my mama."

Ring-a-ling. Ring-a-ling.

I moved to Taddy, watching the tears fall from his eyes like icicles of pain melting into forgiveness.

Mrs. Motes picked up the receiver. "Yes. Really? She's awake? She's responding? And she's hungry? Just a minute, Pastor. Taddy is right here. He's going to want to hear this."

Unknown Soul

Midday of Day Nine

Shoes for You

WITH THE COMMOTION, I FORGOT to meet Imogene. Officer Smoke and Grandma made Taddy sit down for more questions, shushing me whenever I tried to speak. They wanted Taddy's version of what Red and Scar did. He told them just enough to make these horrible last few days almost go away.

The guard from the hall frowned, shuffling his feet every time I grin at him—he hopes for Margo's arrest.

Grandma patted my arm. "You run along to the bedroom. Let us talk to Taddy alone."

"But, I might have something good to add."

The officer raised his left eyebrow. "I'm sure you would."

Taddy sighed. "It's fine. I know what happened. I know what they did. I will tell the truth. I always tell the truth."

I tapped him on the back of the head. "If you need me, I'll be down the hall."

In the bedroom, I grabbed my coat, darted across the hall, searching for Imogene. I hurried to the porch, across the grounds, and saw that the barn doors were swung wide open.

I stomped in the melting snow, jumped over puddles, and ran like a deer set loose from a trap. The warm sun beamed down on the top of my head, warm like hope. I yelled a warrior song racing to find Imogene. "Ya-ha-ha-way. Ya-ha-ha-way. Ya-ha-ha-way. Ya-ha-ha-way."

I skidded to a stop at the barn door. A red-headed bird zinged around my head, darting inside the barn. "Imogene, are you in here? I'm sorry for not meeting you, but you're not going to believe this. The cops are letting Margo go free. Well, I think they will, since Taddy's clearing everything up." I shook snow from my shoe. "Imogene, where are you?"

"She's over here." Boswell's deep voice made me jump. I moved to the rear of the barn to the spot where he keeps his bedding. I stuck my head inside his sleeping-bunk-room, and my ponytail dangled over my shoulder. "Where's Imogene?"

"She's running in the snow behind the barn. Black Dog is with her. War Cat is sitting on the corral fence, swatting at them."

I wrapped my finger around the short post in the middle of Boswell's bunk-room. "So is this a leaning post?"

Boswell laughed a powwow chant, and slid his hand to his hip next to his holster. "It's not leaning. It's pointing to heaven. It's a grand post, huh?"

"Heaven? So are you really an angel?"

"Seems some might say so."

"Chula said you are. How do you become an angel?"

"It's up to God to decide. He does the picking."

I twirled around the post, my hand sliding on the smooth finish. I couldn't wait to get home to ask Slow Tom and Fast Tim if they knew they were angels. I let go of the post and headed to the big swinging doors like the front ones, but these led to a snow playground out back. I turned to Boswell. "If you're angel, then you might want to protect the girls better. Lots of bad things have been happening here."

"I'll see what I can do."

I smiled. "So, why is Imogene playing in the snow? And why are you holding her moccasins?"

"Because she's wearing her black shoes."

"She better hurry. She's going to get in big trouble from the matron."

"Imogene's leaving with her new family, most likely today. The matron isn't looking for her. Go take a look. Imogene's running like she's never run before."

I moved past the doors, stepping beyond the corrals to the open land draped in white. Giggles rose up in invisible clusters of fun, like the sound Chula makes when she laughs at me. War Cat rubbed up against my legs. "Imogene, what are you doing?"

"Watch this." Imogene waved, running in a circle around a big tree, making a figure eight, going faster around the next tree. She stopped, peeking from behind the trunk. "Did you notice anything? Anything at all?"

"No. I just see that you love to run. Run? Show me, again."

Imogene raced for me, tackled me, and knocked me backwards. "I can run like the other girls. I can run!" She grabbed a handful of snow, packing it in her hands. She threw the snowball at my face.

Splat.

I wiped my eyes, and Black Dog darted at us from across the hill.

Ar roof. Ar roof.

Imogene giggled. "Watch me. I can run. I can run without limping."

I dusted the snow from my overalls. "No way. How did your limp go away?"

Boswell came up next to me. "I fixed one of her black shoes. I added a wedge to the bottom, and now she walks without a limp."

"Yes. I walk straight. I can run straight, too."

"Imogene, look at you. This is the best news ever."

Boswell slipped a hand over my shoulder. "Imogene being able to run is good news. Margo being released is good news, too. Shoelace, I suppose you'll be going home soon, which is good news to you."

I turned to him and grinned. "Yes, I can't wait. Taddy's mama is awake. Everything is perfect."

Black Dog jumped at me like a rabbit, barking and leaping like he knew what we were saying. Imogene hugged Boswell and then me. "I'm the luckiest girl in Oklahoma. New shoes. And a new family."

Boswell handed Imogene her moccasins. "Don't forget these. You'll want to keep them. These are the shoes used to save lives."

I nodded, like he was talking to me, but he wasn't.

Imogene pulled me by the arm. "Let's play in the loft. I won't see you after today. I want to climb. I want to run. And play."

"Sure, let's go."

We raced through Boswell's bunk room. I touched the not-leaning post. We rounded the stalls where the mules stood, and Imogene beat me to the ladder, clunking ahead on the rungs.

At the top, her giggles quieted, and Imogene gazed at me with big eyes. "Run! Shoelace! Run!"

I laughed. "I am. I'm running right behind you."

When I stepped into the loft, a hand yanked me by my hair. I landed on my side. "Ouch, what…?"

Red and Scar hovered over us like steeples in a broken-down church. Scar's hand shook and his fingers were wrapped around a pistol. The barrel was pointed at Imogene.

Scar told me to be quiet. He didn't have to repeat it. I moved on my knees toward Imogene. Red squeezed Imogene's arm, making her stand on tip toes.

Imogene's face wrinkled with pain. "Let me go. Who are you? What do you want?"

I yelled. "Take me. Let Imogene go."

Scar scoffed, slapping me with the back of his hand. I whimpered. "Ouch." I rubbed my face.

Imogene cried. "Stop. Don't hurt us."

Red shoved Imogene to the loft floor next to me. I wiped my nose trying to stop the leaky faucet of blood dripping down my overalls. We landed on the hard wood floor. All the hay was stacked on the other side of the loft.

Scar paced in a circle, his hand kept shaking, and the gun pointed at the roof. At the loft floor. And at us. He yelled. "No one is leaving, but us. We came for our horses. We need some money and food to get out of this county."

Red yanked on Imogene's arm. "Is there anyone else in this barn?"

"No one. It's just Shoelace and me. We were playing."

Red pulled his hand back, but stopped in the air when Imogene whimpered. "Please, don't hurt me. I'm going home. I have a mama and a papa who want me. I'm being adopted."

Red backed up, struck a match on the side of his shiny boots, lighting a cigarette. "What do we have here? A little orphan Indian girl is getting adopted. But who wants this blonde? Who wants her?"

I shouted, hoping Boswell heard me. "I've got a family. My grandma is going to come looking for me." I reached for his boots, running my fingers over the toe. "Are these new? They look new. Did you steal these?"

Red kicked my hand away, and tossed the match to the hay. "Leave them be. They're mine. You have no need to know how I got them."

I stomped the hay with the back of my shoe. "You could start a fire throwing matches down like that."

Scar stepped between us, grabbing his leg, grimacing. "Red, don't argue with this child. She's not going to outwit us."

I tossed out another question. "Scar, what happened to your leg? You're bleeding through your jeans."

"You should ask your friend, Margo. That woman sliced my leg with her axe. It's a wonder she didn't kill us."

Red waved his arm.

The ladder on the loft shook. Boswell called to us from below. "Girls, are you in the loft? There's a car coming up the drive. Imogene, I'm sure it's your new parents."

Scar whispered, "I thought you two were alone. It seems we have a visitor."

I kicked at the hay with my feet, hoping loose pieces of straw fell through the cracks in the wood.

Boswell summoned us again. "I know you're up there. Come on down."

Ar roof. Ar roof.

Black Dog barked from somewhere in the barn. A red-headed bird soared up to the loft, diving in circles around Scar's face, and then Red's head. The brothers dodged the bird, swiping at him. Scar's fingers pressed too fast and hard.

Pfffft.

The gun blasted a hole in the loft floor.

Boswell hollered. "Who's up there? What have you done with the girls?"

Scar called down the ladder. "I've got them. One is Indian and one is too smart for her own good. We'll make a trade. We want our horses, some food, and blankets. And you can have them both."

Boswell yelled. "I've got my gun on you. I can see through the cracks in the loft. Send the girls to me. Or I'm taking out a brother. It doesn't matter to me who I shoot first."

Red reached for the rope behind a bedroll, tying Imogene's hands and feet. He tied my hands and feet, too, and rolled us like flour sacks to the corner.

Boswell reminded them of his gun. "I can shoot through the night, through the woods, and through a heart if you make me."

Red pushed Scar like two kids fighting. He whispered, "Why did you go and have to shoot your gun?"

Scar shoved his brother. "It was an accident."

Red grabbed the pistol from Scar's hand, shoving it into his belt, letting his cigarette dangle from the corner of his mouth.

Scar popped Red on the arm. "Who made you the boss? I can carry a gun if I want to, and you ain't gonna tell me what to do."

I shouted from the corner. "Let us go or Boswell's gonna take you both out."

Imogene rocked, breathing with loud sobs. I wanted to cry too, but not in front of these two.

Scar smacked his brother. "I've had it. You took the best boots when we robbed those two men in Swink. Then you think you decide who carries the gun. If you hadn't made us stop at Wheelock for food the other day, we wouldn't be in this mess."

Red socked Scar in the jaw. "What do you mean? You were hungry, too."

They rolled and bumped, screaming louder than Imogene's sobs. Red's cigarette flew into the hay.

I gestured with my roped hands. "Smoke! Smoke! That cigarette has started a fire!"

Ripples of flames raced through patches of hay. The horses and mules kicked at the walls of the barn and neighed.

Boswell's head popped up in the loft. Scar kicked him in the jaw, causing him to tumble backwards.

Imogene whined. "Let us go. Please, don't let us die in this barn."

Red and Scar grabbed their bedrolls. Red hurried down the ladder first. Scar disappeared behind him, but came right back up.

Imogene begged. "Save us. Please."

Scar nodded. "I am. I can't kill two little girls."

I yelled at him. "Hey, I'm not little."

Scar ignored me, sighed, and looked up toward the roof where crackling wood burned. He whispered what sounded like a prayer. "I never meant to hurt any kids."

I was ready to mouth more ugly words, but stopped, whispering to Imogene. "Do you think he's sorry?"

Scar took a knife, flipped it open, cutting the rope on my wrists and then my ankles. I held onto Imogene as Scar cut her free. He climbed down the ladder, whispering sorry words under his breath.

A *pffffft* rang out below, and another bullet landed somewhere in the barn. A thud in the dirt sent a deep hush inside the barn, and a whimpering gurgle came from a body losing its life. It sent chills through my bones.

I hurried down the ladder. So did Imogene. I screamed. "Boswell? Are you alive?"

Imogene coughed, crying. "The smoke's burning my eyes. I can't breathe."

"Mine, too. Follow me. We're almost at the bottom."

The flames jumped and danced a war dance above our heads. Imogene wailed. "I left my moccasins."

Boswell popped up from inside the casket in the wagon, pointing his gun at our heads. "Good grief! I nearly shot you both." He climbed out of the casket. "Where did they go?"

I pointed to the back of the barn, coughed and jumped from the ladder. "I bet they're after the horses."

Clippity-clop. Clippity-clop.

The nose of a horse poked out from the maze of smoke filling up the barn. Red held onto the mane, and the horse galloped out the door.

Boswell jumped from the wagon, barreling after him, firing his gun into the wind. "He's headed toward the lake. He's getting away."

Imogene stood on the last rung of ladder. "I left my moccasins. I have to get them."

Boswell put his gun in the holster, carrying her from the ladder. "No, you can't get them. The fire's growing. The cracking and popping are the flames burning through the walls. We've got to go, and now."

Behind me in the doorway of the barn, Taddy's small voice called to me. "Shoelace, the barn's on fire. Are you in there?"

I yelled at him. "We're here. You can't see me for the smoke." I coughed, tumbling over a warm something on the ground. Imogene fell onto my back.

Boswell stepped up next to us. "It's Scar. He's been shot. He's dead."

Pam Kumpe

Before Day Nine Ends

Streaks in the Snow

I FELL INTO THE SNOW, gazing up at the orange fire spitting flames from the roof of the barn. Taddy shadowed me like a small bush. Boswell's two mules and Scar's horse clopped over to the tree in front of the sweeping porch at the dorm. Scar lay lifeless in the snow at the end of a trail of blood that led to the burning barn.

Grandma, Mrs. Motes, Officer Smoke and the sleepy guard charged across the grounds to us. Grandma reached for me. "Are you burned?"

I hugged her, and my arms smeared ashes on her dress. "I'm fine. The bad brothers came back. They tied me and Imogene up. Red dropped a cigarette in the hay. It wasn't my fault. I didn't start this fire."

Grandma squeezed me like she hadn't seen me in forever, although it had only been an hour or so. I twisted to look for my walking-straight friend. I touched Grandma's arm. "There's Imogene. She can run fast. Is that her new Ma and Pa?"

"Yes. They're here to pick her up."

Mrs. Motes hovered near Imogene, along with the man and woman. The guard and Officer Smoke talked with Boswell, then Officer Smoke hurried to the dorm. "I'll get the Lighthorsemen mounted. We're searching for Red. We're going to put a stop to this."

Imogene pointed to her shoes, holding up the one with the extra piece of wood on the sole. She showed the man and woman how she walked without a limp, running in a circle around a car parked by Pushmataha Hall.

The woman with hair the color of a red bird giggled a squeal. The man in the long dark coat kicked snow from the bottom of his shoe, bending down. He held his arms out, and Imogene ran into his hug. He spun her around in the air. Their laughter rose up. My heart pounded with joy from seeing how happy Imogene was when she hopped into the car.

Grandma moved to Boswell who leaned on a tree, and he wiped soot from his head. I shuffled in the snow toward Scar whose eyes had gotten stuck open. I knelt next to him, on the side where the blood oozed through his shirt.

Boswell called to me. "Get away from him. No need to check. He's gone."

I ignored Boswell who appeared too tired to care if I listened to him or not. I couldn't help but cry. I watched the blood stain grow larger on Scar's shirt, turning the snow pink under him. I closed Scar's eyes, so he would rest better. I whispered to him. "Thank you for saving Imogene. I wish you could see her. This is the happiest day of her life. It's pretty special for me, too."

Boswell hollered again. "Leave Scar alone."

I leaned over, glancing at Grandma and Boswell to make sure they weren't looking. I kissed the prickly hair on the cheek of a dead man. "Scar, you saved two girls today. And I am little, but I like to act bigger."

I sat in the snow crying, not caring if I got wet or colder. I gazed up to the blue sky hidden by patches of smoke. "God, I hope you saw what Scar did for me because thanks to him, I can still talk to you. I don't think he was bad all the way. He did make a bad choice, like I do. As for Red, he's a bad man. You might send him an angel."

Taddy inched closer, plopping down in the snow with me, patting my hand.

Kaboom. Craaa...aa...accck.

The snow-covered roof crackled and tore in half, the stalls crashing to the ground, consuming the barn walls. Flames zoomed higher than a smoke signal as ashes fell into the snow.

I rose to my feet, shaking snow from my backside, pointing at flames sweeping between the cracks in the fallen barn. Boswell's wagon and casket crackled, crumbling in the flames. "Boswell, you're losing your wagon."

Boswell hollered to me. "I can always build another wagon. It's time for a bigger barn, too."

Four men on horses galloped up from the backside of Wheelock, and two pickups roared down the driveway. Grandma ushered me to the dorm. She reached for Taddy's hand, too. "We need to get Shoelace cleaned up. I'm so ready to go home. I'm ready for a good night's sleep. For some peace."

Taddy whined. "Shoelace, I came looking for you because I didn't get to tell you what Pastor Cody told me on the phone. He told me not to worry, but I can't help it. He said mama doesn't know who she is. Her memory is gone for now." He sniffled. "She ... she might not know who I am when we get there."

I reached for Taddy's hand, and moved past Grandma. "Taddy, she'll know you. You're ... you're her son."

He cracked a small grin. "You're right. It's going to be fine. When she sees me, she'll remember me. She'll know me."

Grandma spoke with words to calm Taddy. "Priscilla will never be able to forget who her precious son is. She's the best mama in Texarkana. Maybe a little too protective, but she loves you, Taddy. She will know you. You'll see."

I swung Taddy's hand and mine. "Did Margo leave? Is she gone?"

Mrs. Motes stepped up behind us, answering my question. "Not yet. She's staying here until they can fix her roof at her house. She was rocking Isabella in the front room when we saw the fire. Her two friends were sitting in the front room with her, too.

The four of us rounded the side porch, between the dining hall and Wilson Hall. Dozens of girls' faces were glued to the window panes. I couldn't help but wonder who found the whiskey bottle this morning. Or who found the pictures Doctor Rigghazel scattered on the floor in the auditorium.

Kaboom. Kaboom.

The fire boomed. The last part of the walls fell like a bonfire. Pastor Motes came running up from the chapel, and two men held the crumpled body of Scar. They put him in the back of a truck while Boswell climbed into one of the cars.

The barn crackled and became a heap of ashes. I gave a powwow scream. "We are going home. I don't like it here. Things get way too hot. Too many people die here, too."

Day Nine Lasts Forever

Rock-a-bye Baby Falls

I STOMPED UP THE STEPS leading to the dining hall door, slipping on the third step. "Whew. Slippery ... the snow's slushy."

Taddy pulled me up. "Come on. Let's pack."

Grandma followed us into the kitchen, but she grabbed me by the coat sleeve, smashing me up against her side. She took Taddy by the hand, and slammed him next to me. "Stop. Don't move. Both of you stay put."

I twirled around to her. "What's wrong? It's not lunch yet. I'm getting my satchel."

Grandma used her strong voice. "Shoelace, stop talking. Stay right where you are."

Taddy stepped on my toe. He whispered. "It's the other bad man who kidnapped me."

Red pointed the gun at us. "All three of you. Over here. Sit down next to Officer Smoke. He's called the doctor to patch my shoulder. That casket man snagged me with a bullet. I want to get out of here alive."

Officer Smoke lifted his head. "You're not leaving Wheelock if I have anything to do with it."

Red slammed the butt of his pistol into Smoke's head. His face fell forward to his chest, and his body slouched.

I screamed at Red. "You're mean. You should be more like Scar." I put my hand to my throat.

282

Red charged at me, stumbling over a chair. "I've had it with you. You snuck off in the woods. You won't today."

I jumped into a chair, barreling over one of the long tables, knocking more chairs down with my hands. Grandma hollered at me, but I kept running. I darted down the hallway into the front room, toppled over an end table, and landed at Margo's feet.

Margo bellowed, clutching Isabella to her shoulder. "What's happening? What …?" She handed Isabella to Eliza, which made Pauline grab her belly.

Red stomped into the room, waving his gun. "No one move."

Margo moved in front of me like a mama bird protecting her young.

Eliza begged the man. "Please, put the gun away. Leave us be."

Margo stuck her finger out, waving it. "I should have killed you when I had the chance. Roping you upside down in the tree by your ankles should have taught you a lesson." She stepped to the center of the room. "Where's Scar? Is he in the kitchen?"

I scooted next to her. "No, he's dead. Boswell shot him." I inched behind Margo, peeking around her. "Red and Scar tied Imogene and me up, and they started a fire in the barn, too."

Two shadows stuck their noses into the doorway behind Red, and they shuffled out of sight. It was Grandma and Taddy.

Bam.

Red grimaced, grabbing his shoulder. Blood stained his shirt, seeping through, leaving spots on the hardwood floor. He fell to his knees, taking jagged breaths, and his gun slammed to the floor, sliding to my feet.

I snatched up the gun, and held it with both hands, pointing the barrel right at Red's face. Margo yanked the gun from my grasp. "I'll take the gun. I'm taking this brother out." Red yanked a pistol from his belt. "Officer Smoke's gun will do the job. I don't mind shooting women or kids, unlike my brother." He pointed the barrel at Margo's face, and wobbled. He was having trouble keeping the gun steady.

The front door creaked, and a gust of wind rushed through the opening. Doctor Rigghazel shuffled inside. "What's going on here?"

From the hallway, Mrs. Motes appeared. Her smile faded before she got two feet into the room. She looked at Margo. "Honey, put the gun down. We've had too much death and sorrow this week. Please, hand me the gun. This young man is wounded. He's not going to do any more harm."

Red yelled. "Lady, get over there with the others."

Mrs. Motes scooted next to Eliza and Pauline.

Red eyed her, switching the gun to his other hand, but the pistol swayed up and down. He snatched Isabella with his good arm, cradling her to his chest. "I've got what you want, Margo. Give me the gun, and I'll give you your baby."

Margo jumped forward, her eyes big, her mouth open. Red took a step back, and Doctor Rigghazel came to her side. She ordered the doctor to stay put. "Don't interfere. She's my baby. I'm saving her. She's mine. No one can save her, but me."

Red stumbled into the wall. "Is there anyone else inside this house?"

I yelled. "Don't you know? Wheelock Academy has ghosts."

Red frowned, his eyes popping wide in their sockets. Isabella wailed a baby scream, and Red's arm let the bundle slip through his hold. Together, Eliza and Pauline rushed forward to catch Isabella, along with Margo who dove into the air. Margo dropped her gun, and the *pffffft* blasted a hole in the wall, forcing Red to dodge and roll on the floor.

Isabella was caught. Eliza and Pauline were holding their bellies. And now there's a gash in the wall from the bullet. Doctor Rigghazel sprinted to Isabella, and I dove for the gun Margo dropped. So much so fast. And Red was gone.

I charged like a horse toward the kitchen, carrying the pistol by my side. Margo showed up on my heels, pulling me back by my coat. I let my arms dangle and slide through the sleeves as Margo held on, but the gun got stuck. It clunked to the floor.

Margo reached for it. "Go in the other room and hide."

"I'm not leaving. I'm tough, like my daddy."

Margo shoved me. "You are not tough. Besides, Red will shoot you. He's not thinking in his right mind."

"You don't think in your right mind, either. Let me have the gun." I lunged, and Margo swung at me. She slapped me so hard I slammed into the wall.

Margo shouted. "Get away from me. You are not going to stop me." She ran into the kitchen, leaving me alone in the hall.

I pulled my legs to my chest, rocking, hiding my face between my knees. I sent whispers of sadness to heaven. "Daddy, come get me. Daddy..."

A small hand lifted my chin. "I've heard there could be ghosts at Wheelock. Would you like to be one today?"

I wrapped my arms around Chula's neck. "You pick the oddest times to show up."

Doctor Rigghazel rushed past me, not giving me a second glance. He raced into the dining hall, talking to Red in the other room. "Mister. Let me look at your shoulder. No need for guns. We can sort through this."

Margo shouted. "You can fix him, but I'm holding this gun on him until the police come."

Chula took my hand. "Come with me. We'll sneak into the kitchen through the secret passage near the burial grounds."

I stuck my arms into my coat, glancing toward the dining hall. If I go in there, I might get shot. If I go with Chula, I can see the secret passage. Maybe she has a plan.

End of Day Nine

A Ghost Breaks the Glass

CHULA AND ME RUSHED OUT the door by the matron's car. We danced like Indians on the warpath. We hurried past the water tower. I almost bumped into a brown horse by the back door. I untied him. "Shoo. Go. Shoo." The horse galloped off, kicking like he was free.

Chula danced on a metal covering on the ground. She pointed. "This is it. It leads to the passage. Help me lift the lid off."

I mouthed at her. "This doesn't look like a passage to me."

Chula giggled. "We better hurry. It's a secret way to get to the pantry."

I bent down, reaching for the metal. "Come on. Help me get this up."

A few tugs, one last grunt, and the cover slid into a snow-puddle. Chula reached into the dark hole, felt around, and came up with a flashlight. "I keep one at each entrance. It can get dark in there."

She climbed down the ladder. I followed. "Are you sure this is the right way?"

Chula hollered at me. "Yes, hurry. Stay with me."

I smarted off. "I am. You have the light."

We charged along the tunnel. Chula made a spotlight on the dirt in front of us. The air inside was damp, colder than up above, yet warm on our heads. "What's with the temperature in here?"

Chula pointed the flashlight up. "See those? Those are the pipes warming the buildings from the boiler. They can get pretty hot."

"This is not a secret passage."

"But, it is. Only a few people know. So it's a secret."

"I'm not so sure we're going to make it as ghosts."

"I'm not a ghost. I'm an angel. Remember? And you're a warrior."

I shook my head. Her riddles make me want to hit her.

Chula stopped walking, and I bumped into her. "We're here. Climb those steps and you'll be in the food pantry."

I pushed the half-size door open, knocking a flour sack over. I turned to get Chula. "Hey, where are you?"

Nothing. No answer.

Chula's there one minute, then she's gone. I feel her with me. Then I turn. And she leaves. I don't expect her, and she comes. She's like so many people in my life. Some come. Some stay. Others leave.

Bam. Bam. Crash.

The ruckus in the dining hall brought me to the edge of the half-opened pantry door. I knelt behind a crate of empty canning jars, peeking around the box. Doctor Rigghazel wrapped gauze around Red's shoulder while he wiggled in the chair.

Red knocked the doctor's arm away. "Watch it, Doc."

The doctor moved to his bag. "Let me cut the end of this gauze." He pulled out the scissors, and snipped the extra piece.

I couldn't see Red's gun, but his angry face told me this wasn't over yet. He yelled. "Margo, pack me some food."

I twisted my head, bumping the crate, and saw Margo sitting in a chair, slumped over. She raised her head, standing. She rubbed her blue and swollen face. Her eyelid drooped from the gash on her head. Her dress looked like an axe got a hold of it.

She shuffled to the sink and spit. "I'm not getting you any food. You may have kicked me and beat me down. You got my gun, but feeding you won't happen. Not from me."

Red grabbed the scissors from the doctor, and jabbed Rigghazel in the forearm, right through his heavy coat sleeve.

Ooweeee!

The doctor clutched his arm, stumbling backwards, landing in a chair. "Red, this has to stop."

Red kicked the doctor in the ribs, and two guns poked up from the belt in Red's pants. He put his hand on one. "Margo, pack me some food. Or I'll shoot the doctor."

She screamed. "All right. I'll get it. Just stop."

Red dug the scissors from the doctor's arm, and raised his hand like he was going to stab him again.

Margo yelled. "I said I'll get you some food. Stop stabbing him."

I picked up one of the empty jars, tossing it across the room at an angle.

Smash.

The glass splintered in pieces on the wall, crashing into chunks to the floor.

Red spun around. "What was that?"

I tossed another jar behind him, letting it sail to the window by the back door. The pane splintered, the curtain waved, and the cold air rushed into the room.

Red moved to the curtain. "Who broke this window?"

Margo moved toward the middle of the room. "Ghosts. We have ghosts here at Wheelock, and they kill people."

I chunked two more jars, one in each hand across the room toward the dining hall door, the opposite way. They smashed together in midair, and Red backed up against the wall near the back door. "What's with the glass? It's coming from the pantry. You don't have ghosts."

Margo's eyes saw me. And I saw her. I jumped from the pantry. "Leave the doctor alone. Let Margo go. Get out of here. Leave."

Red crunched glass under his boots, slipping forward, hitting the table. Margo dove toward him. One of the guns crashed to the floor, sliding into the leg of the table. The other gun pounded to the floor under a chair.

Margo was closer to the guns than Red, but I was closer than Margo. I raced for a pistol. Margo did, too.

Red turned around, but tripped over his own boots. "What the …" He pawed his way to the guns.

The running stopped. No one moved. Red held one pistol. I held the other one. We were facing each other across the table.

Margo called to me. "Give me the gun. You have no idea what to do with it."

"So you keep saying. But you didn't do any good with it yourself. I'm not giving it away. I'm ending this."

From the hallway door, a shadow ran inside, a small boy the size of my Taddy. It was my Taddy.

I screamed. "What are you doing in here?"

He hollered. "Grandma's knocked out. She hit her head on the dresser pushing it in front of the door. She's bleeding. She's moaning. She needs the doctor." He stopped next to me, frozen like a snowman.

Margo barreled at me, took the gun from my hand, pushed me to the floor, and shoved Taddy on top of me in what felt like the longest week of my life. Gunshots pinged and rattled in the kitchen. Margo shot. Red pulled his trigger. And I covered my head.

Pfffft. Pfffft. Pfffft.

I looked up. Red tumbled backwards, landing in a pile of ghost-glass. He was bleeding from the mouth, and he let out a moan. His eyes got stuck open like Scar's eyes.

Taddy peeked out from under a table, hurrying to Margo, who was on the floor. "No, Margo. No." He crumpled next to her.

I crawled to Margo. Blood poured from her neck. I pressed my hand over the wound. She took Taddy's fingers, her words gurgling. "Taddy, be brave. Grow up, and make your mama proud."

I put more pressure on the spot on her neck. "No, you can't die. You can't die!" The blood squirted through my fingers.

The doctor groaned, moving to Margo's side. "You have to stay here with me. We have our Isabella. I was going to ask you to marry me, to make things right with us. I love ... love you, Margo. Will you marry me?"

Margo's eyes cracked open. "I bet you don't even have a ring."

I mouthed. "But, I do. It's in my pocket. I have a ring."

Doctor Rigghazel turned to me, his eyes asking silent questions.

I pulled out the blue stone. "Here, use this ring." I placed it into the doctor's hand, and he slipped the ring onto Margo's finger.

She tilted her head, smiling and gasping. "I love this ring. It looks familiar." She choked, clearing her throat. "Yes, I'll marry you."

The doctor kissed her finger. "We'll set a date. Let's get married on the lawn next to the rock church."

Margo's head fell backwards, and Taddy scooted closer, whimpering. He pointed, but no words came out.

Doctor Rigghazel wept. "No! You can't leave me. I've wasted so much time! Now it's too late."

Margo's eyes were stuck open, and mine exploded with tears. I sobbed with Taddy and the doctor. Too many tears. Too much dying. Everywhere I go, someone dies. I melted into the sadness, into a pool of sorrow, clutching Taddy with my arms.

The doctor checked Margo's pulse, and he put his face over her mouth. He checked her pulse again. Taddy scooted away, to a corner. I crawled up next to him. We rocked.

The doctor cradled Margo in his arms. "She's gone. She's the one I loved, if only I had told her sooner."

I whispered, "She knew. She knew."

Someone picked up Taddy. Someone moved Red from the maze of broken glass. Someone said he wasn't shot, that a piece of glass jabbed him in the back. Officer Smoke woke up, trying to figure out what had happened.

Doctor Rigghazel carried Margo somewhere. Someone said something about Grandma getting stitches, and someone moved me from the floor.

Now, I'm awake in the bedroom. Taddy's sitting on the bottom of the mattress, crying. I wrapped my fingers in the quilt. "Taddy, did all of this actually happen?"

Taddy hugged me with his sad arms. "Yes, it's the worst January of my life. Mama gets hit in the head. And she doesn't know me now. Aunt ... Aunt Margo is dead. I never want to come here again."

I nodded. "I'm ready to go home, too."

Taddy wept. "I'm glad you're alive. You're my best friend. You scared me. You need to stop pretending to be bigger."

I smiled. "I can't help myself."

He gave me one of his looks.

"So where's Grandma?"

"She's in the front room. Most of the grownups are in there. Most are sitting there, not talking."

Taddy left the room, and I grabbed my shoes. "I'll be right there."

I plopped down on the bed to tie my laces, and saw a flute on the dresser. I picked it up, and yelled at Chula under my breath. "You kept saying I was here to save the children. Why couldn't we save Margo?"

A hand touched my leg from under the bed.

Day Nine Winds Down

Hiding Secrets in Caskets

CHULA HAS SPOOKED ME MORE than I've scared anyone on purpose. She slipped from beneath the bed, taking a seat on the edge of the mattress. "I see you found the flute. It's yours to remember me by."

I blew air into the tube.

Squeak ... ooaa ...eech.

"You'll get better with practice." Chula laughed, falling onto her back, stretching her arms above her head on the mattress. "This bed is soft."

I put the flute inside my satchel. "Thank you." I plopped down with Chula. "I wish we'd never come."

"But you did. You helped God help the doctor."

"I'm not so sure that I did anything."

"You changed everything. The new babies will live because of you." Chula jumped to her feet. "I came to say goodbye. I'm Doctor Rigghazel's angel now. He's going to need one. His not drinking will be hard. I'll stay until he's stronger."

I touched her face with my fingers, running two of them across her cheek. "If you're an angel, why do you feel like a real person?"

She smiled. "God lets people see us how they need to. If I were transparent, it would scare you more than seeing me as an Indian."

294

I folded my arms, not sure she was an angel, but as far I could remember no one else saw Chula this week—besides Boswell and me. Oh wait, and Bright Eyes. Chula could be who she says she is, or she could be crazy like Margo.

I pulled on Chula's arm. "But why did Eleanor have to die? And Margo?"

Chula sighed. "Eleanor had an accident. A horrible one. And Margo's good days were not-so-good. Her bad days were getting worse. Boswell worried she'd cause more problems than she could solve. You got here when she broke-for-good."

"I will never forget Eleanor." I rubbed my leg. "You know, that night Margo roped me, she talked creepy. Her face had nice parts, but she used a not-so-nice voice."

"She lost a part of her heart every time she buried a bucket-baby. And those buckets leaked sadness into her life. She cried, hit people, and roped strangers coming through the county. Most could outrun her. She would call Taddy's name for hours at the cemetery, too."

"Taddy's name?"

"Yes, her son. But you know that. She told you."

"I wasn't sure Margo was telling me the truth. It's all so mixed up. If Margo wasn't Margo, was she Priscilla? And does this mean Priscilla really is Margo?"

Chula moved to the doorway. "In your heart, you know the truth. But now, there's no need to tell Taddy since Millerton's Margo, who was Priscilla, is gone."

"So much for telling the truth, huh?"

She giggled. "There's no good to come from telling Taddy. He has a mama who loves him. It doesn't matter that her name isn't Priscilla."

"But he saw the letters. He's gonna ask questions. You don't know Taddy. He's not going to let this go."

Chula shuffled to the door. "The less you say, the less he'll talk about it. Goodbye, Nakni Nita."

"Where are you going?"

"It's time to show myself to Doctor Rigghazel."

**

Another funeral. Only this one is at Wheelock Cemetery.

Margo's casket has two red roses on top of it, because Doctor Rigghazel asked for them. He wanted one for Rose, and one for Margo.

A woodpecker keeps flying in and perching on the roses. He's soaring into the bare trees, diving and landing on the casket, making dots in the wood.

I'm sitting in a folding chair wearing Eleanor's dress for the second time. The doctor is sitting to my left holding the sleeping Isabella. To my right, Taddy is weeping, something he hasn't stopped doing since early this morning. It's one in the afternoon. We're catching the train home tomorrow. At least, that's what my ticket says.

Grandma, the matron, and Mrs. Motes are in the row in front of me, wiping their eyes almost as often at Taddy. Pauline and Eliza are sitting to the left of them. Pastor Motes is opening one end of the casket so folks can say their goodbyes. He is doing this at the request of Boswell, who said Margo's face shows such peace.

Ar roof. Ar roof.

"Shoo, boy. Shoo." Pastor Motes moved to the casket and used his preaching hand to get Black Dog's paws off the casket. "Boy, she's gone. Sit. Sit down."

Black Dog crawled to the end of the casket, curling up next to the dotted tree.

The orphan girls are out of school again to show respect for Margo. The matron said they knew her better than most.

I whispered to Taddy. "Are you going to look inside the casket?"

Taddy shook his head. "No way. I don't want to see her. It reminds me of my mama. Seeing her twin in a box isn't something I need to do or want to do."

"I'm going up there. The matron said some of the girls wrote poems to put in her casket, to help Margo rest with kind and peaceful words."

"You know, she's dead. She's not going to be reading poetry."

"I know, but it's nice to give them to her."

Pastor Motes walked in front of the casket, holding his Bible open. "We're here to say farewell to one who wept at the gravesites of many, who wouldn't want us to weep at hers. Let's remember her days of kindness."

I tapped the matron on the shoulder. "Ms. Becky, did she have kind days?"

The matron twisted in her chair. "Yes, the Margo we loved taught the girls how to ride the ponies. The Margo we cared for played basketball with them in the spring. The Margo we'll remember is the one who baked biscuits with Mrs. Motes. Margo loved handing them out to hobos hiding in the bushes at the train station. She had lots of secrets. One of them was her ability to be kind."

I swallowed hard. "Priscilla bakes biscuits too, and she hands them out to people passing through town. I didn't know twins were so alike."

The matron smiled. "It sounds like they had plenty in common. Margo loved to sing with the high school girls at graduation in May, too. She loved to sing hymns. But sometimes she struggled, and thought God's grace fell on everyone but her. On her bad days, things got tough, but God held her. She just didn't know it."

I learned that Margo had days when she roamed around the academy like a puppy, a friend to many. But she must have had plenty of days when she moved like a wolf, too. She's probably the reason the posts lean in the woods. She's knocked them over.

Pastor Motes announced to us. "Anyone who'd like to say a final farewell to Margo, or who wrote a poem, please come on up."

I tapped Grandma on the shoulder. "Will you walk with me to the casket? I don't want to go by myself."

"I would, but I'm exhausted. It must be all this sadness." Grandma blotted her brow with the back of her hand. "Go on now. Walk with the other girls."

A group of orphans walked to the front with papers in their hands, and they placed them next to Margo in the casket. I stood, joined the line, and clutched a folded envelope in my fingers.

Taddy rushed up to me. "Did you write a poem?"

"Yes, I wrote one. You know I write poems." I lied to Taddy, but I had to. The secret had to get buried. It was for his own good.

"Why didn't you let me read it?"

"You would have cried."

Taddy nodded, and went back to his seat.

I stepped to the casket, wiping tears from my face. I whispered to Margo. "I have letter number six. Your secret is safe. Taddy doesn't need to know. I'm giving it to you." I leaned in, kissing her bruised cheek.

I walked to my seat, and Taddy put his head on my shoulder. "I don't like death. Or funerals. I am ready to go home and see my ... see my mama. I hope she knows me."

I patted his leg. "She will."

Ar roof. Ar roof.

Black Dog jumped on Boswell, who walked by the casket. "Down boy. Down."

Pastor Motes shooed Black Dog away again. "Everyone. Boswell has something to say."

Boswell jingled the wind ornament in his hand. "This wind chime will be hung in Margo's forest. The bamboo came from the river bed, and the sparkles you see are from the kitchen floor. We loved Margo, and now our Choctaw girls are once again safe from the likes of people like Red and Scar."

Doctor Rigghazel turned to me. "Because of Margo, I have Isabella, and because I met you, you showed me how to have a heart for God. I've got a new heart for life, too."

My body shook hard, and snot leaked from my mouth. I prayed for the day when I'll get a mama who loves me twice as much as Margo loved Taddy. She loved Taddy enough to give him away.

Grandma moved from her chair, came to mine, and put me in her lap. She kissed me on the cheek. "My little hobo girl. My pride and joy. I love you more than chocolate cake. You make my life complete."

I wiped a tear from my eye. "I love you, too." Seems I already have someone who loves me enough to keep me. That's right, Grandma wants me.

Taddy reached for Grandma's hand, holding her fingers tight. He wrapped his other arm around me. "What will I do if my mama doesn't know me? How will we tell her that her Margo is dead?"

I hugged Taddy back. "Your mama will know you, I promise."

Grandma whispered. "We don't have to tell her about Margo right away. We'll just love on Priscilla for now."

Taddy put his head on Grandma's arm. "I want my mama."

Grandma kissed him on the head. "I know. I know."

At Wheelock Academy, I discovered that secrets float down the river and hide in cemeteries. That they come in surprises and in death, and in auditoriums, and in strange encounters. That secret passages may look like a tunnel, or they could lead to the pantry where life gets preserved. Or the secret gets tucked away, or lost.

Pastor Motes talked and prayed. People cried when he read verses from the Bible. Some of the girls hugged. Some sighed. Others sat like frozen snowmen, while others fidgeted like me.

On the pastor's final amen, the matron jumped to her feet and knocked two girls from their seats with her wild arms. "Eliza's in labor. We're having a baby."

Will the Train Stop?

A Birthday Ride

THE CREAKS AND BUMPS AND noise inside this passenger car make me wish I could sit on some straw inside of a boxcar. This seat is hard, and I can't get comfortable. Grandma and Taddy are sleeping across from me, and my tummy is growling. The man with charcoal hair and a wart on his nose needs to stop staring at my lunch sack.

I unfolded the paper bag, the one Mrs. Motes packed, and looked inside. "Yum. Blackberry cobbler."

Wart-nose licked his lips.

I opened the wax paper, and bit into the purple goo.

The man leaned across the aisle. "The crust on your cobbler looks like the kind my auntie makes."

I twisted and turned my shoulder. "It is good. And it's mine."

Grandma gave me a swift kick, peeking at me with one eye. She took one of her deep breaths. "Give him part of it. I have half a cobbler in the sack under my seat. We have plenty."

"Yes, ma'am." I chomped on a corner of the cobbler and folded the wax paper around the part that was left. The train bumped, clacked, rocked back and forth, and the last jerk sent my cobbler sailing into the man's lap. "Sorry. If you don't hurry, the berries are gonna stain those fancy tan slacks."

The man grabbed a handkerchief from the inside of his jacket, swiping at the purple spot on his pants. "Little girl, you should learn some manners."

"I said I was sorry. I speak my mind."

He gave me a wink. "I expect you do."

Grandma spoke up. "Sir, my granddaughter's had a tough few days. She tends to say things before thinking."

I ran my fingers over my new earrings. "I do not. I mean what I think."

Grandma coughed. "Shoelace, that's enough."

"Yes, ma'am."

Grandma sat lower in her seat, coughing into her palm.

The man rose, and handed Grandma his sticky handkerchief. "Are you all right, ma'am?"

"Yes. Just tired."

Taddy squirmed, opening his eyes. "Are we home? Are we there?"

I motioned for him to sit by me. "Not yet. Sit over here. You can have the window seat."

The man took Taddy's seat. "Let me get you some help, ma'am. Your face is flushed. Your breathing is too shallow."

Grandma breathed her words. "A good night's rest in my own bed. That's all I need, and I'll be fine."

Taddy folded his legs and sat on his knees to look out the window. "Look, we're going over a river. There's a boat." He waved like he thought people could see him.

I joined him, waving with both arms. "Do you think they can see us? I don't. But this is fun." I tapped Taddy's arm. "Hey look, there's a woodpecker hitting his head on that tree."

Swoosh. Thud.

Something soft and heavy landed on my feet. "Grandma? Grandma! Get up. Get up. What's wrong? Get up."

People gathered around us, and a stranger blotted Grandma's face. "She's not responding." He put his ear to her nose. "She's not breathing."

Another man in a black suit pushed through. "I'm a doctor. Let me look. Everyone get back."

People shoved. Others pushed. I was surrounded by tall people who leaned in every direction. Taddy and me were escorted to the back of the passenger car, and I clutched my satchel.

A woman gasped. Another cried. The doctor in the black suit walked toward us, his eyes low, his words awful. "She … she's gone. It looks like a heart attack."

Time stopped. The train rolled on. My life froze. Someone put a sheet over my grandma, but I could see her shoes sticking out from under the seats in the aisle. Four men carried her, and put her next to the last row.

I ran to them, my screams louder than a funeral song blasting sorrow inside my heart. "She's mine. That's my grandma. You can't have her. Don't hurt her."

Someone gathered me up. I glanced into his face. The wart on his nose told me it was the man I'd smarted off to, and he was now holding me like I was his child. He let me soak his jacket with my tears. He cradled me, and sat down in an aisle seat.

Taddy shuffled up to me. His words came like arrows. "Shoelace, you have me. I'll share my mama. She has enough love for all of us." His words sounded strong, but his quivering lip told me he was not so brave.

My heart jumped from my chest to my head. The clickety-clack of the wheels kept the same beat with the pounding behind my eyes, and reminded me of how fast life changes. Secrets become truth. Truth can be forgotten. Life comes and goes. And no one is ever ready to see someone die. Especially not Grandma.

I melted into the man's arms. They felt like a warm quilt, and his humming sent peace through me. He rocked me like I was a baby.

Taddy scooted to the seat next to me, staring out the window.

I got lost in my memories of the last ten days. The pain of losing Eleanor, but remembering the fun in having my ears pierced and laughing with her. I won't ever forget seeing Imogene's limp fade, thanks to Boswell. I'll always wonder if Chula was simply slick at getting around, or if she was truly an angel. I haven't figured out how four angels could look like people from my past, though. Then, there's Bright Eyes. She has my engineer's hat. And I have her dream catcher.

I felt myself fading, and thought about Doctor Rigghazel. He now wants to help mamas have their babies. He loves his baby girl, Isabella, and he's given up the nasty whiskey bottle. He's changed.

Eliza gave birth to a girl last night, naming her Margo Rose. Pauline is still fat, no baby for her, yet. And now ... now ... my grandma has gone to heaven. I can't let her go. Not her. She's the only one who ever really wanted me.

I peeked at Taddy, whose head was against the window. His eyes were closed, but I don't think he's asleep. I thought about seeing Margo's casket. I'm glad I tucked that envelope inside. No one will ever have to know Margo and Priscilla might have changed places. I have to protect Taddy's heart, even if mine is breaking. My head fell, my eyes heavy. I shifted my weight, and kicked Taddy in the side.

Taddy jumped.

"Sorry. My foot slipped."

"You scared me. I was almost asleep." Taddy's hand went to his hip, shoving papers deep inside his pocket.

I climbed from the man's lap. "Taddy, what are those?"

Taddy touched his pocket. "It's Margo's letters. I saved them. I couldn't just throw them away. It's all I have of Margo."

I crumpled to the floor, like a letter that had lost its way. Like a hobo girl without a home. I wanted my grandma back, and I didn't know how I'd live without her. I twisted around on the floor, hoping for the blackberry-cobbler man to put me back into his lap.

Taddy tapped me. "What are you looking for?"

"That man. Did you see where he went?"

"What man? It's just been you and me. The doctor made us sit here after they sent the others to another car. The doctor's over there with … with your grandma."

I marched into the aisle, ready to drill the doctor. I kicked something on the floor. A blackberry-stained handkerchief floated ahead of me. I wrapped my fingers around it, and sniffed the cloth. It smelled like my grandma when she bakes cakes and cookies. I tumbled to the floor again.

The doctor put me into my seat. "We're almost to Texarkana. It won't be long now. We'll get you home."

I pulled on his shirt. "Where'd that man go? The one who let me sit in his lap? He hummed to me."

"Honey, I didn't see him. You're in shock. You just need to sit, and rest. I'm sorry about your grandma. We'll take good care of her until we get her to her resting place."

I let go and shook my head, rattling all the sorrow from my thoughts, letting them land in a hole in my tummy. I could almost hear that man's hum, the tune to *Happy Birthday.*

I grabbed Taddy by the arm. "Today is my birthday. Taddy, today is my birthday. I forgot. I'm eleven."

"I forgot, too. Oh no. Who is going to bake your cake?"

"I don't want one. My first cake was from Grandma last year. I'm done with cakes."

Taddy hugged my neck. "I'm sorry. Birthdays shouldn't feel this sad."

I sobbed with every clack of the train's wheels, wishing that we'd never left Texarkana. I couldn't get the hum of that man's voice out of my mind. And my mouth watered just thinking about Grandma's cakes.

And then … I remembered that new babies will be born in Oklahoma this year. They won't be unknown. They will have names. And faces. And little hearts.

They will grow up and taste Mrs. Motes' blackberry cobbler. And her pudding. They will run and play. They will feel the love of their mama's hugs, too. They will have plenty of birthday parties. And plenty of cake.

I wiped the tears rolling down my cheeks. Taddy's right, this is the worst January ever. Being loved by my grandma was everything, and love will always remind me of her.

Taddy pressed his nose on the window. "I see lights. I see the train station. We're home."

I moved from my seat, inched down the aisle, and knelt beside my grandma.

The doctor reached for me. "You don't want to do this."

I yanked my arm from his grasp. "Leave me alone." I folded the sheet back, and Grandma's eyes were stuck open. I turned to the doctor. "You should have closed her eyes. She can't rest until you do."

"I'm sorry. I should have. I'll fix them." He knelt next to her, and stroked her eyelids. "There. She's resting."

I bent down, kissing her forehead. "Grandma, I'm going to miss you. You loved me more than anyone. I'll never forget you." My arms wrapped around her body, and I put my hand in her fingers. Even now, touching Grandma was like touching God. I looked up to heaven. "You better be nice to her. Make sure she has plenty of flour for baking. She needs an apron, too. And give her a hug from me."

Epilogue

TADDY CAME UP BEHIND ME. "Everyone's already off the train. They want to get your grandma, and Mahlee and Pastor Cody are waiting for us."

I kissed Grandma one more time. "Bye Grandma. No matter where I go, I'll love you."

In the reflection in the window, I thought I saw Slow Tom and Fast Tim. I blinked. I only saw myself.

Pastor Cody caught me in his arms as I stepped from the train. I let him carry me. He would have to do this all the way to the car. All the way to the manor after we parked. And then, he would put me in my bed where I would cry and pet my cat, White Beard.

Taddy would be there in the morning waiting for me. He would sleep on the top of the stairs outside my door, because his mama didn't know him.

Now, I'm sitting with my back against the door listening to Taddy yell at me. "Are you going to let me in? Mahlee's made you breakfast."

I ignored him.

"Let me in, or else."

I didn't respond.

"I'm going to break this door in."

I moved to the balcony, opened the door, and touched the tree limb. A lone train whistle called my name, and freedom waited for me on the rail. No one will miss me if I'm gone. I'm eleven. Once a hobo. Always a hobo.

Taddy's frail voice shouted from below. "I see you. I'm coming up this tree."

"Go away. I'm not leaving my room."

Taddy slipped on a branch, and grabbed the one over his head. "I'm not leaving. You're my best friend."

I leaned over the rail. "Go home. You have a mama."

"I'm not leaving." He stretched his leg to the next limb, his foot slipping again. "Shoelace, I can't hold on. I'm falling."

Taddy's body bounced off the branch, and he thudded to the brown patch of grass beside the manor. He was lifeless.

I scaled down the tree in my socks, and dove to the spot where Taddy's arms and legs were sprawled. "Are you alive? Tell me you're alive." I picked up his head. "Tell me."

He giggled, grabbing his belly. "Now that you're here, let's go eat breakfast."

I slugged him. "Fine. But you're not getting away with this." I would wait for the time to sneak out, for the time to get back to the rail. Things I touch don't live. Without Grandma, I have no reason to stay. It's time to move on. The whistle of the steam engine told me the train was headed west. I think I'll go south this time.

Taddy pulled on my arm. "Stop thinking about trains. I see what's in your eyes. You can't leave. I need you."

I nodded, but my heart didn't. "I'm hungry. Let's eat."

Taddy stopped on the front porch. "I have one question. What happened to letter number six?"

"Why? It doesn't matter."

"Yes. It does. You know what happened to it. So you better come clean."

"I don't know what you're talking about."

"That's what I thought you'd say." Taddy pulled a paper from his back pocket, unfolding the letter. "Does this help you remember?"

"Where did you get that?"

"I took it from your satchel. The envelope you put in Margo's casket was empty. I had already taken the letter out of it."

"So this is how you treat a best friend?"

He pushed me. "You're one to talk. You weren't going to let me see this letter." He shook it in my face.

"It was for your own good."

"Really? Since when do you know what's good for anyone?"

I ran up the stairs, slammed my door, and packed my satchel. I'm not staying. I'm leaving. I picked up my cat. "I'll be back some day. I've got to go."

Mahlee called to me from the bottom of the stairs. "Shoelace, you need to come down here. Mrs. O'Malley found your grandma's will last night. You're not going to believe what she left me."

Unknown Soul

"Undaunted Spirit"
1947. The Call of the Rail

Book 3
The Annie Grace Kree Chronicles
Releasing Late 2015

Pam Kumpe

Discussion Guide

1. Shoelace finds a cemetery can hold pain and loss. Have you ever faced hard times, when someone you care for leaves this earth too soon? How do you find the strength to go on?
2. Priscilla has hopes that her life will come together as planned, but a swift kick changed everything. Where do you run for answers when your heart falls from the pantry shelf?
3. Margo struggles to fit in with normal life. She sifts through the pages of life, unable to rope in hope, unable to sustain her balance. How would you have helped Margo?
4. Mrs. Motes keeps to herself, but helps those she loves. How can you reach out and encourage someone with your touch or smile?
5. The matron's job at Wheelock Academy requires her to be firm with the orphans, but Shoelace discovers a heart of kindness lurking behind that stern voice. Have you ever judged someone too soon?
6. Boswell and Chula show up at the strangest times. Have you ever met an angel? Or wondered if you talked to one?
7. Taddy longs for his mama, and learns Margo is confused about a few things. How would you reach out

to a child who needs help understanding his or her family?

8. Doctor Rigghazel hides his pain inside the casket of anger. Do you know someone who is like the doctor? Will you pray for him or her?

9. Grandma Elsie Kree left a legacy that will live on in Shoelace. What is your legacy? Are you changing the world for God, or letting the world change you?

Do not forget to show hospitality to strangers, for by so doing some people have shown hospitality to angels without knowing it.

Hebrews 13:2 NIV

Pam Kumpe

Wheelock Water Tower / Wheelock Cemetery / Wheelock Mission Church

Books by Pam Kumpe

See You in the Funny Papers—Humor Devotional
A Scoop of Inspiration—Humor Devotional
In the Lick of Time—Children's Book
Things I Learned in Jail—Book of Hope

Annie Grace Kree Chronicles

Untied Shoelace
Unknown Soul
Undaunted Spirit (2015)

www.pamkumpe.com